Iceland Spar

by A W Farmer

All rights reserved.

© A W Farmer 2012

This book is sold subject to the condition that it shall not,
by trade or otherwise, be reproduced, lent, resold, hired out
or otherwise circulated without the author's prior
consent in any form of binding or cover
other than which it is published and without a
similar condition including this condition being imposed
upon the subsequent purchaser.

All characters contained within this publication
are fictitious and any
resemblance to persons whether living or
dead is purely coincidental.

✲✪✯✴

ISBN-13:978-1475271058
ISBN-10: 1475271050

for Diana

for all your help

in this and past writings.

CHAPTER 1

My name is Sam Winter. I'm eighteen years old and I work in a second-hand bookshop in Mendocino, California that is the family business. When I'm not in the shop, I can be found hammering away on the keys of my PC, working on my latest article. Just before I left high school, my dad got sick and I decided that studying for a degree in journalism at home with an on-line tutor was the best way to go. While mom looked after dad, I looked after the shop. Now I'm working on my first novel.

I have a strict workout regime that I employ most mornings. This is because dad, who had been a gymnast and competed in the Olympics at one point, took me at age five to classes hoping that I would follow in his footsteps, but at the school that I attended, I was more interested in literature, reading and writing essays. I even had articles published in the school magazine.

Dad also took me to self defence classes when I had reached my twelfth birthday, where I learned, amongst other things, one-to-one combat and using a handgun, at which I became a crack shot especially at moving targets. As well for my own protection, I carry a small spring-loaded knife in the back of most of my jeans. It's enclosed in a secret pocket and has come in very useful in the past.

The date is May 9, 2000 and I'm on my way to Iceland from San Francisco to visit my Uncle Pete whom I have never met. So, you're probably wondering what my uncle is doing living about as far away from civilization as you could get? When he left the NATO base at Keflavík in western Iceland, he decided to make this country his home. He met an Icelandic woman and married her. He's invited me out for a vacation. He's only ever seen photographs of me as a baby and ten-year old kid.

4

I have no idea where my uncle is. Dad has been corresponding with him for a few years and has provided me with a PO box number and his photograph. All I know is that he lives in Ísafjörður, NW Iceland, and I have to find some way to reach him tomorrow.

I was up and ready for my journey to San Francisco around 5:30 in the morning. Mom and dad were up to see me off. Charley drove me to the airport to catch my flight; a 3 ½ hour drive. There were tears from both of us as we parted and I went to board my plane. I would have to change at Boston for my next flight to Reykjavík.

As I sat in my window seat on the Trans America flight to Boston, I reflected on the visit that I had had with my girlfriend Charley Foster last night. She's the sister I never had and my best friend too. We grew up together and went to the same schools. She had wanted to go on this trip with me but circumstances at work and her mom being sick, made it impossible.

I lay on my front on Charley's bed with my feet in the air and flicking through the pages of my "Icelandic Lessons for Beginners" textbook. Yep, I'm learning the language, well trying to anyway. This is not as easy as French or Spanish that I also speak. I settled on one particular page and began to read it aloud to myself as Charley was still in the shower.

The Icelandic lesson had the English translation opposite. '"Ég elska ost. I love cheese". Yep sure do.'

I could hear Charley moving around in the bathroom now and the shower being turned off.

'"Ég elska þig líka",' I said just as Charley walked in through the door, towel-wrapped and drying out her long golden hair at the same time with a hair-dryer. She's slightly taller than me at five foot three.

I said, translating the text that I just read out, '"I love you too".'

She stopped in her tracks and switched off the dryer for a second. She turned to me. 'Pardon?' She had a smirk plastered on.

I giggled.

'What you got there anyway?'

I held up the book cover for her to see.

'I'm going to miss you when you go away Sam. You phone

5

me when you get there? I want to know you're OK.'

She sat herself down on an upright chair in front of her dressing table mirror; one superbly tanned leg dangling over the floor and the other tucked under her.

'It's OK Charley, I can look after myself. Don't worry about me... ' I trailed off, then added, 'But you will anyway I know.'

She switched on the dryer again.

I said, turning again to where I had left off, '"Þá nota ég sápu; I use soap".'

Charley's eyebrows went up just then and I could tell that she was trying not to laugh. She had a smile there too.

I continued, trying not to laugh myself, '"Rakvél og rakblað; a razor and blade".'

She gave a short laugh and turned off the dryer.

'"Þegar ég raka mig og þvæ mér ég bursta tennurnar með tannbursta, ekki með rakbursta, með tannkremi, ekki rakkremi! When I shave and wash myself...."' I broke off laughing.

She joined in. 'Don't think you'll need that one, unless you're hiding a terrible secret.' She giggled at her own joke.

I continued, laughing again, '"I brush my teeth with a toothbrush, not with a shaving brush".' I broke down laughing and almost rolled off the bed.

She picked up her hairbrush and started combing out her long hair. 'You're mad,' she giggled.

I laughed too and could hardly speak, but was just able to splutter out, '"With toothpaste, not with shaving cream".' We both laughed until the tears flowed. I said laughing, 'Somehow I don't think I'll be needing that one either.'

She sat herself on the bed cross-legged with her back to me. This was the signal for me to brush her hair out. I started on it and I noticed large handfuls of her lovely hair were coming away on the brush.

'You moulting Charley?' I giggled as I showed her the result of my brushing.

She said laughing, 'Yeah I know.' Then, 'Hey, that's my winter coat you got there.'

I sighed. 'Wish I had beautiful hair like this.'

'You've got it.' She laughed. 'You could dye it.'

'Not the same thing Charley. Looks right on you. You suit it.'

When I had finished with her hair she said standing up from the bed, 'Better get home. You've a flight to catch tomorrow girl.'

When I drove home it was just after 11:30. Mom and dad were already in bed. I crept up the stairs to my room. I was asleep before my head hit the pillow.

I had just got home from a visit to Charley's place. Mom had lunch ready on the table. It's my birthday today and I'm wondering what she's bought me. I had mentioned about wanting a pet; a dog or a cat maybe.

She came out from the kitchen. 'Oh, you're here at last. Have a good time at Charley's?' Just before I could answer her, she said, 'I got you something.'

My smile broadened in anticipation. 'Oh?' I followed her into the kitchen. There in the centre of the table was the most enormous birthday cake I had ever seen, with sixteen candles. It must have been all of five feet tall and seven feet in circumference.

'Oh, thanks mom.' I gave her a big hug then pulled away with a puzzled expression.

'What's the matter honey?'

'Em..... ' I hesitated. 'The cake. It's kinda big isn't it?'

'I'm inviting all of your friends around for a party. You do want a party don't you?'

'Oh yeah, but.... ' I trailed off. Who's she inviting, the 5th Cavalry? Gee, I could almost fit inside. I approached the table and tapped the side of the cake. I guess I'm just making sure it's the real thing, and not hollow inside with something about to jump out the top and scare me half to death! Feels solid enough though.

'OK honey, but that's not the real surprise.' She smiled and led me by the arm to the back door.

I couldn't think what was coming next. I'm sure it'll be something nice though. We stepped outside into the yard. I still couldn't see what she had got me. Present? What could it be?

She said, 'You wanted a pet?'

'Yeah,' I squealed in delight. 'Gosh, what have you.... ?'

I broke off as my dad came around the corner leading a.....

7

what? I couldn't think what it could be. It had vague resemblances to a buffalo but with long reddish-golden hair. I almost laughed out loud as visions of Charley's long golden hair came into my mind.

'Gee. What do I do with this? Ride it?' I laughed. 'Mom?' I turned to her for an explanation.

She said, putting her hand into her apron pocket, 'You brush it.' She smiled as she handed a hairbrush to me.

As I took a step forward to have a better look at the animal, I could hardly speak; I could only manage a croak, then, 'You shouldn't have.' My smile had almost gone.

Dad said, 'We couldn't think what to get you, but since you seem to enjoy brushing out Charley's hair, and you wanted a pet, well....' He trailed off smiling.

I was almost speechless. I swallowed hard and said, 'What is it?' I reached out and stroked the soft golden hair. I started combing it out. 'Gee. This could take a while.' I thought sadly.

Dad said, 'It's a yak.'

'Oh. I thought yaks were dark haired.'

'It's a rare breed,' he said laughing.

Mom said, 'And when you're done here....' She trailed off as she took me by the arm again and led me around the side of the house. There in a field as far as the eye could see were thousands of them!

'Oh no mom. What have you done?'

I woke up with a start and soaking in sweat.

CHAPTER 2

I had told dad my plan was to take the airport shuttle to Reykjavík, then fly to Ísafjörður. After visiting the Post Office with the PO box number, I'd find out where Uncle Pete lived and take a bus ride to him. Well that was the plan anyway.

After arriving at Keflavík, Iceland's international airport, I made my way through Immigration to the Baggage Hall where I claimed my soft black backpack. I shouldered it together with my cream-coloured jacket and leather purse, and headed off to find transport to the capital. I did catch the shuttle bus as planned after having stood for some thirty minutes.

The landscape hereabouts closely resembles the Moon's surface. It's very rocky with very little growing. No grass to speak of, just the odd plant clinging here and there into whatever crevice it can find shelter. Along most of the route into the city, there were small stone houses like bungalows, just standing there close to the highway; a wall around the property but no garden at all, and strangest of all, no dirt or lawn, nor any sign of anything growing, so no trees either; just broken rocks. It's very boring! Probably the cheapest real estate in the country.

When I arrived in the city, I made straight for the Tourist Information Bureau. I required accommodation for one night. Once inside the building, I headed for the INFORMATION desk.

'*Hi*,' I said in my usual bright tone to the girl. She was dressed in Icelandic national costume; a black dress with fancy embroidery adorning the front.

'Hello. Velkomen til Ísland.' She pronounced it 'ees-lan'.

I know this one – 'Welcome to Iceland'.

'I need a place for tonight please. Cheap as possible.'

She looked at me inquisitively. 'Are you sure? Well there is the Sjómannsheim, but I'm not sure if it would be suitable for you though.'

'Why? What is that?' I asked in curiosity.

'Seaman's hostel? I'm not sure you'd want to stay there,' she said as her eyes took in my outfit. In my skin-tight, light blue jeans and light green polo-neck sweater, standing only five feet tall; my brown shoulder-length hair in a ponytail and a green baseball cap on my head, I could have been mistaken for a sixteen year old kid. It's happened before.

I said, 'Is there a problem? Seaman's hostel? What's it like?'

'Well, other than tourists and other visitors, they're not going to have many female seafarers. Mostly males stay there, and it's very basic. There's quite a good canteen. We send people there only if they're desperate for a place to stay. OK for one night I guess.'

I smiled and said, 'Sure. It doesn't matter to me. I can handle it OK.' I wondered if I wasn't making a mistake here.

She pulled a sketch map of Downtown Reykjavík from a pile of papers and turned it around for me to see. 'We're here.' She pointed to the Tourist Information Office on the map and marked a cross at the spot, then placed another one in red ink on the hostel. 'There. Not far from here.'

'Thank you,' I said. I was just about to turn away, when a sudden thought occurred to me. It would be useful to have someone who could speak Icelandic to translate for me when I go out tonight. Could be I'll find someone to take me to uncle too. Well, maybe not.

I said, 'Do you know of any clubs Downtown where English speakers can go to meet?'

'Yes. I can take you there tonight if you like, and be your translator too,' she said smiling. 'I was going there anyway tonight and wouldn't mind some company.'

I brightened up on hearing this, 'Oh, that would be cool, thank you.'

'Tell you what. I'll meet you outside the hostel tonight around, say, 7:30?'

'Sure, that's cool.' I nodded. 'Yeah I'd like that, thank you.'

'You from the States?' she asked.

'Yeah, California.'

She asked, 'So where are you heading after Reykjavík?'

'I have to get to Ísafjörður tomorrow. (I pronounced it 'eesa-fjor-thoor'). I've been learning the language.' I gave a short embarrassed laugh. I continued blushing, 'Well, I've been trying anyway.'

'That's very good! Not an easy language to learn.' She smiled.

I nodded. 'Yeah, tell me about it.' I laughed. 'I know a little German and French, and I can get by in Spanish too.'

She said smiling, 'That's very impressive. I speak four different languages too. You have to in my job.' She added, 'Oh, I'm Helga.' She put out her hand.

'Sam,' I said as I shook it. As I turned to go I said, 'Well, see you tonight then.'

I went back out onto the street clutching my map and headed straight for the spot marked with the red cross. I just stood there and looked up at the rather austere-looking stone building. It reminded me of a courthouse I once saw somewhere.

'Well, here goes,' I thought as I stepped through the doorway, my hands in my front pockets. I approached the reception window. It was closed.

An elderly male figure sat in a swivel chair writing at a desk against the faraway wall. I tapped the window for attention. He turned to me with a cigarette hanging on the corner of his lip. There was a slightly puzzled expression on his face as he wheeled himself over to the window. He pushed the glass panel aside without saying anything.

I said, 'Hello? Do you speak English?'

'Komdu sæl,' he said finally.

Sæll if it's a male. He's greeting a female. Well, he's got that right anyway. Maybe he didn't hear me. I'll try again.

'Do you speak English?'

He said shaking his head, 'Nei.' (No).

Great! That's all I need!

He said holding up his index finger, 'Einn?' (One).

One *what*? One night? I'll take a gamble. I nodded.

He said, 'Þrjú hundrað krónur?'

'Easy enough. That's 300 Krónur that I have to pay.' I thought smiling, as I went into my bum bag and handed over the

11

currency. That done, he found a key and placed it on the desk. I took it and looked at the little plastic tag: room number 7. He indicated a flight of stairs and held up his finger again. One floor up, well I assumed that's what he meant.

I said, before I turned away, 'Þakki.' I pronounced it 'thaki'. (Thanks).

I climbed the stairs and reached the second floor. That's first floor in Europe. This corridor was identical to the rest of the building, or what I had seen of it so far. Totally devoid of any soft furnishings, so every sound, no matter how small had a habit of echoing some distance away. A cement floor with no carpeting, tiles on the walls. It was like a prison or an asylum for the insane. I walked down the corridor looking at the numbers on the doors as I went. When I had reached what should have been number 7, there was no number on the door. I put the key in the lock anyway and opened the door. Just before I stepped into the room, I heard the echo of a door farther down the hallway open and close again. It sounded so close, yet I couldn't even see it from my room. Then, another door opened nearby. I turned to see a male figure standing staring at me. He wore rubber boots and a dark green woollen sweater. He was, possibly, fifty-something; could do with a shave by the looks of the grey stubble. He gave me the creeps! I don't like being stared at like that. I shuddered! Those staring eyes! Hasn't he seen a female before? Maybe he thinks it's a kid he's looking at. Did I say something about an 'asylum for the insane'? I think he's one of the inmates! No matter. I turned from his gaze and went into the room. I kicked the door closed with my heel. I dropped my backpack on the floor and threw myself onto the bed. This was the best piece of furniture in the room. I bounced up and down several times on the bed and squealed in delight. I was a kid once again! Then I caught myself. I should be keeping a low profile here, I think. Maybe not a good idea to attract too much attention. Jesus, why am I thinking like this? I'm getting paranoid over one small incident.

The room was sparsely furnished with a sink at the left on the far wall, a dresser in the middle, under the window, and the single bed on the right-hand side next the wall with a bedside cabinet, and a small red lamp with a red shade.

Helga was right, it's basic, and cold, in fact it's freezing in

12

here. I think if I take off my sweater I'll turn into an icicle.

'Well,' I thought, smiling to myself. *'It is Iceland after all so what do you expect?'*

I found a radiator on the left of the dressing table and put my hand on it; it was cold. I tried turning the circular heating controller, but without success. It refused to budge.

'God,' I thought. *'I could do with a hot shower before I go for a lie down, then I'll look for something to eat.'*

I took off my cap and removed the hair clasp. I sat down at the mirror and ran my fingers through my hair.

I thought with a sigh, *'I need a wash badly, and wouldn't mind a soak in a tub if there was such a thing here. Maybe that's too much to hope for though.'* I've had a long journey today from California and I'm feeling very exhausted. I went to the bed and lay down for about thirty minutes lost in thought. I'm looking forward to doing some sightseeing if I get the chance. Maybe Uncle Pete will show me around. He should be well acquainted with the country I would think, then I'll get the chance to take some photos of this beautiful country. How many people ever get the chance to come here? I'm so lucky to have a relative living here. He'll be able to speak the language too, and maybe I can learn some more of it from him.

'OK, time for that shower,' I thought as I visualised myself standing under the hot water. I opened the door cautiously and looked out into the corridor. Coast is clear I think. I don't want that creep looking at me again. That face would give the goosebumps, goosebumps! There's a possibility that he might follow me to the shower. No! I have to stop thinking like this. Calm down girl, get a grip for goodness sake!

I took a blue t-shirt and blue panties from my pack and rolled them up in one of the two bath towels that were draped over a radiator next to the sink.

'Cold towels too,' I thought. *'Oh well.'*

I returned to the door and looked out again. Satisfied that there were no eyes staring at me, I ventured out into the unknown. I turned briefly to the door to close it and stole a glance over my shoulder; so far so good. I turned to the right and made my way down the corridor to find the bathroom – the female one? Would there be such a thing here, in a hostel mainly for males? I walked down the corridor, looking at all the doors. Presently, I came upon one that was painted green with no number, and it also looked different from the others. Not so unusual since I had noticed that many doors didn't have a number anyway.

I took a quick look up and down the corridor then tried the handle. It opened, and Eureka, it *was* a bathroom! No! Stop! It's not a bathroom at all, but a shower room! For males? It's impossible to tell who it was for. No latrines here. Lockers on the left; showering cubicles on the right-hand side of the room. I went to the one farthest from the door and threw my towel over the top of the cubicle, then I returned to the door and – it had no lock! *Damn*! I'll just have to work quickly then. I took off my sneakers and my pink cotton socks and put them into the first locker opposite my cubicle. Then I stepped into the shower and stripped off the t-shirt, jeans, bra and panties, and then I wrapped my towel. I took my clothes to the locker and put them with my sneakers and socks.

Back in the shower, I noticed two controls here, one hot and the other cold. The cold first. I stepped aside to let the water shoot past me to the wall. It's cold enough in here as it is. Now I turned on the hot! *Whew*! What's that *smell*? Rotten eggs? Of course, I remember reading about it; sulphur from the hot springs. This is where they get their hot water from. It was overpowering; it took your breath away. Once I had the temperature the way I wanted it, I just stood there under the water and revelled in the warmth.

While standing there under the shower, a quick thought past through my mind. *'What if someone should come in now?'*

After a few minutes, I thought I heard the sound of footsteps somewhere in the hallway and the door open, behind the roar of the water. I stood with my back pressed against the wall so that there was no chance that I could be seen through the curtain from the door.

My heart was thumping as I thought, *'This isn't a good idea. I should have waited till tomorrow and a shower at the hotel. What difference would a day make anyway?'*

Too late now. I was tempted to take a peek through the curtain to see who it was – male or female, but that would only draw attention. Presently, I heard the sound of water hammering down – a shower had just been turned on. I think it was coming from the faraway cubicle. Good; the farther away the better.

Some minutes passed, and the shower was turned off, then coughing and grunting. Yep, a male. No doubt about it. I *was* in the wrong place! Don't they put signs on doors these days? How's a person supposed to know? I have to maintain my anonymity. I heard the door open and close again. I waited a few minutes, just to be sure he was gone, then I looked out through the curtain and the coast appeared to be clear. He *was* gone.

I dried my hair and the rest of me followed. I breathed a big sigh of relief as I stepped carefully out of the cubicle suitably wrapped in the towel. I tiptoed lightly to the locker. It's mighty cold in here, so I have to work fast, and there's always the possibility that someone might come into the room. I'm beginning to regret having come in here at all. I turned my back to the door and picked out my bra and placed it to one side together with my panties. I picked up my t-shirt and placed it with the other two.

'I'll wash them later,' I thought as I dropped the towel at my feet. I took out my fresh blue t-shirt and panties from the locker and prepared to put them on. It was then that I was suddenly aware that I wasn't alone! I turned my head to the right and saw the creep with the 'eyes' standing there beside his cubicle staring at me! How long had he been there? I turned, clutching my t-shirt to my front and gave several loud screams!

He made a quick dash for the door and disappeared down the hallway. He must have been waiting for me as I came out of the shower. He had only pretended to have left the shower room, but instead, stepped carefully back behind the curtain so that when my guard was down, he could get a good look at me, no doubt from his cubicle. He was probably watching me enter the shower room earlier too.

I just stood there trembling, some of this was from the cold. I pulled on my panties and jeans, and was just about to start on the t-shirt when I heard voices and running feet coming down the hallway. I didn't have time to pull on my t-shirt before the door opened suddenly and two males entered. I still clutched my shirt to my front.

First in the door was a well-built, middle-aged, full bearded guy with black hair pulled back into a ponytail. He wore a two-tone green woollen sweater and rubber boots. His companion, a blue sweater and was much younger; possibly thirty-something with black, close-cropped hair.

The bearded one saw me redden as he entered the room. The incredulous expression that he wore asked, 'What are you doing in here?' He said, 'Talarðu Íslenzku?' (Do you speak Icelandic?)

I just stood there staring at him 'Em....?' I had *no* idea what he said. I'm wishing I had access to my phrasebook and dictionary. I looked from him to his companion and back with a question mark over my head, then I began to feel tears forming.

'Do you speak English then?' he said in perfect English.

'Yeah.' This is all I got out before I felt a tear running down my left cheek. I wiped it with the top of my shirt.

His younger companion asked, 'Was that you screaming?'

I just nodded as more tears fell, and also this time, down my front too.

'Are you OK? Sound travels far in this place,' the bearded one said. 'I'm staying two doors along that way.' He pointed to the right.

His companion said, 'I was visiting him when I heard you. Can we get you anything?'

'Thank you. No. I'll be OK now.' I sniffled and tried to regain control of my emotions.

'Want to tell us what happened? My name's Björn by the way,' the bearded one said putting out his hand to me.

I shook it and said, 'Sam.' I sniffled again.

The other one came forward and introduced himself as Jón. He said he was the manager here. I shook his hand too. I told them the story about the 'eyes' watching me from the doorway and finishing up with the shower room.

'Would you know him again?' Björn asked.

I nodded.

Jón said, 'If you get any more trouble from him, we'll get the police. His name will be in the register in Reception.'

'There are some homeless people living here. Maybe he's one.' Björn said. He continued, 'You shouldn't have come in here at all, but it's not your fault the door wasn't marked.'

I just smiled at them and felt sorry for myself. I wiped my

nose with the back of my hand.

'I'll get the door sorted out shortly. Make sure this doesn't happen again,' the manager said and turned to go.

'Thank you,' I said to his back.

'See you later maybe Sam,' Björn said as he turned to go.

As I made my way back to my room, I kept looking over my shoulder, but no more eyes watching me thank goodness. Once in, I looked at my watch: 4:30. I'm meeting Helga at 7:30. I'm going for a lie down now, and then I'll look for a bank. I have some traveller's cheques to cash. After this I intend to return here and about 6:30, I'll look for something to eat. I set my watch alarm for 5:30. It's gold plated and does everything but make the breakfast, and who knows, maybe even that, if only I had the time to study the instructions. I have to have time to fix my hair before I go out. I went to the sink and washed my face.

I lay on the bed fully clothed after kicking off my sneakers, but was unable to sleep for some time due to that creep, the adrenaline still flowing. I know I have only myself to blame. I shouldn't have been there. Then there's the bathroom....! I dozed off.

CHAPTER 3

My watch buzzer sounded. I sat bolt upright, not entirely sure where I was, then I remembered. I have to remember to call my dad on my cell phone later. I got up and brushed out my hair. I twisted into its usual ponytail and fixed the clasp in place. I dug out mom's perfume that she gave me some time ago. It's nice, and it gets me noticed. I sprayed it around my neck, and then found my 'bum bag' in my backpack. I strapped it on my left hip. It has its own belt, because I don't normally require one for my jeans, as they have an elasticated waist and cling tightly to my hips. I fished out my short-sleeved, white woollen top with its low-cut neckline. The top stops just short of my navel. My California tan is on show now as it contrasts with the white of my top. I finished off with the baseball cap. As I closed the door on my way out, I made sure that it was locked. This action did not require a key, just pull it closed.

As I walked down the corridor towards the head of the stairs, my hands thrust into my jeans front pockets, I heard the soft clicking of a door opening behind me. I turned quickly to look over my right shoulder and saw the 'eyes' following me *again*. He would hear my door opening and decide to follow. I don't like being stalked. The last time that someone did that to me I was at high school. By the time I had finished with him, he wished he hadn't picked on me!

When I reached the top of the stairs, I almost ran down them. I could hear his footsteps behind me. At the foot of the staircase I headed straight for the exit. I'm hoping he won't follow me outside, but if he does, I may be able to lose him. I turned right when I got out onto the sidewalk and just continued walking along the street. I turned briefly to see if he was still following, and he was. I turned right again at the next corner and stopped when I had reached a clothing store. I pretended to be interested in the contents of the window, then I stole a glance to the right. He was standing looking in a shop window too. He turned and stared at me. I just stood there and gave him my stare too. *Ooh!* He didn't like that. He turned his head away from me and that's when I stepped back into the shop doorway. When I put my head around the corner again, he had gone, no doubt back to the hostel. I found a bank on the next corner and cashed my cheques. I returned to the hostel myself now and in no time, was walking in through the front door and relieved to get back into the warmth, or at least, out of the cold.

I glanced at my watch: 6 o'clock. I could hear voices and the smell of food coming from straight ahead, so I headed there. I just wanted to be with people. I'd feel safer that way. He's unlikely to follow me in here. I don't want to risk going back to my room just yet. With my hands thrust into my front pockets, I walked through the open doorway. It was a canteen with plenty of tables and chairs scattered around. There were about twenty-odd males in here, all looking like they had just come off a boat; rubber boots and woollen sweaters appeared to be the order of the day. Fishermen probably. I turned around to see if the 'eyes' had followed me in here, but thankfully so far they hadn't. However, other eyes were on me, in fact they were the moment I walked in. They were friendly though, unlike my stalker. I wasn't intending to eat here but I will buy a drink, if only to escape from him. I joined the end of a short disorderly line that had formed for the self-service counter. While I stood there, I glanced up at the chalkboard on the wall displaying the menu. It was almost meaningless to me.

In a short while, it was my turn to make my choice. I took a cardboard tumbler and chose a diet coke, and then I picked up a straw from the counter. I paid for it and approached the first of the tables. All of them were occupied. I looked around the faces sitting there, as many were turning to look at me anyway. I smiled back at them and continued to sip my coke.

I spotted a young guy sitting by himself close to the wall. He had red, close-cropped hair and a nice smile. Cute comes to mind. He couldn't stop smiling at me. I wove my way through the tables and chairs and stopped at his, looking down on him. Now that's a new one; me looking down on someone. He indicated that I should sit down opposite. I did and smiled shyly into my coke.

I looked across at him over my drink and said, 'Do you

speak English?'

'Yes.'

'Are you from Iceland too?' I asked looking at him over my coke again.

He nodded. 'You from America?'

I nodded. 'California.' As I leaned my arms on the tabletop, I could see that his eyes were fixed on my neckline. I smiled again.

'They don't get many females in here. But they used to have a few. Long-term residents you know...?' He broke off.

No I don't, but I can hazard a guess at this one. Surely he didn't think...! Prostitutes? With my low-cut neckline and the rather short top, my navel on show, and the skin-tight jeans....! No, silly, it's the fashion! Maybe he's mistaken me for a fifteen or sixteen year-old kid! Females appear to be thin on the ground here! No wonder there wasn't a sign on the shower room door!

He asked, almost in a whisper, 'What's your name?'

'What? He's asking my name.' I spluttered through my coke, then coughed twice to clear my throat. 'Sam.'

He put out his hand for me to shake. 'Magnus.'

I shook it, then looked at my watch again: 6:15. 'You working on the boats too?' I'm leaning my arms on the tabletop now.

'Yes. We fish all around the coast of Iceland.'

I brightened on hearing this. Maybe he might know Uncle Pete. Well it's worth a try anyway. I produced the photo of my uncle and placed it on the tabletop in front of him. 'Would you know him at all?'

He picked it up and examined it. He shook his head. 'No. Sorry.' Then he added, 'Someone you know?'

'Yeah. He's my uncle. I'm supposed to be staying with him for a few weeks, but I don't even know where he's staying.'

'So how are you going to get to him then?' he asked.

I shrugged. 'I honestly don't know. Have to find somebody to take me to him I guess.'

He said sounding concerned, 'You'll have to be careful. Careful who you accept a hitch from.'

I nodded. 'Yeah, I know.' I took off my baseball cap and laid it on the tabletop. 'But I can't think of any other way to do this though. Well, maybe bus for part of the way?'

'Well, you're right of course,' he said in agreement.

I glanced at my watch: 6:30. I don't think I will have time to eat out. Maybe I'll eat here after all, now that I have company.

'You waiting for somebody?' he asked curiously.

I nodded. My coke was almost finished. My straw made a slurping sound. I almost giggled out loud, but just managed to stifle it in time. Heads turned. I smiled at them and turned back to Magnus.

I looked over at the chalkboard and puzzled over the menu. He saw me look. He said, 'You going to eat something?'

I nodded. 'Yeah. Not sure what I'll have though.' There were about ten items on there, but I didn't have much idea what they were. I pretended to read the board.

'So, what are you going to eat?' he asked.

I searched my memory banks for anything that matched the items displayed there on the board. 'Em....' I'm still thinking. My memory ran into a stone wall!

I turned to him and smiled. Keep it up girl!

He stood up and led me across the room to the board. Yes! At last! He's taking a liking to me I think. I felt my face flush red. We stood at the board. I looked up at it with my hands in my front pockets, him standing at my back.

'Any excuse to look over my shoulder,' I mused. I turned and smiled at him, but didn't say anything.

'Can't you decide?' His hand was on my right shoulder now, then he quickly removed it.

I made up my mind eventually and chose the third one down. 'That one?' I pointed to it.

He said laughing, 'Súrsaðir hrútspungar.'

I turned to him with a smile. 'What's so funny?'

He said, still laughing, 'Sour ram's testicles.'

I said, 'Pardon?' then I dug my elbow into his ribs. I chose again and pointed to the next one down.

He said, 'Steikt ýsa. You don't read Icelandic?'

I shook my head. 'Well, I'm learning.'

'It's fried haddock.'

'O-K,' I said slowly. 'And soup first?'

He chose fried cod.

We went to fetch our food.

Back at our table, I kept looking at my watch. When it had reached 7:15, I was getting worried about missing Helga.

I was about almost finished my meal when it happened my stalker strolled into the canteen together with three other males dressed in sweaters and rubber boots. One smelled of fish as he passed me on his way to the counter. The 'eyes' spotted me sitting with Magnus.

I looked down at my food, avoiding his stare. I looked up at Magnus. My smile had gone.

I must have looked concerned because he asked, 'What's wrong?'

The 'eyes' moved forward to the end of the line. He's still staring. I can't stand it any longer.

I whispered, as I leaned close to him across the table, 'I'm being stalked.' My eyes are quickly filling with tears, causing my vision to blur. I sniffled.

He said, 'Who's doing this? Is he in *here*? Can you point him out?' He was looking around the room.

'At the end of the line there.' I wiped my nose with the back of my hand.

'*What*? That's Einar! Are you *sure*?' He couldn't believe it.

I just nodded. The tears were running fast down my face now. Some of them were dropping down my front too. Just then, I was aware of a figure approaching our table. I looked up into those 'eyes'! How the hell did he get so far down the line? He must have changed his mind or something.

I screamed, '*No*! Keep away from me!' I stood up quickly, knocking my chair over backwards.

As I ran from the canteen and down towards the front door, I almost collided with Helga who was coming in. She was dressed in blue jeans and a light-blue sweater and carried a leather purse on her shoulder.

'Whoa!' she said holding up her hands to me. 'Slow down. What's going on here Sam?' She wore a troubled expression.

I told her the whole story, including the incident in the shower room.

She said concerned for my safety, 'You're not staying here any longer. You can stay with me instead. I insist!'

I protested, 'No, I couldn't.' More tears running down.

She said, taking me by the hand, 'Let's get you to your room and get your things together. You're leaving here tonight.'

'But....' I knew it was pointless to argue with her. And she was so nice to me.

Just before we ascended the staircase, Magnus appeared. Einar wasn't in evidence, thank goodness.

I said to him in what amounted to a whisper, 'He watched me in the shower room as I came out of the shower and about to get dressed!'

He said angrily, '*Did* he? I'll kill him - the pervert! Don't worry.'

Helga said, 'She's leaving tonight with me.'

I said, 'The manager knows about the shower and the stalking, and they threatened to get the police if something like this happened again.' I was sniffling again.

'I'll tell them myself.' He patted my arm.

Helga led me upstairs and we headed straight for my room.

As we stood outside the door, I fished in my pocket for the key.

I turned to her and said pointing down the hallway, '*That's* where that pervert is.'

She looked to where I was pointing. 'I'm sorry I got you into this Sam. It's the first time that anything like this has happened here that I know of.'

I felt I needed the bathroom, and I don't want any problems this time. We can go find it together. No more mistakes.

I said, 'I want to go to the bathroom Helga. Will you....?' I trailed off. I'm walking backwards away from her.

'Sure,' she said following me down the corridor.

As we proceeded down towards the shower room, I pointed it out to her. 'There! That's it! Notice the lack of a sign. How are you supposed to know what it's for?'

'Manager's responsibility,' she said.

'You said it.'

Presently, we came to the bathroom, and it was too. It said so on the door this time. We went in and used the facilities and just generally freshened up. Thank goodness Helga was with me. I just wanted to get out of this place and get on with my vacation.

She said, when we were ready to go, 'Let's get your stuff

together and get out of here. I'm going to have a word with the manager tomorrow. We don't want any other females having to endure what you went through. Next time it could be more serious. You don't know what people like him are capable of.'

We went back to my room and I just stuffed everything into my pack, then, when I put my coat on I said, 'Let's get out of here. I don't want to stay another second.'

I checked out and left the key, and in a few minutes, we were out of the entrance and heading for a car park across the road. Oh, the relief! Thank goodness I'm out of there at last.

Once inside Helga's car, a Japanese Suzuki 4x4 I think, I said, 'Thanks Helga. I don't know what I'd do if you hadn't offered.'

She started the car and began to back out of the parking lot. 'It's the least I can do. I shouldn't have directed you there. There are other places.'

'Not like that I hope,' I thought looking at the buildings we were passing.

This is not a city of skyscrapers. The tallest building, standing on a hill overlooking the town, is Hallgrímskirkja. It's a cathedral. Took almost thirty years to build using only volunteer labour!

We merged into heavy traffic on a main street and got stuck behind a city bus that had stopped to set down and pick up passengers.

'It's not your fault. No-one could have foreseen what happened there,' I said.

We drove for about five minutes without any real conversation, and in no time, we were heading into the suburbs of Reykjavík.

I said to Helga, 'There's something odd about this set-up. That guy Magnus? He knew that pervert. Must have known what he was like too, so why did he act as though he was surprised at me being stalked and the incident in the shower room?'

'I don't know Sam. Probably trying to protect him for some reason. Maybe the guy was his father or something, or maybe they worked on the same boat. Who can say? Anyway, you don't have to worry about it,' she said smiling, 'you're off to Ísafjörður tomorrow.'

She turned the car into a quiet street of two storey stone

24

houses, all with identical red-tiled roofs. She pulled up outside one of them. 'We're here,' she said switching off the engine.

With my backpack on my shoulder, I followed Helga along the side of the house, then we ascended a flight of steps to the door. She produced a key and opened it. We stepped into a short hallway. I took off my coat and baseball cap and hung them on a peg. She showed me into a spacious living room with Swedish-style wood-panelled walls. A window on the left looked out of the back of the house and the front window on the right. A leather couch together with two large matching armchairs provided the seating in the room. A TV with a stereo hi-fi unit in one corner, and a coffee-table taking up the centre space opposite the couch. It was cosy here.

'It's lovely Helga. Nice place.' It didn't look like much from the outside though.

'Thanks. I'll just show you where you will be sleeping,' she said as she led me into a small bedroom.

A child's room? I don't know why I was surprised to find that the sleeping accommodation was a bunk bed! I haven't slept in one of those for a while.

I turned to her and said with a smile, 'Looks cosy Helga. I like the bed. Reminds me of when I was a small kid.'

She smiled and said, 'I'm glad you like it Sam. You get yourself settled and I'll make us something to drink. Coffee, tea...?'

'Oh it doesn't matter. Whatever you're having.'

'OK. I'll see you shortly then.' With that, she turned and closed the door.

I dropped my pack on the floor and just collapsed onto the lower bunk in exhaustion. I've travelled far today from California and then all the trauma of the last few hours was taking its toll too. If I put my head down now, I'll surely not waken for a week! I kicked off my sneakers and pulled my legs up onto the bed and just lay there. That's all I remember.

I awoke with a start and sat bolt upright as I felt a hand shaking me by the arm and in the process, banged my head on the overhead bunk. 'Ouch!'

It was Helga. She said, 'Tea's almost ready Sam.' She sat on the edge of the bed. 'And try not to break the bed.' She laughed.

'How long have I been asleep?' I said as I removed the hair

clasp and ran my fingers through my hair.

Could do with a shower, and get my hair washed too.

'About an hour. I didn't have the heart to waken you. You deserve a good sleep after your ordeal,' she said empathetically.

'Thanks,' I said standing up from the bed. I added, 'I could do with a soak.'

She said standing up from the bed, 'I don't have a tub, but you can use the shower if you like. The tea can wait.'

'Thanks. I'll just do that then.'

She showed me through to the bathroom. I had my shower and stayed in there for about ten minutes, then, suitably wrapped in a bathrobe and carrying my discarded clothes, I made my way back to my room as Helga busied herself in the kitchen. I combed out my hair and twisted it into its usual ponytail, then fixed the clasp in place. I put on a fresh thong and pulled on my cream-coloured jeans that cling tightly to my hips with an elasticated waistband. My push-up bra followed, then a light-blue woollen, close-fitting top that stops just short of my navel, with its low-cut neckline completed my outfit. I stood in front of the dressing table mirror and admired my slim figure side-on.

'At least I don't have to diet like some people,' I thought smiling to myself. *'And, I can eat most things without fear of putting on weight.'*

This is probably because I workout most mornings. I like to think it keeps me trim and fit anyway. I'm the envy of some of my girlfriends back home, and, it attracts the guys too! They can't keep their eyes off me!

Satisfied with my attire, I returned to the living room to join Helga who was just about to pour the tea. She was seated on the couch when I came in.

She looked up from her pouring. 'Gosh! You look stunning Sam.'

I just smiled and sat down in one of the armchairs opposite. I said with a big sigh, 'Don't think I feel like going out again tonight Helga. I could sleep for a week.'

'It's OK Sam. I don't blame you.' She said changing the subject, 'Thought you might like some of this jam sponge that I bought yesterday. It's very tasty. Err, you don't mind sweet things? You know, weight...?'

I shook my head. 'Not really a problem Helga. I don't worry about it. People who get fat only do so because they eat too much of the wrong things too often. Everything in moderation.'

As I helped myself to the sponge, I could smell cooking smells coming from the kitchen. My nose was getting the better of me.

Helga saw my expression. She said, 'It's chicken tikka masala. Tómas' favourite.'

I was too busy pushing cake crumbs into my mouth otherwise I would have asked her who she meant.

She saw my look and said, 'That's my brother. He's staying here for a few days. He's manager of a tourist agency in Hveragerði.'

I had a question mark over my head as I sipped the hot tea?

She spotted it. 'It means "place of hot springs". They have lots of glasshouses there where they grow tropical fruits for the home market.'

'Really? You wouldn't think you could grow anything like that here in Iceland.' I was surprised and impressed. Is there nothing those enterprising Icelanders haven't tried?

'Oh yes. They grow bananas and oranges too.' Suddenly there was a loud hissing sound from the kitchen. She said abruptly, 'Excuse me.' She got up and scurried into the kitchen to fix something.

I sat there sipping my tea and contemplated the day's events. I'm lucky that Helga saved the day. She rescued me from that place just in time. I'm grateful to her of course. Pity I'm not staying here for longer. She's proving to be a good friend.

Presently, I thought I heard a key being turned in the lock at the front door. Tómas, I wondered? Just then, a male figure dressed in a blue jacket and shirt and black pants materialised in the living room doorway. He was taller than me – so what's new? He was twenty-something, with short, black wavy hair, a prominent nose and generous lips. He removed his jacket and threw it over a chair back, then froze to the spot when he saw me stand up from my chair. He looked me up and down, drinking in the view. His eyes were fixed on my bust, or at least that's the impression I got anyway. Just then, Helga came into the room.

Tómas' expression changed to puzzlement. He's wondering who I am.

She said, 'It's a long story Tómas.' Then she introduced me to him. His name was Hallgrímsson.

He was speechless. He couldn't take his eyes off me. She retreated back into the kitchen.

I just stood there with my hands in my back pockets and a grin plastered across my face. Eventually I approached him with my hand outstretched and said, 'Hi.'

He shook it then planted a kiss on my right cheek. I felt myself redden. I thought, *'Oh, I'd love to kiss those lips.'* But I digress!

I returned to my chair and the tea, all the while watching Tómas. He was worth watching. He sat in the armchair just beside me. We were only inches apart. I could smell his aftershave from here. He could probably detect mom's perfume from me.

He helped himself to some tea and sponge. 'Well now, which cloud did you descend from?'

I giggled and almost choked on my tea. I spluttered out, 'Excuse me?'

He heard my accent. 'Oh, from America? OK,' he said answering his own question.

I just nodded and smiled.

'What part? Let me guess....' His eyes were taking in – I think – my navel and the tan, oh, and my bust. He continued, 'California, or Florida?'

I was just about to tell him when he interrupted with, 'California? I used to know someone there.'

'OK Sherlock,' I thought. *'What else can you tell me about me?'* I was smiling broadly.

I had just put my cup down when he asked, 'More tea?'

Without waiting for an answer, he lifted the teapot and filled my cup to the top. Now I'll just have to eat more sponge. I smiled to myself. Hmm, yummy. Watch your figure girl! Even I have my limits! At this rate, even my morning workouts may not be enough!

I coughed, or was that another splutter? My mouth was partially filled with sponge crumbs. I just managed to stifle a giggle.

He said, 'You like Iceland? Impressions so far?' He leaned closer to me. *Yes*!

I'm trying to swallow the cake. I started to speak but coughed instead. I think it's gone the wrong way.

'So you like it here then? Seen much of the country, or have you just arrived?' He actually paused long enough to take a gulp of his tea.

I thought, *'If you let me speak I'll be able to tell you!'* It seems Mr Holmes is short on answers. I drank down some more tea.

'Em....,' is all I got out before he interrupted with, 'Are you familiar with hot springs and geysers?'

'Em....' This is frustrating!

He interrupted again with, 'I could show you around if you like? Go on a little tour of the thermal areas of the south?'

I coughed again to clear my throat of cake crumbs. When I had recovered I said, or at least I tried to, 'Em...'

He cut me off again with, 'We could start with the geysers or a swim in the hot thermal lake.'

I thought with horror, *'No we won't! I don't have a costume to wear!'* I managed a smile, then put my cup down. 'Thanks, but I'm leaving tomorrow.'

'Oh,' he said sounding disappointed. 'Where are you going?' He took another slice of cake.

'Ísafjörður?'

'O-kay,' he said slowly and drank down more tea. 'How do you intend to get there?'

'Fly?' I suggested and grinned.

He said laughing, 'Not with your own wings I hope.'

'What is he on anyway?' I thought and smiled.

'You could put it off for a day couldn't you? So much to see here Sam. So much to experience.' He finished off his tea.

'The reason why I came here was to see my Uncle Pete, but I guess I could put it off since he doesn't know when I'm *actually* arriving. It's meant to be a surprise.' I finished off with a smile and put down my cup.

'Right. OK. Can we make it a date then? Hot springs, geysers?' he said smiling.

I said laughing, 'Been there, done that, I've even got the t-

29

shirt.'

'*Oh*? Where? Not in Iceland?'

'No. Yellowstone. Old Faithful?'

He bent closer to me. *Yes*! I like it when he gets close. He said, before rising from his chair, 'Excuse me for a second.'

He crossed to the kitchen and disappeared inside. He only partially closed the door, so I could hear something of a conversation in English. He was discussing me in a low voice. 'Helga, she's gorgeous. Where did you find her?'

I'm blushing now!

'I didn't. She found *me* in the Bureau, you know?'

There was some clattering of plates and utensils, then the conversation lapsed into Icelandic.

I'm looking forward to tomorrow and Tómas' company. He's nice. It's just a pity that I can't stay around longer. I'd really like to get to know him better, and maybe get a chance kiss those lips too. I'm dreaming again.

Tómas reappeared from the kitchen and sat himself down beside me again. 'Helga told me what happened in the hostel.' He sounded concerned.

My smile had vanished temporarily. 'Yeah. I'd rather not discuss it, thanks. I just want to get on with my vacation and put it behind me.'

I poured myself more tea.

I indicated the teapot. 'You?'

He said, shaking his head, 'No thanks. I'll be eating shortly.'

Helga came in and started setting the table. 'Oh, nothing for me thanks. I've just had a meal at the hostel, oh, and the sponge. It was lovely Helga.'

She said smiling, 'Yes, I thought you'd like it.'

'Em..... are you planning a family? I just thought.... The room with the bunk beds?'

'No. I haven't been here long. They belonged to the previous owner.' With that, she headed back into the kitchen.

I got up and followed her. 'I'll give you hand with that Helga.'

She handed me an ice bucket and said, 'My boyfriend is living in the north. We only ever see one another every now and then.' She whispered, 'Tómas has certainly taken to you, but I guess you know that already? He said he thought that all his birthdays had arrived at once.'

'Oh, sure.' I blushed and sighed contentedly before I said, 'Yeah, that's obvious.' I laughed.

I carried the ice bucket into the living room and placed it in the centre of the table. As I made to return to the kitchen, Helga was already carrying the wine into the room. She handed it to me and I placed it into the bucket. She returned to the kitchen and fetched the soup for Tómas and herself.

I sat next to him on his left, and Helga opposite me. He opened the wine and poured mine to the top without asking.

I nodded my thanks and said, 'I'm looking forward to tomorrow.' I smiled then continued, 'Thanks for the offer Tómas. I probably wouldn't have gotten the chance to see those sights if I hadn't met you.'

He smiled back and placed his hand on mine as I was about to raise the glass to my lips.

I almost choked on the first sip as I thought, 'He's a fast worker, but I'm loving every second of it.' I coughed to clear my throat. It's gone the wrong way again.

He said, 'It's a pleasure. It'll give us a chance to get to know one another better.'

I had been taking a gulp of wine when he had made that last statement. I coughed and spluttered as the wine went the wrong way once again. I seem to be doing this a lot recently. I just smiled back and drank down some more wine. My glass was about halfway down now. He filled it to the top again without asking.

CHAPTER 4

In the morning, after I arose and showered, I pulled on my blue jeans, two t-shirts and my green polo-neck sweater, my hair in its usual ponytail, oh, and I mustn't forget my baseball cap. My pack goes with me and my camera too. I'm looking forward to our trip to see the thermal areas in the south of Iceland. It sounds so exciting. I remember the exhilaration that a hiking trip to Yellowstone with my dad when I was a kid of 12 had on me, the thrill of watching Old Faithful spouting into the air, the mud pools and the hot springs; hot water gushing out of the ground. Then, when I was 15, I returned there with friends around my own age, and the same sense of adventure. Oh, the memories!

We left Helga's place early after breakfast and in no time, were cruising onto the main highway heading south-east. The traffic was light here. The weather didn't promise to be kind to us unfortunately; grey skies threatening to open up and drench us in a torrent of rain at any moment. Now and then the sun would emerge from behind the clouds and caress us with its golden rays.

One of the first places that we visited was Gullfoss. He pronounced it 'gootle-foss'. It means 'Golden Falls'. It's a large waterfall, well actually a series of three cascades ending in a very fast-flowing river. This is a very small-scale version of Niagara Falls, but without the boat trips.

There were no cars in the parking lot when we arrived around 10 o'clock. We alighted from the car, me with my camera slung diagonally across my shoulders and no jacket as the sun had decided to make an appearance at last, so I felt quite warm here. I left my baseball cap in the car too. Tómas wore a green waterproof jacket and a dark green woollen sweater.

A brisk breeze accompanied us as we walked from the parking lot along a gravel track towards the waterfall, Tómas leading the way. The track ran alongside the river that had carved a deep ravine into the living rock. I paused to look down over a sheer drop into the raging waters below. Such a dangerous place with no guardrail to protect you. When we had gotten to within about 100 yards of the viewing platform, I stopped in my tracks and readied my camera for action. I took a few shots of the waterfall and its tumbling into the river.

I said to him brightly, handing over my camera, 'Take my picture here?'

I ran to the guardrail, turning my back to it and leaning against it. I rested my two hands on it behind my back, my legs crossed and a broad smile plastered on. The breeze was blowing my hair around my face, so I tucked a few strands behind my right ear and hoped they would stay put for the photo. Tómas just stood there looking at me with a smile on his face.

'What?' I asked with a puzzled expression.

'You look gorgeous Sam. Ever thought of becoming a model?' He turned the camera vertically and pressed the button.

I just smiled ever more sweetly and brushed some strands of hair behind my ear. He turned the camera horizontally then took another shot. He stood there for a moment studying the result, a smile appearing on his face. I came over to him and he handed me the camera.

I asked inquisitively, 'What is it?' Then I saw the screen. I liked the result. I nodded and said, 'I like it Tómas, thanks.'

He said, 'I wonder if I could use this picture for one of our brochures? And maybe the other one too?'

I smiled and said, 'Well, maybe. OK.'

I thought I'd take some wide-angle shots of the river and waterfall together plus some of the other scenery, like Tómas. He was standing admiring the waterfall close to the guardrail when I stepped backwards towards the river. What I didn't realise was that I was too close to the edge and I lost my footing on the rocks. I stumbled and lost my balance and found myself falling in the direction of the river. Tómas made a dive towards me and was able to catch me around the waist before I fell down into the ravine.

He was still holding me as I said looking up into his face, 'Thanks Tómas. I think I'm going to throw up.' I was feeling positively sick and was trembling inside. I could feel some tears forming. *'Jesus! That was a close one!'* I thought as I tried to recover from the shock.

'What? So that's what you think of Helga's breakfast efforts?' He laughed.

I turned in his arms to face him with a big grin and punched him on the chest. 'Oh, shut up!' I laughed too, although I was still shaking.

I sniffled. A tear ran down my right cheek. He saw it and wiped it away with his finger. I sniffled again and wiped my nose on the back of my hand.

One or two cars had come into the parking lot I noticed. Maybe I can ask someone to take a picture of us together.

An elderly gentleman came along the track walking his little dog. I said to him, 'Could you take our picture please?' I indicated Tómas who was standing a short distance away from me.

The guy didn't say anything to me. Instead he tied his dog to a post, then took the camera from me and Tómas and I stood at the guardrail waiting to be snapped. He put his arm around my waist and we both produced our broadest smiles. Click went the camera, and the guy handed it back to me without saying a word.

When I got it back I looked at the result on the screen. 'I like that. Thanks,' I said to him. He just smiled and walked away.

We walked along the track again just enjoying the freshness of the air. I sat down on a rock and tried to compose another picture of the waterfall. Tómas joined me but only just managed to sit himself down with a squeeze. I was in danger of falling off my end of the rock. He put his arm around my waist and pulled me close. Yes! I like it when he sits close!

'When you come back to Reykjavík later at the end of your vacation, will you look me up?' he said looking at me intently.

'Yeah, of course.' I smiled at him, then I thought I felt something wet drop onto the top of my head. I'm hoping it's rain and not a bird! I guess it's rain, because it was cold. I looked up at the sky and all I could see were grey clouds. Then another drop and another.

I thought sadly, *'And me without a jacket.'*

The rain started falling in earnest. Big lumps. It bounced off the stones and gathered quickly in little pools all around us. Tómas took off his jacket and put it over our heads. Yes! I'm smiling again. We just sat there and listened to the pitter-patter of the raindrops.

When the rain had stopped, I said, 'So where to next Tómas?' I was composing another shot, because I had been watching a rainbow forming over the falls. 'Look!' I pointed to it. It was bright with vivid colours.

I turned on my camera's 'saturation' facility to make the colours more pronounced.

We're still sitting under his jacket; still very close and I'm loving every second of it! I have a plan forming now. I want to get closer to him, feel his arm around me, his breath in my ear and smell his aftershave.

He said, 'Where would you like to go?'

'Em..... the restroom?' I laughed at my own joke.

He said laughing too, 'That's not what I meant. What place would you like to go to?'

I said smiling, 'Oh, I don't care so long as you're with me.'

I stood up and pretended to have hurt my foot.

I shouted in pain, 'Ah! My foot's hurting.'

I leaned on his shoulder for support. He put his arm around my waist again.

'Are you OK?' he asked sounding concerned and studying my expression.

'I think I must have twisted my ankle when I stumbled.' I was trying to keep a straight face.

I leaned my head against his arm and looked up into his face with a coy expression, then I winced.

He said in a concerned voice, 'Sit down and take off your shoe.' *Yes*! He's bought it!

I sat down again and removed my right sneaker and pink cotton sock. He lifted my foot up onto his lap. *Yes*! I like it!

'What part is sore?' He was massaging my toes, then he started working his way up my foot. Ah! It felt good having Tómas touch me...... *anywhere*, I don't care!

I pointed to the left side of my ankle. 'There, oh, and there too,' I said smiling to myself and pointing to my leg just above the ankle.

I've got a large grin plastered on, and I almost giggled out loud.

He massaged the 'affected' parts, then he spotted my grin. 'What is it?' he said smiling himself.

'Nothing.' I'm still grinning. I think he's suspicious.

As he ran his finger along my sole he said with a grin, 'How about here?' It tickled, and I giggled out loud.

By now, several other visitors had arrived at the viewing platform. One of them, an elderly lady gave me a disapproving look and turned away again.

I said to him smiling, 'Can I have my foot back please, thanks?' I put on my sock and sneaker and stood up, forgetting momentarily, my 'sore' ankle. I said, 'Can we go find the restroom now?'

He said standing up, 'We'll have something to eat there too and you can rest your foot at the same time?'

I hobbled alongside Tómas, his arm around my waist again, until we reached the tearoom. I wanted this to last forever, but alas, it wasn't to be as we were fast approaching the building now. We pushed through the door and I sat down at a table next the window.

Tómas fetched the tea in the shape of a teapot and two mugs, and a selection of sandwiches.

When we were well into our first cup, I asked, 'Do you speak any other language besides English?' I had just finished off my third cheese sandwich. I didn't realise I was so hungry.

'*Yo hablo español también, et je parle français aussi.*' (I speak Spanish, and I speak French too).

I was impressed. I said, not to be outdone, '*Vous n'êtes pas les seuls qui peuvent parler français!* (you're not the only one who can speak French!). I grinned over my cup.

'OK,' he said, 'try this: *¿dónde usted viene de?*' (Where do you come from?). It was Spanish this time.

'*Un pueblo pequeño en California.*' Spanish again. (A small town in California).

'*¿Usted tiene un novio?*' Spanish. (Do you have a boyfriend?).

'*No. Pas au moment. Pourquoi est-ce que vous demandez?*' French. (No. Not at the moment. Why do you ask?').

'*Ninguna razón.*' Spanish. (No reason), he said finally.

'No wonder you went into the tourist business to work.' I

smiled. Then I said, 'I'm off to the restroom.'

I had spotted it while Tómas was speaking just then. I forgot again, my 'sore' foot, and walked normally towards the restroom. When I returned Tómas was already standing at the table waiting for me.

He said with a smirk, 'Your foot OK now then?'

I looked up at him with a coy expression and said, 'Hmm.'

He put his arm around my shoulders and we walked back to the car.

I asked him after I had settled myself into the passenger seat, 'Where to now?' I donned my baseball cap.

'Hveragerði. Place of Hot Springs. You'll like it,' he said starting the car.

I just smiled and looked forward to getting there.

About thirty minutes later, we pulled into a parking lot beside the tourist bureau. Tómas said that this was where he worked.

I wore my camera slung around my neck, leather purse on my shoulder. We walked down a street that consisted of nothing but glasshouses. It stretched as far as the eye could see. I stopped walking and stared in awe at this unusual sight.

'Gosh, Tómas. What do they grow here?'

I was trying my best to see in through the glass of the nearest one. We were standing just outside it. I went right up to the glass and put my face close to it, and shielding my eyes with my hand. Difficult to see anything in there due to the glass being dirty. I think they were tomatoes, but I wasn't entirely sure. If it was, they were still green.

I turned to him. 'Tomatoes?' I pointed inside.

He nodded. 'Want to go in?'

'Sure,' I said and followed him through a door on the side of the glasshouse. I said to his back, 'Sure it's OK to come in here?'

I was looking around at all the tomato plants hanging from supports; row upon row of them. There must have been thousands of them here.

'Yes, it's OK. They know me here. We take visitors through here every day. Well, I don't, my staff does.'

I took a few photographs in here. This was something different to look at.

I turned to Tómas and said, 'It's impressive. Any more surprises for me?'

He turned to me. 'Through here.'

He walked to the far end of the glasshouse and opened another door. We went in and.... bananas! *Thousands* of them growing in here! There was a difference in the atmosphere as well. It seemed more humid than in the previous one.

I sauntered down the first aisle admiring all the plants there. It was *awesome*; all those bananas grown at this latitude! There was a basket lying on a bench full to the brim with bananas. He picked one out and handed it to me.

I took it and examined it. 'Looks like the real thing, eh?' I laughed.

'Eat it,' he said smiling.

I peeled it and took a bite.... yummy, but then a banana is a banana wherever you go right? It's the thought that it was grown here that matters.

I nodded my approval and said through a mouthful of fruit, 'Where to now?'

Tómas turned away and headed towards the exit with me in pursuit. Once outside, we went back to the car. I was just about to get into the passenger seat when I spotted a shop selling Icelandic handicrafts etc. I heard Tómas sigh when he saw me looking at it. I just smiled cutely at him and marched off to see what I could find there.

Once in the shop, which was full of handmade craft objects, I spotted jewellery under glass. Some items were displayed on the counter top; they included necklaces. I chose one; a gorgeous ruby-coloured pear-drop shaped stone, about a quarter inch across and an inch long on a silver chain. I heard the door open behind me. Tómas arrived at my side now. I picked up the necklace and turned my back to Tómas. 'Could you fasten this for me please?'

He fixed the necklace in place around my neck. It nestled just inside the top of my cleavage. Perfect! This'll set off my top with the low-cut neck-line just nicely. Get me noticed.... well, my cleavage anyway! I removed the necklace again and handed it to the assistant behind the counter.

I said to her, 'Don't bother wrapping it, thanks.'

She told me how much it was.

'Whew! Was that expensive or what?' I thought.

Lots of things are here in Iceland, but it's usually because they have to be imported. This item is home grown isn't it?

When I was handed back the gift box, I opened it again and turned to him whilst reading the little booklet that accompanied the necklace, 'It says here that it's rose quartz.' I took it out of the box and placed it on the back of my arm to see how it looked against my tan. *'Yep, I like it.'* I put it back in its box and slipped it into my purse.

I turned to Tómas. 'I'd like to have a look round, see what else is here.'

I turned to study some handmade pottery, then I noticed another part of the shop through a doorway on the left. I strolled in through to have a look. I found the most lovely geodes lying on a shelf. They were every colour that you could imagine, and they were *massive!* Some were as much as nine inches across! Those beautiful crystals; just right for my living room. But they're too big to take back with me. The baggage handler who got my luggage, would end up with a rupture for sure!

Tómas, I'm sure, was waiting patiently for me in the other part of the shop. I thought I spotted him purchasing something. Maybe he's buying Helga a present, so no doubt he'll show me what he's got her later.

After a few more minutes, I decided that I had spent enough time in here, so I headed back to Tómas. He was indeed waiting for me.

I smiled up at him and asked, 'You get what you wanted?'

'Yes I did,' is all he said and turned to go.

'Think that's all I want in here. Where to now?'

'Geysers?' he asked as he made for the door.

In about thirty minutes we were heading towards the distant mountains across a vast plain of sand and lava desert. I could see a curtain of steam being pulled across the landscape in front of us. It appeared to be getting thicker as we approached it. I could also smell that now-familiar odour of sulphur hanging in the air. Yep, there was no doubt about it. This was geyser country all right. There was no mistaking it.

As Tómas looked for a suitable place to park the car, I

noted that there were no other visitors about. So far we had the place to ourselves. He parked the car just off the road and we alighted into a brisk cool breeze and warm sunlight. We both wore our jackets here against the wind.

A large column of water shot up into the air some distance off.

'Look!' I pointed to it excitedly, then I spotted something. Well actually I heard it before I saw it. A boiling pool of grey mud just off to the right of the road, in fact there were several of them. I sauntered over to them and stood close to the edge of the nearest one. The mud was boiling furiously here. Not a place you'd want to fall into. I could feel vibrations through the ground on which I stood.

'Oh the power! What raw energy there must be down there,' I thought as I got down low to train my camera on the mud pools.

'Don't get too close. It's dangerous there at the edge,' he said as he watched me standing there.

I straightened up again and turned to him with a smile. 'It's OK. I've been here before. Well not *here* exactly....' I laughed.

He cut in laughing too, 'Yeah, I know. Yellowstone.'

It was just then that I felt it; a tremor! I could feel it through my feet. This was just before the dried mud at the edge of the pool on which I stood seemed to crumble under my weight. Everything appeared to happen in slow motion, and the ground simply wasn't there any more! I lost my balance and tried to throw myself backwards, then suddenly I felt strong hands grasp me around the waist and I found myself in Tómas' arms yet again!

I looked up into his face with a smile, although I was trembling inside. 'You seem to be making a habit of this Tómas.'

He looked down on me laughing. 'You seem to be making a habit of falling into my arms.'

'Oh shut up!' I said laughing as I pulled out of his embrace, then my smile vanished as I could feel tears welling up.

I turned to him again and threw my arms around his neck, then kissed him on the left cheek and just held on to him tight.

He asked inquisitively, 'What was that for?'

'For saving me again!' I said this as I felt a tear running down my left cheek. That was quickly followed by another.

He must have felt them too because he said, 'Hey, what's the matter?'

He pulled back a little to examine my face. He would see tears running down *both* my cheeks now, then he pulled me close again and rubbed my back. 'It's OK Sam. Just be more careful where you go.'

I pulled away and made for the car. I wanted a Kleenex from my pack. Whilst sitting in the car, I cleaned up my face and blew my nose. I took off the baseball cap and removed my hair clasp. I wanted to get the wind through my hair. Just before I opened the door, I grabbed my camera and returned to him minus my jacket as the sun was warming things up now. Well I felt warmer anyway.

He reached out and took my hand.

'What's he doing?' I thought as I felt a sudden surge of electricity run through me. Tómas has that effect on me.

He said pulling me along with him, 'This way.'

We moved towards the geyser which at this point was not performing for us.

'How long before it goes?' I asked excitedly. I was still sniffling a little, but I had my Kleenex in my hand, so that's OK. I stood with my camera at the ready, waiting for the geyser to go. I turned it vertically so as to emphasise the height of the column when it eventually erupted.

He waved me to silence. What was he doing? I guessed he was counting the seconds before the geyser blew. Then it did! And what a spectacular performance it was too! Click, went my camera as a column of super-heated water shot up into the 'cold' air for about five seconds before dropping back to Earth again.

I turned to Tómas. 'That was spectacular. How high does it go?'

'It's about 180 feet or 54.8 metres,' he said.

He took me by the hand again and we walked for about five minutes, then he stopped when we had reached a large pool of hot water. I know it was hot because there was a lot of steam rising from it. It was a gorgeous turquoise-blue colour. He said this was due to the mineral content of the water. Another photo here I think.

I turned again to him. 'Take my picture here?'

I handed him the camera and stood back a little in front of

the pool. I tucked some strands of hair behind both my ears, and with hands in my back pockets, produced one of my broadest smiles. Tómas turned the camera vertically and snapped me. I returned to him and looked at the result. Yep, I like it. Maybe I could be a model after all. I'm dreaming again of course.

I thought I'd like a photo taken against the geyser. I suggested this to Tómas. He agreed and we returned to the spot. I stood there with my back to the large pool while we waited patiently for it to erupt. Again, I stood there with hands in back pockets, my broadest smile plastered on and hair getting into my eyes. I should have kept my hair clasp on. I could hear the water's surface behind me bubbling and getting louder, and as a result, didn't hear what Tómas was saying.

'Pardon?' I cupped my right ear with my hand in order to hear better. The geyser spouted and all I could hear was a tremendous whooshing sound as the water shot up into the air! What I didn't hear however, was him telling me that I was standing too close to the geyser, and the next thing I knew, I was drenched with a very warm spray of water as the geyser returned to Earth again.

'*Damn*! Look at me, I'm soaked!' I said as I felt the water seep into my clothing and my hair soaked too. I'm a mess. I'm starting to feel cold now.

Tómas held me close and said, 'Let's get back to the car and a change of clothing.'

I started to walk back with him to the car, then he stopped and asked, 'You do have a change of clothing don't you?'

'Oh yeah,' I said confidently.

When we reached the car I got in the back, Tómas the driver's seat.

I pulled my sweater off followed by the two t-shirts. I was now down to my bra. He handed me a towel from the bag. He pulled a plastic carrier bag from his bag and said, 'You can put your wet things in there Sam.'

'Thanks,' I said. I pulled on my long blue t-shirt. It comes down past my waist, then I removed the wet bra.

He asked, 'Where will you go tomorrow?'

'Ísafjörður.'

'Why there?'

I started stripping off my jeans. 'My Uncle Pete is there, or at least somewhere in the area,' I said with a sigh. I put on another bra.

'You mean you don't know where he is? Don't you have an address?'

I started pulling off the thong. 'No. Get a bus perhaps, or if there isn't one, I'll have to get someone to take me to him. That should be fun.' I sighed again.

'Be careful Sam,' he said concerned.

I pulled on another thong and started on my cream-coloured jeans. 'It's OK Tómas. I can look after myself, thanks.' I zipped up and reached into the front seat for my jacket.

I heard him sigh, then he said, 'Yeah, I'm sure you can.' Then added, 'Your hair?' he asked.

'Yeah. Would you?' I reached into my pack and found the hairbrush. He got out and came into the back seat beside me.

'So, what does your uncle do for a living?'

'Fishing, as far as I know. He has a boat. I think it's a fishing boat.'

He said, 'Maybe he has another job too. Most Icelanders have more than one job you know?' He was making good progress with my hair now.

'So I've heard. Going to be difficult to track him down though I think.'

He said, changing the subject abruptly, 'Sam?' He was still brushing my hair.

'Yeah?' I asked absently.

'Could you put your hand into my jacket there?' He had a grin on his face when he said it.

I turned and looked at him with a puzzled expression. 'I'm sorry?'

'Put your hand into my pocket? In there.' He indicated his inside pocket.

I frowned at him and said, 'Sure.' I couldn't think what he had in mind. I reached into his pocket as instructed. My hand found a small box wrapped in paper by the feel of it. I took it out and held it in my hand. It was wrapped in gold paper.

He just smiled at me.

'Em.....' I hesitated, then I asked quizzically, 'You want me to open it for you?' A sudden flash of electricity passed through me as I thought that this could be for me! I'm not sure why I thought so, but I'm dreaming again of course.

He didn't reply, but smiled instead.

My heart was racing as I unwrapped the rectangular-shaped box. I smiled as I saw it, then I tried to read the expression on his face as I was just about to open the lid. He nodded his approval and I lifted it. I realised then that it *was* for me because Tómas wouldn't buy himself a bracelet, or, it could still be for Helga!

I asked, holding my breath, 'For *me*?'

He nodded with a smile.

It was gorgeous; Norse symbols engraved in gold and with semi-precious stones, blue, green, red and yellow, all held together with little chains.

'Oh Tómas, it's beautiful, thank you.' I started to cry and buried my face in his chest, then I pulled away and indicated that he should fasten it on my wrist. So that's what he was buying in the shop.

He put it on my right wrist and kissed me on the left cheek. I threw my arms around his neck and kissed him full on the lips. Eureka! At last, I did it! I kissed those lips! Then I couldn't stop myself. I just hung onto his neck and we kissed there like there was no tomorrow.

He pulled away finally and said smiling, 'Anyone ever tell you that you look gorgeous?'

'Yeah. Frequently,' I said with a smirk. Then I decided to wind him up. 'Tómas, you shouldn't be spending money like this on me. It must have cost you quite a bit. It looks expensive.'

'Don't be silly, it wasn't expensive,' he said as he pushed some strands of hair behind my right ear.

'What? You mean you bought me some cheap jewellery? And here was I thinking that you really liked me and....'

He cut me off abruptly by placing a kiss on my lips and we stayed in that position for some minutes before pulling away again.

A few minutes later and Tómas had finished with my hair. 'Fancy trying again for your picture with the geyser?' he said grinning. He didn't wait for an answer.

He was already stepping out of the car when I finally

answered him. 'Sure. Why not?'

I joined him in front of the geyser again. By this time there were quite a few other visitors there, all trying to get pictures of girlfriends and boyfriends, aunts and uncles against this unusual backdrop. Gosh it was cold here, at least it felt colder now that I only had my t-shirt and jacket for protection. I was shivering visibly, but Tómas held me close and tried to keep me warm until the water in the pool began to bubble fiercely. This was the sign that the geyser was about to erupt again. Whilst everyone was concentrating on the action about to unfold, I took off my jacket and posed for the camera, remembering not to stand too close to the water this time.

With my hands in my front pockets to show off my new bracelet and a broad smile on my lips I said to Tómas, 'Can you take it *now* please? I'm *freezing* standing here.' Then I heard it the whooshing sound as the geyser faithfully performed for us yet again. Click went the camera.

'Whee!' I shouted excitedly as I turned to watch it race skywards. Click! He took another one.

CHAPTER 5

On the way to the thermal lake, we stopped off at a shop selling woollen goods. Tómas said it was part of a farming co-operative. I wanted to get another polo-neck sweater. I chose a blue one this time to go with my blue jeans.

As we approached the lake, all I could see was tremendous volumes of steam rising from the surface of the water, and I could smell that now familiar, ever-present odour of sulphur hanging in the air again. A power station stood about a mile away on the banks, the only man-made structure for miles around in this moon-like landscape. Tómas parked the car in a parking lot just beside the lake. I just sat there staring through my window at the water. I could see lots of people in the water some distance from us, in fact so far away that they were almost completely obscured by the curtains of steam that drifted across the lake. I half expected to see bubbles on the surface of the water as it boiled away into the cold air, but of course, the temperature wasn't that hot, it just looked that way. Its colour, grey, reflected literally, that of the sky, and the mood of the afternoon in general; most uninviting. I was beginning to regret having agreed to bathe in the hot thermal lake. I gave a big sigh and turned to Tómas.

He heard it and asked, 'What is it?'

I turned to the window again. 'I don't have a bathing suit.' I turned back to him again.

'You don't?' A big grin appeared on his face just then.

'I can bathe without one back home, if I can find some secluded cove, but this is too public.'

'Really?' he said smiling. 'Wouldn't mind seeing you in your birthday suit though,' he said with a smirk.

I turned to the window again and said, 'Yeah. In your dreams.' I pulled off my sweater and said, 'This is as close as you're going to get.'

He was watching me in curiosity as I started stripping off my top-most t-shirt, but his eyes almost popped right out when I began to undo my bra. I let it fall down then threw it into the back seat. Then I unzipped my jeans. A smile appeared on his lips now.

I said to him with a smirk, 'Could you help me get them off please?' Silly question really. I thought, *'How to get a guy's attention; ask him to take your jeans off for you.'*

'Sure,' he said brightly as he took hold of my jeans. He began to pull them off me, and once he had that done, he just sat there and stared at me. I'm wearing a white thong.

I asked him what he was looking at.

'You look even more gorgeous in that outfit.'

I just smiled and stared through the windscreen at the water, clouds of steam billowing across the surface.

He said, 'Towels in that bag there.' He pointed to a blue plastic carrier bag on the back seat, then he got out and came around to my side. He opened my door and began to pull me out by the hand. I just stood there rooted to the spot; I was freezing. There were several changing booths nearby. Tómas went to the nearest one and disappeared inside. When he emerged less than a minute later, he was wearing swimming trunks. He looked so handsome and strong, oh, and I have to admit, very sexy too standing there.

I went back into the car and fetched the towels, then just sat there on the seat and shivered. I wasn't looking forward to this venture at all.

He said, 'Come on now, it's not *that* cold.' He was standing by the water's edge now watching me.

'I know. It's OK.' I stepped out and just stood there, my bath towel in my hand. *God*, it was cold, but perhaps not as bad as I had thought it would be.

'*Ah*! Oh! *Ouch*!' The stones on the ground were destroying my feet as I made my way towards Tómas. There was some grass here too, so I was stepping from tuft to tuft to reach him.

He turned when he heard me approach, 'Ah, at last. Well, jump in!'

'Yeah, right,' I thought. He knows that I've only got my t-shirt on top. I'll let him go in first, then I'll follow.

He asked looking at me curiously, 'What's the matter? It's not boiling although it might look like it!' He had a smirk on his face.

I just stood there and shivered even more. I said, 'I'm freezing here.'

He came to me and held me tight. He would feel that my nipples were hard as they pressed against his chest through the t-shirt.

He said finally, 'Yeah, you *are* cold aren't you?'

'You can say that again,' I thought, as I stood there waiting for him to make the first move. *'Hurry up Tómas; I'm freezing!'* He must have read my thoughts, because he suddenly took a headlong dive into the water. That was my cue. I had a good look round to see that no-one was watching me, then I stood up quickly and dropped my towel at my feet. I jumped into the water feet-first making a loud splash that completely swamped him.

He said laughing, 'You make an awfully big splash for such a small person.'

I was at this moment, about five feet from him. I made a face and put out my tongue. Then I dived under the water and swam around to his back, but keeping my distance. I put my head above the surface again.

He was looking for me. 'Sam?' He turned to face the power station, still searching for any sign of my head above the water.

I dived again just as he was about to turn in my direction, then came up behind him. 'Hi!' I said to his back.

He jumped visibly in the water and said, 'Sam don't do that.' Then he started laughing. He moved towards me.

I backed off away from him and dived, then came up behind him again. 'Hi!' I said to his back.

'Hey!' he shouted.

I giggled as I dived again and this time I stayed down longer. I decided to go for a swim.

We must have spent an hour at least in there. It was very refreshing and relaxing in the water. I think I'll come back to Iceland some time and do this all over again.

I resurfaced and looked around for Tómas but he was nowhere to be seen. Where had he got to? I resurfaced just then to find him sitting on the bank with his towel about to dry off. He hadn't see me approach, so I dived again and swam towards him. I could see his legs dangling in the water. Without resurfacing, I grasped his ankles and pulled him quickly down into the water with me, then I made a hasty retreat in the opposite direction. The water was very murky in places where the sediment had been churned up by passing swimmers. I turned to look for Tómas but I couldn't see anything for muck. As I was about to turn away, strong arms grasped me around the waist from behind. I'm hoping this is Tómas! We resurfaced together. He was still holding me, then I turned and kissed him full on the lips. I just held on tight to him.

I could see the bank was quite close so I struggled out of his embrace and headed for it. I pulled myself up out of the water and had just started to wring out my hair, when something grabbed both my ankles and I found myself toppling backwards into the water again. I screamed and screamed out as I fell. I hit the water with a big splash.

He was laughing. I was too. He was kissing me again. I escaped his embrace once more and climbed back out of the water, rather more quickly than last time and snatched up my towel quickly. I started to dry off. *'God, it's freezing!'* I thought.

I thought I'd do a quick change in the car, so, once in the back behind the driver's seat, I started stripping off my wet t-shirt. That done, I wrapped my towel and I began to take off the thong. It was proving more difficult to do than usual because it was soaked and clinging to me. I had only just managed to get it halfway down my legs, when with peripheral vision, I realised that I was being watched! Tómas had arrived at my window and was watching me. He was laughing. My towel had slipped a little! I gasped and gave a short shriek and quickly pulled my towel up to cover myself again! How long had he been there? I don't think he saw much though, at least I hope not!

'Tómas!' I shouted at him. 'What are you playing at?'

'Sorry,' he mouthed apologetically through the glass. He went to the booth and disappeared inside. Seconds later he emerged beside the car, opened the driver's door and slid behind the wheel. By this time, I had only just managed to pull on my fresh thong when he appeared, but I was well hidden from his view behind the driver's seat.

I finished off with the bra and sweater. I said, 'I'll be back in a tick. Just want to get my jeans on.' As I stepped out of the car I said with a smirk, 'And no, you can't come and watch.' I giggled as I snatched up my jeans from the seat. I retreated into one of the changing booths and pulled on my jeans, then I went back to the car. Once in the passenger seat, I started on my hair with the brush.

'Where to next?' I asked as I attempted to twist my hair into a ponytail.

'Horseback ride?'

What? I have never been on a horse before. I expressed this fact to him.

He said, 'It's easy. Nothing to it. I'll show you how it's done.'

'OK,' I said with a smile as I clipped the hair clasp on. Then came the baseball cap. I saw his eyes brighten.

'What now?' I asked grinning.

'That cap takes years off you,' he said looking at me intently.

I said maintaining my grin, 'I know. That's why I wear it silly.'

I saw his eyes go to my waist. This is probably because at this moment, my navel and California tan was on show, as I was sitting with my left leg tucked under me. My sweater only just makes it to the top of my jeans. It's tight, and shows all the curves in all the right places.

He had a smile plastered on.

'What?' I looked at him curiously.

'Your outfit?'

'What about it?'

He leaned closer with a smile. 'I thought maybe you might want warmed up a little. All that bare skin there, and you mentioned about being cold earlier?' He laughed.

I shifted in my seat and removed my left leg from under me. 'I'm quite comfortable thank you very much,' I said with a smile, then added, 'Could you start the car please?'

50

CHAPTER 6

We arrived at the riding stables around 4 o'clock. As we alighted from the car, we were approached by an elderly guy about my height wearing a red sweater, jeans and rubber boots. He wore a woollen cap on his head. He had small pig-like eyes and a grey beard.

'Is that the only footwear that they wear here in Iceland?' I thought as I looked him up and down.

Tómas said something to him in Icelandic and he turned on his heel and disappeared into the stables.

I just stood looking around the place and wondering what my horse would be like.

Presently, the guy reappeared leading two horses without saddles.

'Oh,' I thought suddenly and with some disappointment, because I thought I'd be riding with Tómas; me on the front of the horse and his strong arms around my waist, or maybe I could be on the back with my arms around him holding onto him tight. But, I guess it's not to be. I sighed inwardly and looked forward to my ride anyway.

Two young kids appeared from the stables now, each carrying a saddle; a boy and girl. They could have been twins. I guessed they were about twelve years old. The elderly guy left us and went back into the stables. The teenagers saddled the horses and disappeared again briefly, then the elderly guy returned to us.

I wondered if we would be introduced to our mounts. *'I guess not,'* I thought sadly, as the elderly guy indicated that I get on the nearest one.

As I stood next to it, I noticed that its back was almost as high as I was tall. *'This horse was made for me I guess,'* I chuckled to myself. Then I noticed that Tómas' horse was also small. *Gosh*!

He looks like a giant beside it. They're smaller than the average horse back home in California. I noticed also that mine had a little white diamond shape on his forehead. I'll call him diamond from now on.

I hesitated. I wasn't too sure how to get on him. I know how to put my foot into the stirrup, but can I get my leg over? Tómas has ridden before and he showed me how, and I just sat there waiting for something to happen. Tómas mounted his horse and started moving away from me, impatient to get going.

The elderly guy showed me how to turn right and left just pull the reins to the left or the right.

'Easy enough,' I thought, *'but how do I stop him?'* Well, that'll come later I guess. I don't think the guy had any English as he hadn't said a word to me.

I noticed the two kids were back, this time riding their own mounts. Looks as though we'll be moving soon. Good. I'm looking forward to it. I stroked Diamond's neck at the side. Did he even notice?

The kids moved off ahead of us and then Diamond started moving too without even a word from me. How did he know to do that? Well, at least we're moving.

Tómas was well ahead of me, following the two kids. I saw him looking back over his shoulder at me. I don't know whether he saw me smile or not. Probably not from that distance, but as he turned away again, I had replaced it with a frown, as I thought I felt the saddle move under me. Then I began to panic as I realised that it was indeed moving; slipping to the right. I can't stop him since I haven't been shown how. I can't signal to the kids either, they're too far ahead and they'll never hear me anyway. Besides, the wind is blowing the wrong way, and Tómas has lost interest in me it seems. As if by telepathy, Tómas turned and waved to me. I waved back then realised that I should have given him a signal that something was wrong! Too late, he had already turned away again!

The two kids broke into a gallop, Diamond did likewise, and I, with my saddle in danger of slipping further, hung onto my horse's mane for dear life since there was nothing left for me to hold onto! He's getting faster and my saddle has slipped again! They started to slow down, thank goodness, then one of them turned round. I waved, and they waved back then proceeded on their way. Probably thought I was just being friendly. Diamond slowed down now too thank God. I'll have to attract their attention somehow. Shouting is of no use here; the wind is wrong for a start. If I fall off Diamond, I'll surely break something. It's a long way to the ground for me to fall.

It's very rocky here in this sandy lava desert, with nothing growing at all. It's a very bleak landscape. I know there must be something growing *somewhere* in Iceland because they have horses, and they have cattle and sheep too, but so far I haven't seen any signs of vegetation except in Reykjavík.

I'm beginning to wish I hadn't come on this trek now. When I first realised that my saddle was moving, I was aware that my right foot was in danger of slipping out of the stirrup, my left getting higher. This state of affairs only got worse as the saddle continued to slip round.

The two kids began to gallop again.

I thought in alarm as Diamond broke into a gallop too, *'I'm going to come off this horse for sure!'* I tried pulling the reins tight, but he didn't appear to notice. Am I doing this right, or am I pulling too hard? I have no idea how to stop him. I try pulling the reins to the right, to go right. *Nothing*! He doesn't respond to that either! I tried pulling to the left; again nothing. Does this horse not obey *any* instructions at all?

My left foot was now so high up in the stirrup that the calf of my leg was hurting and I was getting cramp in it. I removed it from the stirrup, my right was barely in it anyway, so I removed it too.

The kids slowed down again. I could breathe a sigh of relief, at least for now, as Diamond slowed too. He's simply copying what the others are doing it seems. I wondered if he has been trained just to follow them and do as they do for the benefit of beginners like me.

I noticed that Tómas' horse was not behaving like mine, he has control there. He turned round to look at me briefly. I waved back with both hands in the air in a frantic bid to attract his attention. He obviously realised that something was wrong because he stopped and turned his mount around and galloped back to me. Diamond had stopped in his tracks. Was he confused? I tried slipping off his back but I was afraid that I might simply fall off him onto the stony ground, so I changed my mind and just sat there waiting for Tómas to put things right.

By now, Tómas had reached me. Without dismounting, he took Diamond's reins and let him walk behind his own horse, then he stopped.

'Now what?' I thought as I looked at him in curiosity.

He dismounted and helped me down off Diamond.

'What are you doing?' I asked wondering what was coming next.

He said, indicating his own horse, 'Get up.'

I just smiled at him and put my right foot into the stirrup, then hauled myself up and into the saddle.

He said, 'Take your feet out of the stirrups.'

I did as instructed, but I wondered if it was safe to do this, then he got up behind me and immediately grasped me around the waist with his strong arms. Eureka! At *last*! He did something with the reins and we galloped off after the two kids, who were by this time well ahead of us.

It's nice to feel Tómas' arms around me again. I looked up into his face and he just smiled back as he concentrated on the terrain ahead. I felt somewhat giddy travelling at this speed. This is probably how the Pony Express riders used to feel when they travelled between towns back in the days of the Wild West.

When we reached Helga's place, she had a nice meal prepared for us. We were going to eat about 7 o'clock. I was famished and was ready for anything that Helga could dish up.

Tómas carried my damp clothes from the soaking of the geyser and the swim into the kitchen for Helga to put in the wash while I went off to have a shower. First I went to my room to take off my clothes. There is no lock on the door, this being a child's room. With my back to the door, I began to hum the striptease tune and strip off my clothes slowly one by one, starting with the sweater. I pulled it off slowly, swinging my hips from side-to-side in a real sexy way and twirled it round and round in the air a couple of times before throwing it across the room and into the audience. They cheered and called out for more. Then came the jeans. I unfastened the stud and slowly pulled down the zipper. I pulled them down slowly then stepped out of them. That was thrown to the audience too. More cheering! Swinging my hips and gyrating on the spot, I turned to the door and pulled off my t-shirt and twirled it around my head a few times then threw it backwards over my right shoulder and into the audience once again. Cheers from the audience. I unclipped my bra and threw it into the audience too. More cheering and clapping. I turned my back to the door again and now I'm down to my thong. Swinging my hips ever more slowly, I began to pull it down my thighs and that is as far as I got, when I was interrupted by the door opening behind me. I jumped with fright and gave a loud shriek and pulled it up again quickly. Of course I knew it was Tómas even before I turned to the door, as I could hear Helga messing around in the kitchen still. I instinctively threw my arms across my chest as I swung around to face him. 'Tómas!' I screamed. 'What are you doing in here?' I was angry with him.

'Sorry. Didn't know you were undressing.' He said with a smirk on his face, 'And *you* should keep your door locked girl. You never know who might walk in.'

I said breaking into a grin, 'You know there's no lock on the door, and you must have heard me humming that tune. Come on admit it!'

'OK, I admit it,' he said with a broadening grin. 'It was all part of a devilish plan to catch you unawares.'

'O – K,' I said slowly with a smile. 'Can you get me a bathrobe please, oh, and a shirt?' I grinned up at him.

He said, 'It'll have to be one of mine. Helga doesn't wear shirts.' At that, left the room and returned moments later with a shirt and bathrobe. As soon as he had left, I donned the bathrobe and made my way to the shower. I told Helga I would be out shortly as she was just about to serve the meal. We were starting with melon. Grown in Iceland? I hope so.

I dropped the bathrobe on the floor and stepped under the hot shower, now oblivious of the strong smell of sulphur. I had just finished lathering myself from head to foot when it happened. I thought I heard someone shout something but I could have been mistaken. It's difficult to hear anything with this water hammering down. Then I was certain I could see someone on the other side of the shower curtain, but just before I could react, it was pulled aside quickly. Again I instinctively threw my hands over my important bits and gave out several short screams. It was Tómas again! He is so determined. I swear to *God* I'll kill him if he does that again.

He said laughing, 'Tea's ready. You didn't hear me shout did you?'

'Go *away* Tómas!' I shouted and quickly closed the curtain again. I waited till I was certain that he had left before I washed off the soap and stepped out. After drying off I threw on the bathrobe and made my way back to the bedroom where I put on a push-up bra, a pair of panties and the white shirt that Tómas had left me. It was, of course, miles too big for me, with the sleeves coming down passed my fingertips and extending well down my thighs. I put on my new necklace, making sure that the stone nestled between my breasts, and left the top three buttons unfastened. Then I put the bracelet on my right wrist. I opened the bedroom door slowly and walked in the sexiest manner that I could muster at this time in the evening. I'm trying to wind him up of course. Helga and Tómas were already seated at the table; she at the head and he with his back to me. They both turned as I entered the room. Helga smiled at me. Tómas just stared and gasped, his eyes almost popping out. He was speechless. I just smiled at them both and sat down beside him. I sat with straight back and my chest thrust out. Tómas' eyes were fixed firmly on my necklace, at least I think that's what he was looking at!

Helga's eyes, I could see, were drawn to the necklace too. 'That's a beautiful necklace Sam. Where did you get it?'

'Hveragerði. There's a gift shop close to the tourist bureau.' As I fondled the stone with my right hand, I could see Tómas' eyes were still fixed to the spot. The bracelet was on my right wrist, and naturally Helga's eyes caught that too.

'I like your bracelet Sam. Expensive?'

I extended my arm across the table in order for her to see better. I shook my head with a smile as I turned to Tómas then back to Helga. '*I* didn't buy it.' I was still smiling.

She held up my hand and looked at the bracelet closely. 'It is nice. Wouldn't mind one like that myself.'

Helga had put an ice bucket in the centre of the table. There were two wine bottles in it. I reached out and handed one to Tómas to open. As he was doing this, Helga got up and scurried into the kitchen to fetch something. She reappeared with the melons. As she handed two of them to me she said, 'Grown in Iceland.'

I took them from her and held one in each hand, feeling the weight of them. '*Really?*' I said. 'I'm impressed Helga. That's quite an achievement.'

Tómas said, 'That's a nice couple of melons you have there Sam.'

I turned to him. Did I hear right? 'I beg your pardon?'

He blushed slightly and laughed. 'I was referring to the fruit.'

I blushed too. '*Sure* you were. You couldn't wait to get that one out, could you? You and your jokes,' I said laughing. I handed them back to Helga and turned to Tómas. 'So, you like my necklace?'

'I do..... ' he hesitated. 'Before I forget Sam; can I give you my cell phone number? Call me any time.'

'Oh, yes thanks. I'll just go get my cell phone.' I got up and went to the bedroom. I put my jeans back on plus the blue woollen top, my navel on show, oh, and the necklace. I returned to the living room with my cell phone. I sat down beside Tómas and we exchanged numbers.

In bed that night I could hardly sleep for thinking about Tómas. I couldn't get him out of my mind, and I just had to tell someone. Charley will be jealous for sure. Yeah, I'll give her a call.

My cell phone was lying on the bedside table, so... I found her number. I waited and waited for the phone to be answered. I looked at my watch: 2 o'clock. I'm thinking, *'Must be around 6 o'clock there. Maybe her phone's switched off.'*

'Come on Charley. *Answer* it!' I whispered impatiently.

A voice said, 'Yeah?'

Before I could answer I heard a squeal of excitement. 'Sam?'

I whispered, 'Hi Charley, how's things with you?' I could hear water noises. I thought quickly, *'Swimming pool?'*

'Hi Sam. How's it going? You meet anyone yet?' More water sounds and this time a splash.

'Great.... em.... you at a swimming pool or something?'

'No, I'm in the tub having a soak. So, what's he like then?'

She's giggling.

'What's who like?' I'm trying to stifle a giggle.

'Come on Sam. I know you too well for that. I want to hear *all* about it. You've met a guy right?'

'Yeah, OK....' I broke off, then I couldn't stop myself. 'Oh, *Charley*, he's so *cute*. We only just met on Monday.'

'And you've done what since then?' She laughed.

'*Oh*, you wouldn't believe the places we've been to Charley. It was so *cool*.'

'Yeah? I meant what did you *do*? You know?'

'Pardon? Oh, nothing really.' I hesitated. 'He's a good kisser though.' I laughed.

'So that's as far as you've got then? Kissing?'

'Charley! *Stop* it!' I whispered. 'What do you think I am?'

'So where did you go? Get up to anything interesting?'

I told her about the places we went to including the thermal lake.

'*Ah*! So you had a swim together?'

'Not exactly a swim. More like bathing.' I gave a short embarrassed laugh.

'And you without a swimsuit, right?'

'Yeah. You know I don't own one. Hey, what are you trying to say Charley?'

'Nothing. But you could have bought one there before the swim couldn't you?'

'Too short notice. Well, I guess I could have. Anyway, I wore a t-shirt and thong and it did the job OK.' Well *I* was satisfied with my explanation anyway.

'So what *did* you two get up to? You keep evading my question.'

'You really *are* jealous aren't you?'

'No I'm not. Well....' She broke off, then, 'Yeah, well maybe I am just a *little* bit. Send me his picture Sam.'

'You mean take it with the phone?'

'Yeah. Well I'll have to go. Going out tonight. You phone me again and tell me what progress you've made, you know?'

'Oh, and we didn't get up to *anything* if you must know.' I sighed. 'I'll have to go too. Catching a flight tomorrow.'

She sighed. 'You *are* slow Sam. Catch you later, bye.'

CHAPTER 7

In the morning, Helga had made a nice breakfast for us and gave me back my clothes that had been in the wash. I wore my new blue polo neck sweater, my necklace on the outside of it and my bracelet on my right wrist. With my backpack on my left shoulder I was all ready to go. Helga gave me a big hug and I started to cry; she did too, 'You come back here Sam when you're finished your vacation and Tómas will take you to the airport.'

'Oh no, he doesn't have to Helga. He'll be working. I'll find my own way there. Thanks anyway.' I was looking at Tómas.

'Let's get you out to the car. You've got a plane to catch.' He opened the front door and took me by the hand. I rescued my coat and baseball cap from the peg in the hallway and followed him outside to the car.

About ten minutes later and we were standing in the departure lounge at Reykjavík Airport, watching my Arnarflug (Eagle Air) aircraft being readied for take-off.

Tómas stood at my back, his hands clasped at my waist at the front. I pulled my sweater up a little and put his right hand onto the skin just above my jeans. It felt good to have Tómas touch me there. He hugged me tighter and I started to cry again as I turned to him, burying my face in his chest. Tears were falling fast now.

An announcement was made in Icelandic only and I looked up into Tómas' face enquiringly.

'That's your flight Sam.' He hugged me even tighter and then let me go. 'Keep in touch. Let me know how you're doing.'

I nodded. I went into my pack and removed my camera and purse, then stood in line at the check-in desk. I turned and waved to Tómas with a smile, still sniffling and wiping my nose with a Kleenex. In no time I was going through the door to the outside via a flight of steps that would take us onto the tarmac and the aircraft. I turned momentarily to the departure lounge window and I could see him standing there waving to me. I had to go into my pocket again for the Kleenex as I could feel another tear coming.

We had now reached the aircraft steps and were climbing aboard. A girl in uniform checked our tickets and we went in to find our seats. I had a window seat. I could see Tómas standing there at the window waving again, a smile on his lips. I waved back as the engines started up, propellers spinning, getting faster and faster until it became a deafening roar, then the door was closed and the aircraft began to taxi down the runway. In no time we were in the air and heading for Ísafjörður – Ice Fjord.

When I came off the aircraft I headed straight for the luggage trolley, as there was no carousel here, in fact there was no terminal building at all, just a waiting room and no doubt a control room too. The trolley was being loaded up with baggage directly from the plane. There were few passengers on this flight from Reykjavík so picking out my soft backpack wasn't too difficult. I climbed up briefly on the trolley to have a look inside. I pointed my bag out to the handler. He picked it up and handed it to me.

'Þakki,' I said, and dropped back down to Earth again.

I have to find a taxi now. I could see other passengers standing waiting on transport arriving. Private cars came and went, but I didn't see anything resembling a taxi. I'm thinking, *'What? No taxis in this country?'* I found a telephone in the waiting room, but there was no telephone directory. I thought I'd call Hotel Ísafjörður on my cell phone to ask where I could get a taxi. 'Hello? Hotel Ísafjörður?'

A male voice said, 'Já?'

'Can you tell me where I can get a taxi from the airport?'

'No taxi here. You got the wrong number.' He hung up again.

'Jerk,' I said under my breath. I thought, *'Damn! Try again.'* I dialled again and waited.

The phone was picked up on the sixth ring. 'Já?'

'Look, I need transport from the airport. I'm supposed to be staying at your hotel? I have a reservation?' I'm beginning to lose my cool.

60

He said with a sigh, 'You should have said. OK, I'll be right there.'

'Thank you,' I said with a sigh of relief and switched off. I found a bench and sat down with sandwiches that I had found lurking in a dispensing machine.

After about fifteen minutes, a car drew up. The driver introduced himself as Þórsteinn Magnússon. He pronounced it as 'Thorstain Magnoo-sonn'. I and my bag jumped aboard. I was in the back seat and leaning forward to hear what he was saying. He was forty something with black hair cut short and a small moustache.

I said, 'Sam Winter.'

He asked, 'Good journey?'

'Fine thank you. Nice view from the plane. It's beautiful here too,' I said as we headed towards town. This small town is largely built on a peninsula on the fjords of north west Iceland. It appeared to be built beneath a table mountain.

'Weather's been cold recently and we've had some snow, but it's OK for the time of year I guess,' he said.

'I don't mind the cold,' I said. 'I just wrap up warm and get on with it. Vacations are for enjoying yourself after all.' I couldn't help thinking about Uncle Pete and how I was going to find him. How was I going to get to him?

Another ten minutes and we stopped outside the Hotel Ísafjörður, close to the centre of town.

We alighted from the car and Þórsteinn carried my backpack into the hotel. I don't know why he did because it wasn't particularly heavy. He carried it upstairs to a room at the rear and dropped it onto the floor. Before I could say anything, he had turned on his heel and disappeared downstairs again.

'Charming,' I thought. *'Friendly sort. I can see we're going to get along just fine.'*

I headed for the shower, then I decided to have a soak instead, so I ran the water in the tub. While I waited for it to fill, I pulled the curtains back on the window to reveal floor-to-ceiling windows. They looked out onto – I don't *believe* it - a large outdoor swimming pool! I slid the glass door aside and stepped onto the wooden deck. A high wooden fence surrounded the pool so that it couldn't be seen from any direction, not even other guests, since this bedroom was the only one at the rear of the hotel. No-one to see me here. Just as well as I don't have a bathing suit.

I smiled to myself and thought, *'This is the life.'*

I could hear the tub filling just nicely. I'm thinking I just might go for a swim instead, now that I've found this pool. I went back into the bathroom and turned off the water. The tub was half full now and I could, if I so wished, have my soak. I'll just leave it there for the moment and go for a dip. Maybe I'll decide that I still want that soak after I come out of the pool. How right I was!

I went back to the bedroom area and strolled outside clutching a hot bath towel that I took from the radiator. I stood on the wooden deck and looked forward to my swim. The air temperature at this time, 4 o'clock, was cold, in fact it was only 30 degrees! The wind was blowing from the north; no wonder it was so cold! I kicked off my sneakers and took off my pink cotton socks, then I stepped off the deck, and...! My *God*! My bare feet were freezing when they came into contact with the stone flagging of the steps that led down to the pool's edge. I just stood there on the top step and started stripping off my clothes. First the sweater, then the t-shirt. I gasped when the cold wind struck my skin, but I almost died when my bra came off! I shucked out of my jeans, and took off finally, my panties. Jesus, it was cold. I was freezing all over now, and my goosebumps had goosebumps.

'Well here goes,' I thought as I ventured forward.

I was now at the edge of the pool, with the warm towel in my hand, but my feet were frozen! I dropped the towel where I stood. The water looked so inviting! Curiously, there wasn't any steam coming off the water. Maybe I should have thought of that sooner before I took a step forward and dived headlong into the..... icy cold water! I gave a big gasp as I resurfaced! The only thing that this water lacked was a sheet of ice on the top! I got back out of the pool in a hurry, but as I sat myself down on the cold stone flagging, I found that my teeth were chattering and I was trembling all over. I thought my bottom would freeze solid when it came into contact with the now-wet marble edge of the pool.

I thought, as I took deep breaths, *'Jesus, it's cold! I'm freezing! Have to get warm quick!'*

I just sat there on the pool's edge, my knees drawn up to my chest and feeling very foolish. This is when Þorsteinn decides to make an appearance. I heard a voice shouting from behind the bedroom door. 'Hello?'

'Oh no,' I thought. I should have locked the bedroom door. Then I remembered that I had. Luckily, I have a towel to hand. I wrapped it as best I could and was relieved to find that it was still warm! Thank goodness. I stood up and made immediately for the bedroom door. I opened it and put my head around it.

I think I may have been showing off a little more than I had intended because he said in a shocked voice, 'Oh, sorry.'

'What did you want me for?' I asked, 'You were going tell me something?'

He said, 'Sorry. I was going to warn you not to use the pool. It requires maintenance.'

I thought, *'Great! Now he tells me.'*

I didn't say anything to him. Instead I gave him a quick smile and retreated behind the door, kicking it closed with my heel, then I went straight to the bathroom and the hot tub. Once inside the door, I stepped into the beautiful hot water and sat down. I just lay there till I dozed off.

I awoke with someone knocking on the bedroom door, and the water temperature lukewarm.

I called out, 'Yeah?' I looked at my watch: 5:30.

It was Þórsteinn again. He shouted, 'Would you like something to drink before your meal? It won't be ready for a while.'

'Sure.' I'm standing up now in the tub.

'OK, come down when you're ready,' he called out.

'Yeah,' I replied absently.

I stepped out and dried off, then wrapped myself in the towel. I went into the bedroom and opened the glass door and began to retrieve all of my discarded clothes. The wind was even colder now: 25°F or minus 3°C if you prefer. I scurried inside again to the warmth of the bedroom.

I had to get dressed ready to go downstairs. Before I did so, I had to dry my hair, so after using a hair drier that I found next to the sink in the bathroom and combing it out to my satisfaction, I twisted it into my usual ponytail and fixed the clasp in place. I pulled on my slim-fit, cream-coloured jeans. They cling tightly to my hips with an elasticated waistband. Then I changed into my white, short-sleeved, close-fitting woollen top with its low-cut neck-line. It only just makes it to my navel, and finally, my baseball cap on my head. I stood in front of the dressing table mirror and admired my figure.

'Yep, perfect!' I thought in satisfaction. Happy with my mode of dress, I made my way down to the restaurant.

I went straight to the counter where I found Þórsteinn busying himself with looking through some stationery. He was looking for the menu as it turned out. He said as he handed one to me, 'You can study that while you have your drink.'

I took it from him. 'Thanks. Em...?' I was wondering about the drink.

'Oh yes. Sorry. What would you like to drink? Tea, coffee, soft drink, alcohol....?' How long was his list?

'Coffee, if it isn't too much bother. Thanks.'

'It's always ready to drink.' He poured it into a mug from a coffee maker. 'Mug OK for you?' he said as he placed it on the counter.

I nodded with a smile as I took the menu and my coffee to the nearest table and sat down, crossing my legs. I studied the menu and sighed. *'Not again,'* I thought. The entire menu was printed in Icelandic! I turned to ask Þórsteinn, who was by now, messing around in the kitchen, if he had one printed in English. I was just about to get up from the table, when I happened to glance at the back of the menu; it was printed in English. 'O - K!' I said slowly to myself as I dropped it onto the tabletop. I took my time studying it and enjoying my coffee. I settled on lamb soup followed by roast lamb.

Þórsteinn materialised beside me as if by a Star Trek transporter. He asked, 'Have you decided yet?'

I drank down the remains of my coffee and gave him my order. He took the mug and the menu away and retreated into the kitchen to mess around with the pots and pans in preparation for the meal.

I'm wondering why he appeared to be the only member of staff; taxi driver/chauffeur, bellboy, cook, waiter, cleaner, kitchen hand, chief bottle washer....! How many jobs does this guy *have*? I chuckled to myself at that last one. I think I'll ask him. I got up from the table and leaned my arms on the counter.

'Þorsteinn?' I shouted. I tried to make myself heard over the clattering of pots and pans.

He came out to me.

I said, 'How come you have no staff here?'

He replied, 'I can't get them. In Iceland we have more job vacancies than people to fill them. It's crazy. Sometimes I can get students in the summer, but so far none.'

'*Really?*' I said surprised. 'That would never do back home.'

'And many people have more than one job too!' he said, and retreated back into the kitchen to finish whatever task he had been engaged in.

I wanted to take some photos in the town. I'm determined to get some pictures here too. I don't know when I'll get the chance to return to Iceland.

I called Þorsteinn again. He was making a racket with dishes and I had difficulty attracting his attention. Eventually he heard me and came through from the kitchen.

'When will the meal be ready Þorsteinn? I'd like to go out for a while.'

'Come back in about thirty minutes, and I'll have a hot bowl of lamb soup waiting for you,' he said with a smile.

'OK, thank you.' I bounced out of the restaurant and headed for the exit. Once on the street, I decided to head down to the harbour and photograph some of the fishing boats and other activity around there. My digital Canon SLR is fitted out with an 'image stabilising' zoom lens to cut down on 'camera shake' that would normally lead to fuzzy photos. I must have a sharp image; it's very important to me. I like to enter photographic competitions at my local camera club back home in California. I have my own website too where I can sell the odd photograph.

First to take my attention was the string of fishing boats standing alongside the quay. I spotted a fisherman standing at the bow of the Siggi with a fishing net in his hands. He wore a green polo-neck sweater and rubber boots and appeared to be about thirty-something. I raised the camera to my eye and, 'click', he was transformed into a digital image on my camera's screen. I moved along the line of fishing boats tied up there. I spotted a young guy on the next boat dressed in rubber boots and a green sweater pulling on a fishing net. I stepped forward and raised the camera to my eye and click! Another one. I moved on down the quayside, and as I turned to take another shot of the same guy I had just snapped, someone gave a wolf whistle. I turned to see two figures standing on the next boat along. I smiled back at them and moved off in their direction, then I turned again to my previous subject who had, by this time, discovered me watching him. I snapped him too. I turned again and walked on to the next boat. One of the two who had whistled I saw was smiling at me. I deliberately took my time as I passed his boat. Then I had an idea. Maybe they would know how I could get to Uncle Pete, maybe they might even know him. I retraced my steps back to their boat and looked up at them with a broad grin plastered on, my hands behind my back. One of them came forward to the rail and looked down smiling. He wore a dark green sweater and rubber boots, and had fair, close-cropped hair and a broad smile on his face. He looked to be twenty-something. His companion looked younger and shorter and was of dark complexion, with shoulder length black hair.

I called to them, 'Hi! Do you speak English?'

The fair-haired one called back, 'Yes.'

'Can I come up?' I shouted back still maintaining my posture.

He nodded and indicated a short plank that was propped against the side of the boat. I was too short to get up onto the boat in the normal way, so I assumed that this is what the plank was for. I picked it up and placed it against the side, then walked up it towards them. They couldn't take their eyes off me. As I reached the top of the plank, I pretended to lose my balance. The fair haired one leaned out and grasped me tight by the arms and with help from his companion, was able to literally lift me up and onto the deck.

'Thank you,' I said smiling broadly. I introduced myself immediately.

The fair haired one must have been about six feet tall. His name was Sigurd. The black haired one was Páll.

Sigurd asked smiling, 'What did you want?'

I said suddenly, almost forgetting why I wanted to speak with them in the first place, 'em.... ' I hesitated. I went into my back pocket and took out the photo of Uncle Pete. 'Do you know him?'

Páll couldn't take his eyes off my figure.

Sigurd said, 'No, I don't think so. You could ask in some of the taverns in the town. Someone there is bound to know him.'

Páll said, 'Let me see.'

I came forward to him with the photograph in my hand for him to see. I think he just wanted to get a better look at me. I showed it to him.

'I think I've seen him around the quayside.' He smiled, then continued, 'If it's the same guy, he keeps himself pretty much to himself.'

'Would you know how to reach him?' I'm standing by his side now.

'No, I'm sorry.'

'He's my uncle and I'm supposed to be visiting him but I've no idea where he is at the moment.'

Sigurd said, 'Sorry we can't help. Can we assist you with anything else?' He had a big grin on his face.

I smiled back and said, 'No thanks.' Then I thought suddenly, *'I wouldn't mind a photo here.'* I said, 'Could I get a picture?' I indicated my camera.

Sigurd thought for a moment. 'Sure. The two of us?'

I nodded and took a few steps back to enable me to get them both into the frame, then pressed the button.

Páll said quickly, 'Can I get one of you too?'

I was just about to hand my camera to him when I thought, *'How do I get the picture to him?'*

He must have seen my puzzled expression because he said, 'I'll just get my camera.' He dashed into the wheelhouse and came back almost immediately clutching a small digital camera.

Sigurd took the camera from him and I stood beside Páll. He snapped us standing there together. Then it was Sigurd's turn.

He put his arm around my waist and said, 'You OK with this?'

I nodded.

Páll snapped us and I giggled as Sigurd kissed me on the right cheek.

'Thanks,' he said.

As I turned to go, I said, 'Thanks again. See you guys later

67

maybe.'

They both waved as I turned back to them briefly as I made my way down the plank towards the quayside again.

I thought I'd try to get some candid shots of the people who make their living here off the sea. I stood behind a telephone pole and framed my first 'victim'; an elderly guy dressed in dungarees carrying a box of fish across the street from the quayside. I snapped him just as he was passing one of the fishing boats that were tied up there. I spent the next ten minutes taking more candid shots, then a sudden thought flashed through my mind. Something else I have to do immediately. I don't know why I didn't think of this sooner. Uncle Pete's Post Office Box number. This might give me a clue to where he is located. If I find out where he is, I will have to see if there is a bus going anywhere near to where he stays, if not I'll have to hitch.

As I made my way back to the hotel, I was on the lookout for the Post Office. I spotted it on the corner of a street; I headed there now. Just before I pushed through the door, I spotted a sign there displaying the opening times. It was almost closing time; I had just made it. I went in the door and made straightway for the counter. There were no customers here, so I went up to the first window and.... there was no clerk there either, in fact there didn't appear to be anyone around at all. There was a buzzer on the counter, so I pressed it and I waited for a response. Shortly, a tall elderly male figure appeared from a back room looking irritated. I asked him if he had English. Yes he did, thank God! I produced a slip of paper with Uncle Pete's PO box number on.

I said, 'Do you know where this place is? This person's house I mean? I have to reach his place somehow.'

He replied as he read the note, 'It's not on a bus route, and the Post Office won't deliver there either.'

'Oh? Why not?'

'Too remote. It's in the mountains. Not many houses there.' He turned to go then added, 'We're closing soon.'

'Yeah, OK.' I tried another angle this time. 'When was the last mail picked up from here?' I may get the chance to meet him here if and when he comes to collect it. Maybe that's hoping for too much though.

He went back into the room from where he had just come, and messed around for something, then he returned to the counter. 'About two weeks ago?'

'Oh. Well, when is he likely to be back in here again?' I asked wondering if I wasn't wasting my time here.

'Couldn't say. Any time I suppose. He doesn't come in at any specific time or day. Just turns up whenever. Sorry I can't help you there.'

I sighed disappointedly, 'OK. It's not your fault. Thanks anyway.' At that, I turned on my heel and bounced through the exit to the street. Looks like I will have to hitch after all.

I made my way back to the hotel and just in time for Þórsteinn to serve my meal. I tucked in immediately and enjoyed my bowl of lamb soup. I thought over the day's events and how much I was enjoying this vacation so far. Apart from the unpleasant episode in the hostel, I'm feeling OK for the most part, but at the same time, if it wasn't for that particular event, I would never have met Tómas or Helga. Most importantly though, it was going out with Tómas yesterday and being in his company that I liked the most so far. Saying my goodbyes this morning to Tómas and Helga was the most difficult part, but I'm looking forward to seeing him again when I return to Reykjavík at the end of this vacation. Then they'll be more tears as I have to say goodbye yet again. We'll write to each other and keep in touch until I can get back here, or maybe he can come to California and visit. Oh well, I'm dreaming again.

I could feel a few tears forming now as I finished off my soup. I sniffled as I put my spoon back into my empty bowl. I was wiping my nose on the back of my hand as Þórsteinn appeared with the next course. He placed two plates, one with the roast lamb and the other one with the roast potatoes and veg on the tabletop.

I looked up at him with a smile and said, 'Thanks. That was lovely soup.' I sniffled again. I'm trying my best to hold back the tears, but they appeared anyway and began to roll down my cheeks. I tried wiping them away but I don't have a Kleenex to hand. I reached across the table for a paper napkin and began to wipe my nose and clean up some of the tears.

He just stood there looking down on me with a slightly puzzled expression. 'You OK?' He sounded concerned.

'Yeah. I'll be OK. Had to say goodbye to someone today, is all.' I helped myself to the roast potatoes and peas.

'Boyfriend?'

I nodded. 'Something like that.' I sniffled again as I spooned up the broccoli from the plate.

He said, 'I'll just get the gravy.' He returned seconds later with the gravy boat and placed it in the centre of the table. 'Enjoy your meal.' He departed before I could express my thanks to him.

That evening I decided that I was going to have to find a lift for tomorrow. I have to get to Uncle Pete, but I have no idea where he is. Some of the locals must know him; know where he lives.

Back in my room I went to the bathroom and freshened up. I decided not to take my purse or my bum bag with me; too tempting for pickpockets. I think I'll wear my jacket tonight; it could be cold out. I picked it up from a chair back and headed downstairs. Þorsteinn was around somewhere. I could hear him moving about.

A door opened suddenly and he came out from the kitchen wearing a blue apron. He smiled and said, 'Can I get you anything?'

I smiled back and said, 'No thanks. I'm on my way out to find a club or just any place with someone who speaks English.'

He just looked at me in curiosity.

I said, 'I have to find my Uncle Pete and I don't have any idea where to start looking. I thought maybe some of the locals could tell me.'

'Maybe. You'll have to ask around though.' He wiped his hands on the apron. He had been baking I think. It looked like he had flour on his hands.

'This is why I came to Iceland,' I said with a sigh. Then I suddenly remembered the photograph. I pulled it from my pocket and thrust it under his nose. 'Do you know him?'

He took it from me and studied it closely for a few seconds then he shook his head. 'Sorry. Can't help you.'

'OK.' I said disappointedly and put it back in my jacket pocket. 'I'll see you later then.' With that I put on my jacket and left the building.

I walked briskly down the street heading for the centre of town. I'm looking for a men's club or just somewhere that seamen, fishermen, or even servicemen, ex or otherwise would hang out. After some minutes, I spotted a building on my side of the street called Regnbogi (Rainbow). Several people, mainly fishermen and some in uniform – all males – were popping in and out of the joint. I'll try in here. Unfortunately, I had no luck there at all even after showing the photo to a number of different people. Disappointed, I left and headed down the street once again until I saw another club. I'll try this one. I pushed in through the door and, with hands in pockets, approached the bar. It was dark and smoky here, with the smell of stale booze. It was also fairly crowded with males, many in rubber boots and sweaters, one or two in sailor's uniforms. The barman didn't see me at first as he had his back to me. He turned as he polished a glass with a cloth and studied me. Then he turned away to serve another customer on my left.

As I perched myself on a stool, I could feel that the place was overheated. I felt too hot, so I began to loosen the buttons on my jacket starting from the top. A guy - thirty-something with short, black hair and a lot of stubble on his chin, sat on my right someways down the bar. He too wore a sweater and boots. He watched me as I slowly unbuttoned my jacket. As I loosened the last one, he could, no doubt, see my cleavage there, as his eyes suddenly brightened. I pulled it closed quickly and looked away to the barman avoiding his gaze.

I said to the barman, 'Talarðu Ensk?' (Do you speak English?)

He shook his head, then pointed to the guy who had been watching me. *'Oh God. There must be someone else in here who speaks English,'* I thought turning round to look at the clientèle.

The guy on my right moved closer to me up the bar. He said, 'You looking for something?'

I thought with disgust, *'Not what you're looking for anyway.'* I didn't look at him, but fixed my gaze on the glasses behind the bar just beyond where the barman stood. I said, 'Not you, that's for sure.'

He got up off his stool and came to stand behind me. The smell of booze and stale tobacco off of him was nauseating.

He asked, 'You got a problem, just say. Maybe I can sort it

out.' He looked into my face.

I sighed in resignation. I reached into the inside pocket of my jacket for the photo of Uncle Pete and quickly closed it again.

I showed it to him. 'You know him by any chance?'

He took it from me and studied it. He thought for a moment. 'Maybe. Your boyfriend or something?' he said with a sneer.

I ignored his remark and snatched the photo from his grasp. I got up from my stool and said, 'I'll find somebody else.'

I was about to turn away from him when he said, 'No you won't. That could take some time to do and you might never find him in the end.'

I'm wondering what he meant by that? 'Listen, I need someone to take me to him. He's my uncle and I'm supposed to be staying with him for a few weeks, that's why I have to find him.'

He moved closer to me. I drew back a little. I could smell foul breath and stale sweat.

He said, 'I know someone who might take you. He's got a truck.'

'Oh, does he?' I'm not sure why I said that. I visualised myself sitting in the back of the truck on my own.

'Yeah. You still want to go?'

'Sure,' I replied although I wasn't *really* sure if I wanted to ride in a truck with a stranger or not. I continued, 'Where is he? Is he in here?' I looked around the faces.

He nodded and pointed across the room to the far corner. A monster of a guy with a full black beard and wearing a thick red-chequered jacket sat hunched behind a table drinking what I took to be scotch, and playing a game of cards for money with his mates. He looked to be fifty-something, but then I could be mistaken. Every now and then he paused to light a pipe that appeared to have gone out.

The guy beside me said, 'I'll take you to him.' At that, he took me by the right arm and led me across the room. I shook off his hand. He put his hand round my waist instead. I unfastened his fingers and removed his hand quickly. I was now standing before this monster's table. He was a bear of a man. He was big and broad. I judged him to be over six feet tall. He didn't even look up. His two companions though were looking at me intently. I pulled my jacket closed speedily with my left hand. One of them was thirty-something and had a red scar running from his left eye to his jawline. The other one was about the same age group and was badly in need of a shave.

The guy behind me said, 'Jack? Somebody to see you.'

Blackbeard looked at his pipe. 'What do you want?' He said this without looking up. He wasn't smiling. His voice was as rough as sandpaper, and the accent was North American; I couldn't place it immediately. He turned to me and spat on the floor.

'Uncouth bastard,' I thought. I was unable to speak. I had a lump in my throat.

The guy behind me pulled a chair from somewhere and I felt myself being pushed down into it. I looked up at him and back to Blackbeard.

'Well?' he demanded examining his pipe. He pulled a box of matches from his pocket and started to re-light, then he looked up. 'Oh *God*, a woman. That's all I need right now!' The match went out. He struck another one. He sucked and sucked on the pipe stem. This time it caught.

I indicated the guy standing at my back, his hands now on my shoulders. I couldn't shake them off.

'He tells me,' I said and coughed nervously, clearing my throat, then I continued, 'that you can help me? You can take me to this guy? Do you know him?' I placed the photograph of Uncle Pete on the table.

He picked it up and looked at it, then back to me. 'Yeah, I know him alright; and you want to see him, right?' He threw the photo onto the tabletop.

I nodded. 'I'm willing to pay for the trip.'

He examined me again. 'I don't want your money.'

'What? You mean you'll do it for nothing?' I don't believe this guy.

He spat on the floor again. 'I don't do *anything* for nothin' babe.' A wry grin played across his lips.

I demanded, 'What do you mean by that?' I snatched up the photograph and pocketed it.

He said blowing smoke at me, 'Stand up and take off your jacket.'

He turned to his two companions with a grin, then

sniggered.

'I beg your pardon? I will not!' What's he playing at?

He gave a signal to the guy behind me. I was made to stand up, and the next thing I knew, my jacket was being pulled off of me. He let it drop onto the chair. I just stood there staring at the tabletop; it was intimidating. I have to keep my cool. I was now being scrutinised from head to foot by all three of them. His two companions made whistling sounds with their lips.

Blackbeard just stared, then smiled. 'You can sit down,' he said. He dragged on his pipe and blew smoke across at me.

I thought, *'His Highness has just given me permission to sit in his presence. What a jerk! What a nerve he has. Who does he think he is anyway? Mister High and Mighty indeed! I'll find a way to cut him down to size.'*

The guy behind me pushed me back down into the chair.

'What now?' I thought.

I'm beginning to wish I hadn't come in here. I'm going to ride in a truck with this animal? Anything could happen.

He said, 'We could start right away.'

'What? I *can't*,' I said in alarm. 'I have things to get first from Hotel Ísafjörður.'

'Oh yeah. I know, woman's things,' he said hoarsely and laughed. He took another puff of his pipe.

'What would *you* know about women?' I don't know why I said that! He might just tell me! He did!

'Listen here babe. By the time we're finished, I'll be able to tell you things about you that you don't even know about yourself!' He laughed out loud and his two companions joined in. They were about as disgusting as himself.

I didn't know what to say. I've surely made a mistake here. I stood up quickly and was about to turn to go when he said, 'I'll see you here about 5 o'clock tomorrow morning, OK?'

I said angrily, '*What*? Why so early?'

'That's it babe, or the deal's off!'

He stood up. He must have been about seven feet tall. I couldn't believe I was doing this.

He leaned close and ran his finger along my jawline. I moved my head away. 'Get your hand *off* me!' I was almost shouting at him now.

He said with a snicker, 'I make the rules around here babe. Do as I say and we'll get along just fine. Know what I mean?' His hand went to my left arm, but I withdrew it quickly. Then his right hand went onto my skin just above the jeans.

I pulled it off rapidly and stepped to the left out of the way. I said slowly and deliberately to him with a raised warning finger, 'If you touch me again......!'

He interrupted me with, 'Did you hear *that*? She's threatening me.'

'You go to *hell*!' I raised my voice just then, and was on the verge of screaming at him, when I caught myself. The other two were obviously enjoying this too. They didn't appear to have an ounce of brains between them; just doing as they were told. And I thought all Neanderthals were extinct! Just goes to show how wrong you can be.

Blackbeard shouted at them. 'Shut up!' They obeyed immediately. He turned back to me. 'Listen babe. No-one threatens me. I could snap you in two at the blink of an eye.'

He probably could too. I thought, *'My one-to-one combat would be of no use on him. The other two though...'* If it comes to the bit, I'll put my knife in his guts.

I turned away from him and made for the door clutching my jacket. My bare middle was now exposed to the cold night air. There is no sunset here in the summer, so it was still broad daylight as I stepped outside. There were deep shadows though between buildings, where the sun was hidden from view, low on the horizon.

I stopped briefly to put on my jacket and, as I retraced my steps back to the hotel, I reflected on the events of the last hour. Blackbeard was an animal. He was a bear of a man. All he lacked was a fur coat. The closest thing to a grizzly in human form that I have yet seen. I shivered at the thought of sharing a truck cab with him. Maybe I'll just forget about tomorrow. I'll think up an excuse to get away from him. I plan to tell Þórsteinn about this incident and maybe he can warn me in the morning if Blackbeard appears.

CHAPTER 8

That night I couldn't sleep for worrying about the next day. I tossed and turned all night. Sleep just wasn't happening for me. I was perspiring greatly, and my shirt was clinging wetly to my back. I got up and paced the room. I'm only wearing my nightshirt and my watch. I opened the glass door and stepped out onto the wooden deck. God, it was freezing! My bare feet were cold too! I'm wondering why the temperature of the water was cold last time I tried it. Of course, I remember now; he said it required maintenance. Well that was only hours ago so it's not likely to have been fixed already. A slight breeze blew my shirt up briefly and I shivered even more. I retreated indoors quickly and headed for the shower. I stayed there for the next ten minutes, then it was back to bed, but this time, without anything on. I just slid between the sheets, and this time I must have drifted off, because the next thing I knew, there was a hammering on my door.

I looked at my watch; 5 o'clock! *'What the hell?'* I thought.

I stepped out of the bed then suddenly realised that I wasn't wearing anything but my watch. The banging started again.

I called out whilst searching for something to wear, 'What? Who's there?' I found a bath towel and wrapped it around myself for quickness.

'Who do you think it is?' It was Blackbeard.

'Oh no,' I said to him through the door. 'I slept in.' And I did too!

'Open the door,' he demanded, 'or I'll break it down!'

I didn't have a choice here. I opened the door cautiously and put my head around it. I said, as he pushed it open further, 'I'm not dressed.'

He ignored me and came into the room anyway. I backed away from him, holding onto my towel tightly, lest it should slip.

He sat on the edge of my bed and sized me up.

I said, 'Can you let me dress now please?'

I was still backing away. My clothes – the ones I took off last night were ready to hand, but I would rather be wearing something not too revealing today for obvious reasons.

He spotted my looking at the clothes draped over the chair back where I had dropped them.

'Put them on,' he said tossing them to me.

I caught them and retreated into the bathroom closing the door behind me and turned the lock.

He shouted through the door, 'Make it quick. We don't have all day!'

I dressed hurriedly and used the toilet. Then I opened the door and stepped into the bedroom. He was standing there, arms folded across his massive chest.

He said, 'OK. Get your things together quick; we're leaving now.'

'Why the big hurry?' I thought. *'Is he escaping from something?'*

I grabbed all of my possessions including my camera and stuffed everything into my pack. I was only just able to shoulder my pack and grab my jacket in time, as he took me by the right arm and practically dragged me out of the room. My arm was hurting. His grip was vice-like.

'*Stop* it!' I shouted.

He ignored me and said, 'Hurry up, or I'll be forced to do this the hard way.'

'What does he mean by that?' I thought.

I didn't want to find out, so I struggled to keep up with him. He might be big, but he can move fast when he feels like it. I made a mental note of that for the future.

We had now reached the foot of the stairs. Þórsteinn appeared from the restaurant. He just stood there and stared in disbelief. Blackbeard stared back at him with a scowl, as he continued to pull me towards the door.

I shouted at him, 'I have to pay the bill!'

He shouted back at me, 'Shut up and behave yourself!'

He's treating me like a kid! He turned to Þórsteinn and slapped a sum of money on the reception desk. He ushered me outside then let go of my arm. It was still hurting. He pushed me forward towards a battered 4x4 truck across the road.

He said hoarsely, 'Get in.'

Just then, the cab door opened and one of his two companions – Scarface – sat there, a wide grin plastered across his ugly face.

I struggled to climb up onto the step. Blackbeard gave me a hand – literally – on my bottom, pushing me up into the cab. Scarface reached down to me and grasped me around the middle with both hands and I was lifted up into the cab.

I thought, *'That's the last time that you get your hands on me!'* Well, maybe that thought was just a mite premature; wishful thinking on my part.

He moved himself across the seat a little, just enough room for me to sit down. He reached round behind me and pulled the door closed. Then, he put his arm around my waist and his hand on my skin at the front. I fixed my gaze on the world outside and slowly removed it.

Blackbeard appeared through the driver's door. He saw Scarface sitting close, and with his arm around me.

He said in a voice that sounded like thunder, 'You! Get in the back!' He moved aside to let Scarface get out of the cab, then he started the truck. Scarface clambered into the back and we moved off slowly down the street.

I'm thinking, *'I thought he was in a hurry!'*

Where had the other Neanderthal got to? Then I spotted him, at least I thought I did, carrying something across the road towards us. It was, as it turned out, a large box of groceries. Was this for all of us, or just themselves, or maybe...? Oh, I don't care any more. I just want to get to Uncle Pete and the safety of his house, wherever that may be.

Blackbeard stopped the truck briefly to allow the other Neanderthal with the grocery box to jump aboard, then he hit the gas hard and we shot off like a bullet up a side road heading for the mountains; at least the road appeared to be going in that direction. This one was gravel!

Blackbeard reached into his pocket and took out a tin of tobacco.

'Christ', I thought, *'he's going to fix his pipe now! We'll go*

78

off the road for sure.'

With one knee pressed against the wheel to prevent the vehicle from wandering, he began to cut strips from a block of tobacco. At least at this point, the road was straight, but I could see a bend some distance ahead. He opened his window and tapped his pipe on the glass to empty the bowl of ash.

He said to me without turning, 'Well babe. You can relax now. We're on our way.'

'No I can't. Not so long as I have *you* for company!' I said in the most sarcastic voice that I could muster at this time in the morning.

'You'll get used to it babe.' He began to light his pipe, drawing hard on it until it caught. Tobacco smoke began to fill the cab.

I opened my window a little.

I said, 'Quit calling me that name please.'

He took the pipe from his lips and said, 'OK babe.' He grinned.

He took his knee off the wheel and concentrated on the road as we approached the bend. He said, without turning, 'You got a name babe?'

I ignored him.

'Come on babe, don't be shy. Speak to me.'

The truck slid dangerously to the right across the road towards the edge. I thought we were going to go off. I held on tight to the door handle although I was strapped in.

I said angrily, 'Shut up!'

He just laughed. 'You'll get to like me in time. When you get to know me better.' He winked, then laughed.

'Never! Not if I can help it,' I said sarcastically.

We started climbing, leaving the green fields and farms behind. No barriers here of any kind. Sometimes a sheer drop on the left or the right. If we should go off the road at any point, there's no hope for us.

He said, 'You're a feisty little number aren't you babe? But we'll soon sort that out.' He laughed as he negotiated another right-hand bend.

'*Excuse* me?' I said turning to him. 'What did you call me?'

'I've got you pretty well sized up babe. I've met your sort

before. Your dress wear says it all.' He laughed.

I turned to him angrily, 'What the hell do you mean by that? What's wrong with my dress wear?'

'Look at you?' He puffed on the pipe and blew smoke at me.

'It's the fashion stupid!' I spat out the words.

'You don't have to follow fashions babe. Would you walk around in a bikini?'

'For your information, I don't own one. Anyway, it's none of your damn business!'

'Ooh! I've really got her hackles up now!' He laughed again.

I said, 'I'm glad you think it's funny. I can see you're easily amused.'

Am I seeing things? I thought I saw a snowflake drift across the windscreen. That's all we need. God knows, it was cold enough for it. I shivered although it wasn't cold in here. Just looking outside was enough to give you the goosebumps.

He saw me shiver. 'You cold? I can warm you up good. We'll stop somewhere and.....!'

I cut him off with, 'Don't even think about it. Don't you dare touch me or you'll regret it.' I was serious.

'I make the rules around here babe, remember?'

I refused to acknowledge him and stared through the windscreen. I tried to concentrate on something; anything but this mess that I had gotten myself into. I thought of Tómas and his strong arms around me, and those lips. If only he was here now. Then I suddenly remembered that I hadn't called my dad. I was going to do that while I was in the hostel in Reykjavik, but it didn't happen, did it? I went into my pack and rummaged around for my cell phone. Would it work here?

Blackbeard saw me. He said, 'Don't think that'll be any use here babe.' He smiled.

I ignored him and switched it on then dialled dad's number. My screen said, 'NO SIGNAL'! Great! I hope he's satisfied.

He was. 'I told you babe,' he said with a smug look on his face.

'I told you babe.' I echoed his words. 'You're *pathetic*!' I

80

put the phone away and stared ahead.

He just laughed.

I heard a knock on the rear window. I turned to see Scarface grinning at me. I turned away quickly. Was he trying to get my attention? If he was, he failed. Oh *God*, I can't stand these people; uncouth, ill-mannered, common. I have to watch my back all the time. I don't know what their intentions are! Blackbeard would no doubt love to get me into his bed, if he has one. Pigsty would be more like it! Not if I can help it. If he so much as puts a finger on me, I'll do him an injury he won't forget in a hurry!

He said to me, 'We're going to eat now babe.' With that, he pulled the vehicle over to the side of the road and parked it. There was room enough for other vehicles to pass.

I continued to stare through the window.

He said staring into my face, 'Did you hear what I said babe?'

I ignored him.

He said finally, 'OK, suit yourself.' He opened the door and jumped out. He went to the rear of the truck and climbed aboard.

I thought I could smell food. I felt hungry, but I didn't want to dine with that lot! They were enough to make you want to throw up. I turned to look through the rear window. They were eating something alright, but I wasn't caring. I turned away from the window and continued to stare through the windscreen. I'm wondering what Uncle Pete will be like, if I ever see him at all!

I snapped out of my dreaming with someone tapping on the rear window. I turned to see Scarface grinning at me again. He was gesturing at me to come join them. Not on your life!

I turned away from the face at the window, then I thought, *'How am I going to eat, if I keep this up?'*

I think I'm going to have to trust them. Well at least till I have something to eat; I was hungry after all.

I opened the door and put on my jacket, then jumped down onto the ground. God, it was cold here. A chill wind was blowing which didn't help matters. I went to the rear of the truck. I couldn't see them on the back; I'm too short at 5 feet to see over the tailgate, so I had to jump up to get my head above it!

I heard a voice shout, 'Look, there she is there!'

The next thing I knew, the tailgate was being dropped.

Scarface bent and started pulling me up by one arm, then Blackbeard came to help too. He went under my jacket at the back and grasped my jeans tightly, pulling me up without effort.

I thought, *'My God, he has some strength there.'* I actually said thanks to him.

He smiled and said, 'Come on and get warmed up.'

I hope he doesn't mean..... ! He led me to the little alcove that projected from just above the rear window. I couldn't decide if this alcove was part of the original design of the truck or not. No matter; it was welcome on a day like this. They had a gas stove there in the alcove with a bottle. Stubble Chin was cooking the food.

I was watching Blackbeard all the time. I daren't turn my back on *any* of them. I just don't trust them.

He pointed to a pile of sacking on the floor just under the alcove. 'Come on. We'll get you warmed up good in no time.'

I looked at it in horror. What are they going to do to me here? I can feel panic building up inside me. No! I think I want to get out of here fast. Just as I turned to go, Blackbeard caught me around the waist.

He said, 'Come on babe. It's OK. Just sit down there and make yourself comfortable.'

That's about the last thing that I'd want to do in present company!

'Come on now. Sit!' he insisted.

I refused to sit and stubbornly stood my ground.

He pushed me backwards and I fell heavily on my bottom onto the sacking.

I cried out, 'No!' Tears began to form. They were running down my cheeks fast.

He saw them and said, 'What's the matter now babe?'

I didn't reply. I'm losing control already, and we've only just started the journey. At this rate I'll be a total wreck by the time I get to my destination. What will Uncle Pete think of me if he sees me in this state.

Blackbeard said to me, 'Take off your jacket?'

I cried, 'Why? I won't do it! You can't make me!'

Tears are forming even faster now. He could see them running down my front too. My top was soaked. A wet stain was

82

beginning to form on the front of my white top just above my navel.

Blackbeard took off my jacket, ignoring my protests and more tears.

He said, 'You don't want to get your jacket dirty do you? Now eat this and you'll feel better.'

He handed me a paper plate with fried chicken in breadcrumbs. I ate it and, surprisingly, enjoyed it.

I was sitting with my back to the wall. I feel safer like that. This way, no-one can get behind me; take me by surprise. These two I could take on one at a time, but both together? I don't know. With my knife in my hand I could be a formidable opponent!

He asked, 'Drink?'

I nodded. I sniffled and tried to recover my composure. I wiped my nose with the back of my hand.

He pulled out a can of beer from somewhere and thrust it under my nose.

I shook my head.

He shrugged his shoulders in resignation and moved away from me. He helped himself to more food.

He said to me, 'I'll be in the cab if you want me.'

I thought, *'In your dreams.'* I stared at the floor.

Blackbeard walked away and jumped off the tail of the vehicle. I heard him get into the cab and close the door. The other two opened cans and drank greedily.

I ate more of the chicken and almost choked on some breadcrumbs.

Scarface came over to me and sat on my left. 'Are you warm now?' he asked, his speech a little slurred. I noticed that he had had two empty beer cans on the floor beside him and was now working on a third!

I nodded, still sniffling and staring at the floor.

His companion came over to us and held out a dish to me. It had French fries in it. Before I could say anything, he had emptied them into my plate. I didn't look at him, but sniffled instead. Are these the ones that he didn't want himself? No, it couldn't be that. They looked perfectly OK. I tasted one; then I couldn't stop myself. I finished them off in no time. I didn't realise I was that hungry, but then I had no breakfast this morning.

Scarface offered me some beer from his can. I shook my head. I'd rather be shot than poisoned. He took another can from a box beside him and offered that to me instead.

He said slowly, 'That's all......,' he hiccuped, then continued, 'we have to drink here.'

I took the can from him. I don't drink beer. Oh what the hell. I pulled the ring-pull and drank the liquid down. It was refreshing. I spluttered and almost choked when a sudden thought struck me. *'Is he trying to get me drunk or something?'*

He said, looking into my face, 'Are you cold?' He put his arm around my shoulders, and his left hand on my left arm.

I prised his fingers off and tried to move away from him, but I couldn't due to my nearness to the stove on my right.

He put his right hand on my neck, his left on the top of my left arm again and said, 'Can I kiss you?' He hiccuped again. 'Just a little one?' He definitely sounded drunk now.

'I beg your pardon?' I said in alarm. Did I hear right? No way! I prised his fingers off my arm and attempted to stand, but he pulled me down again. '*Stop* it! Go away please! Just don't *touch* me!' I was on the point of screaming at him.

He leaned over and pulled my head towards his own, then kissed me on the lips before I could do anything. I didn't like it. It was disgusting, especially when I didn't want it. He put one hand on the back of my head and pushed his face into mine, his lips smothered me. He wasn't even doing it right. He was obviously stupid drunk, the jerk.

I made as if to stand up, then turned and slapped him hard across the face. He was taken completely by surprise. He was speechless. I had made my point, and forcefully too! I stood up, taking my jacket with me.

I turned to him and said slowly and deliberately, 'If you touch me again, I'll take off the offending arm at the shoulder and shove it up your ass, OK?'

I just wanted him to know, and his accomplice there too, that this girl means business and is not to be messed with! With that, I marched to the rear of the truck and jumped onto the ground. I went back to the cab and climbed in.

Blackbeard looked at me curiously. 'What are you looking so smug about?' He was smiling.

I wasn't when I replied, 'I just wiped the floor with your friend there.' I indicated the rear window with my thumb.

'What are you talking about?' He couldn't believe his ears.

'He kissed me on the lips, and he got a slap for it.'

'Did he babe? I'll sort him out later. He was probably drunk.' He turned and said, sounding concerned, 'You all right otherwise babe?' He put his hand on my arm and caressed the skin.

I removed it quickly and said, 'Next time he touches me, the offending arm will be sticking out of his ass, and it'll take a surgeon to remove it!'

A wry grin worked across his lips, then he laughed, and laughed. 'I'm impressed! There's a side of you I hadn't bargained for. Got more surprises for me babe?' He started lighting his pipe again.

'You'd better believe it!' I added, 'He's lucky I didn't put him in the hospital. I can do it you know!'

He blew smoke across at me, then examined the pipe stem as though seeing it for the first time. He said starting the truck, 'We'd better get going. There's bad weather coming. Snow.'

I turned to him and asked, 'How do you know that?'

'Trust me I know. It's snow all right. Didn't you see the snowflakes earlier babe?' He hit the gas pedal hard and we shot off up the road again.

'That's all we need,' I said with a sigh.

He was driving fast.... well, about 45 mph. That's fast on a gravel road, especially in Iceland. We hit a left-hand bend at speed.... 50 I think. I thought we were going to go off, but Blackbeard managed to regain control of the truck in time.

After a few more minutes, we began to see snow on the ground; not a lot but enough to cause concern. Snowflakes began to fall too. They were quite small and insignificant at this point.

He said turning to me, 'What's your name?'

Hey that's a new one. He didn't call me babe this time. Has he taken leave of his senses? Maybe he should see a doctor!

Snowflakes were falling faster now and getting larger.

I said almost reluctantly, 'It's Sam.' I said this without looking at him.

He smiled and said, 'OK Sammy.'

I turned to him and said, 'Are you doing this deliberately?'

I was angry now. 'My name is Sam, OK?'

I fixed my gaze on the now snow-covered landscape outside.

'Damn!' he exclaimed suddenly. He shifted gear.

I looked at him in alarm. 'What the hell is it *now*?'

'We're losing traction. Should have snow chains on!'

'*Great*! So what happens now?'

I'm holding on tight to the door handle as he takes a right-hand bend. We slid across the road then came to an abrupt halt.

'What the hell *now*?' I said in alarm.

The snow was deeper here. Well, what do you expect in the mountains?

Blackbeard said, 'Think we've got a flat. I knew it didn't feel right.'

'Oh God no. What next?' I'm feeling ill. Didn't get much sleep last night. All I can think of right now is climbing into a warm bed..... by myself, or Tómas...... if only!

He opened his door and jumped out. It was now a white-out out there. You couldn't see anything at all through this snow. It was a curtain of white with seemingly nothing beyond. Blackbeard jumped into the rear of the truck and rummaged around for something. In the meantime, the driver's door opened and Scarface appeared.

I said to him, 'Oh *no*, not *you* again.'

His blue-chequered jacket was covered in snow.

He said to me with a grin, 'Warm me up babe. I need a cuddle.' His speech was slurred as usual.

I turned to him and said, 'Not on your life!' I put on my jacket, opened the door and jumped out. Preferable to being in close proximity to this animal.

It was cold out here; very cold! I looked at my watch. It was minus 10 degrees! My hands were freezing. I went to examine the flat.

Blackbeard was already on the job. He had a jack in place and was in the process of taking off the wheel when I appeared.

He turned to me in alarm, 'What are *you* doing here? You'll catch your death. Get back inside now! The last thing I need is a *woman* interfering!'

I said to him, '*Excuse* me? I am trying to help!'

He shouted back at me, 'You can help by staying out of the way!'

I screamed at him above the howling wind, 'Do not shout at me please; I'm only here!'

He had the wheel off now. 'Get back in the cab. You're not dressed for this weather. Look at your footwear? As for your clothes....' He trailed off.

The wind was rising and I was getting colder. I looked at my watch; the temperature had dropped to minus fifteen! I said through now-chattering teeth, 'Once you've fixed this wheel, what then?'

He rolled the spare into place and began to fix it. 'I have a summerhouse on this road. We'll try to make for there and weather out the storm.'

'Oh God no!' I thought. *'Houses have bedrooms....!'* I shouted, 'I'm not staying under the same roof as *you*. Forget it!'

He turned to me and shouted back, 'Behave yourself and do as you're told! Now get back in the cab!'

I shouted back, with hands on hips, 'No I won't! You cannot and will not dictate to me, understand?'

He shouted, 'Perfectly!' He turned and lifted me up bodily and carried me to the cab.

I resisted and struggled to get out of his arms, but all attempts to get free were futile. He was too strong. He shouted to Scarface. The door opened and I was pushed up into the cab.

I shouted back at him, 'You'll regret this!'

Scarface grinned at me. He was sitting up close.

I said to him, 'Keep *away* from me.'

He just sat there and grinned. Then he said with slurred speech, 'Come here babe and give me a cuddle.'

I couldn't get away. Where could I go? I was trapped here with this animal. He put his arm around my shoulders, then tried to remove my jacket. I shouted at him, 'Go *away*!' I tried to push him away, but he insisted on pulling at my jacket. I shouted at him, 'No!' He ignored me and kept pulling at the jacket. 'Go, *away*!' I screamed.

'Come here babe. You know what I want and I know you want it too.' He hiccuped, then he put his arm round my waist, caressing the skin at the same time! Then he kissed me on the cheek.

I turned and slapped him hard across the face.

He slapped me back!

I screamed at him, 'What the *hell*!' I've just about reached boiling point!

He put his hand on my right shoulder and pulled me down onto my back. One hand went under my top and cupped my left breast; his lips onto my neck. He was kissing me there. His hand then started groping; moving under the cup. He had now found my breast under the bra and was caressing it. Enough!

I shouted, 'Remove your hand or I'll break your bloody arm!'

He ignored me and continued with his groping.

'OK, you *asked* for it!' I said in exasperation. I grasped his wrist with both hands, and in one swift movement, I had twisted his arm up his back until I heard a crack! It's not broken, but next time I'll take it off!

'Ah!' he cried. 'You little *bitch*! I'll get you back good. You'll see!'

I said to him slowly, 'If you touch me again I'll *kill* you! You'd better believe that!' I meant it too.

Blackbeard appeared through the driver's door. At this moment I felt myself losing control again. I covered my face with my hands as I could feel the tears coming.

He saw me and asked, 'What's going on Sam? Has he done something to you?'

Jesus, he's using my name again! Is he taking a liking to me? I hope not! I can't let my guard down no matter what. I just nodded.

He opened his door again and grasped Scarface's jacket, pulling him out of the cab with him, then he threw him onto the ground.

He shouted at him, 'If you so much as *look* at her again, I'll break both your legs. You hear me?'

Scarface said in a pleading voice, 'She was leading me on boss. She encouraged me.'

I heard Blackbeard say, 'Why don't I believe that? You're going in the back for the rest of the journey.'

I saw him lift Scarface up bodily and throw him into the

back of the truck, then he got back into the cab. He started the truck again and we moved off, then, about thirty minutes later, another problem. As we approached a slight gradient, the wheels started spinning. He engaged the four-wheel-drive and we moved off again, then another few minutes later and we stopped again!

'Hey, get these two in the back out of there and tell them to start pushing,' he said.

I turned to him in disbelief. 'Who, *me*?'

'Yeah you. Tell them I sent you, and that it's an order. Any problems and you come to me, OK?'

'O – K,' I said slowly. I said under my breath as I was leaving the cab, 'Anything you say boss.'

I jumped down and hurried around to the back of the truck. I had to jump up and grasp the top of the tailgate in order to see over it, then try to attract their attention. I guess getting their attention is the easy bit; it's getting them to *do* something that's going to be the problem! The top of my head is all they would see of me at first. I pulled myself up, then I put my leg over the tailgate. Well I made it here, now to attract their attention. I opened my jacket and just stood there with hands on hips. The wind was blowing hard now and the snow falling heavily. My bare midriff was freezing and I felt myself chilled to the bone!

Scarface turned and stared, then looked away again quickly. I guess he's learning. The other one awoke with a start on being prodded by Scarface. They both stared again.

I said, 'Get your asses down there and start pushing. We're stuck!'

They both stood up and just stared at me.

I shouted at them; it was almost a scream. 'Come *on*, we haven't got all day!'

The other one shouted back, 'We're not taking orders from you!'

Whoa! Where did *that* come from? That's the first time that I've heard him speak. The accent was foreign. I couldn't place it. European?

I shouted back, 'OK suit yourselves, but you'll answer to him.' I pointed to Blackbeard in the cab.

Oh they didn't like that. They approached me in a threatening manner, their body language said it all, but I stood my ground. My left hand was slipping into the back of my jeans, searching for the knife, just in case.

I stepped aside to let them pass. Scarface dropped the tailgate and the two of them jumped onto the ground. I joined them there, then I shouted to Blackbeard to start moving. He hit the gas hard, and the two of them began to push. I stood back out of the way as I thought, but unfortunately, I miscalculated and I found out when it was too late, that I was standing in line of fire. The dirt off the road; mud, snow and gravel hit me full in the chest. I tried to shield myself from this shower of dirt and snow with my hands, but it was no use. Freezing mud and water coming at me at speed; I didn't have a chance! I just stood there and cried. My top and my jeans were soaked through. I was a mess! I just dropped to my knees and cried hysterically, and thumping the ground with my fists. I felt as though my sanity was slipping away. I was truly freezing now and my body so cold, I thought I would surely pass out. I could hear the wind howling loudly in my ears. This only made me feel worse, then the hysterics of the two Neanderthals standing laughing at me, Scarface in particular.

Blackbeard was on them in a trice. 'I thought I gave orders for you two to start pushing?' he bellowed at them.

'We *were* pushing boss,' Scarface shouted back through the howl of the wind. It was blowing a real blizzard now.

Blackbeard approached me, still on my knees and crying. I wasn't sure what to do next.

'You're cold. Come back inside,' he said as he picked me up.

I just stood there with the tears running down my face and my front, making me feel even colder.

Blackbeard went back to the cab and started the truck. The two Neanderthals started pushing and eventually the vehicle was able to free itself.

Blackbeard jumped out again and led me to the truck by the arm, but instead of helping me inside, he pushed me quickly against the side of the truck and his right hand went under my top and onto the skin just under my left breast. His left he tried to push down the back of my jeans, but I managed to remove it quickly. I'm wearing a thong anyway. Then he caressed my bottom through the jeans instead; his right went between my breasts under the bra and touched me there.

'*Stop* it! What are you *doing*?' I cried and gasping with the cold.

I tried to push him away but I did not have the strength, and he was too strong for me anyway.

'Stop it *now*!' I screamed at him. What was he trying to *do*!

I heard him mutter, 'I haven't been with a woman for *ages*.' He buried his face between my breasts and his tongue started exploring there.

'And forgotten your manners too!' I said through gasps. This was due mainly to the extreme cold. My hands and feet were freezing too.

He was making groaning and grunting sounds and kissing me on the neck and shoulders. It was like being with an animal. Beside this seven foot giant, I was only an elfin-like figure.

I felt myself being crushed against the truck; I could hardly breathe! I tried pushing him away again, but it's impossible! I'm panicking. My teeth are beginning to chatter! I've never felt so cold in my life; not even when I took that plunge into the icy cold pool! Tears are running down my cheeks.

I said to him through sobs, 'I'm very cold. I'm freezing, and I have to get warm now. Can you let me go *please*?'

As he pushed his lower body against me, I could feel an ominous bulge press against my stomach. Just as well it was still inside his pants!

I could feel his hand cupping my left breast; his fingers caressing the nipple. At this point – excuse the pun – he could feel that I was cold because it was hard to the touch. I pulled his hand from under my top, then his lips were on my neck and working their way down again. More groaning sounds. He was warm, and I could feel the heat from his body cross to mine. That was the only welcome part of this whole episode. Would it not have been better to have waited until I had a wash? I was a *mess*! I must have looked a sight in my muddy clothes; some of it on my face and neck. I don't like being touched like this and I want it to stop now!

I cried, '*Stop* it! I want to get warm!'

He held me tight whilst his hands wandered up the back of my top towards my bra clip.

'Oh *God*,' he said through gasps. 'Can't get enough of this babe!'

'No!' I cried out. 'Don't do this please! Get *off* me!'

I don't know where I suddenly found the strength, but I surprised myself too by being able to squirm out of his embrace. I ducked down quickly beneath his arms and out of the way, then broke into a run towards the back of the truck and away from them. I of course knew that this little show of mine couldn't last, as I had nowhere to run to. I fell to my knees and just broke down again. I've just lost control for the third time today!

He came after me, but I didn't have the strength to resist. I was too weak with the cold. He picked me up bodily and I was carried to the cab and laid to rest on the seat, in an upright position I hasten to add! The other two got into the passenger side and Blackbeard sat with me. I was warming up now, with the heat coming off the engine. Blackbeard put his arm around me and I leaned against him. *What*? What am I *thinking*? He's just fondled my breasts; kissed me on the neck and tried to get into my jeans....! I must be delusional to let him get this far, when earlier I couldn't bear to have him within ten miles of me. I still don't trust him though. As for the other two wastes of space....! I fell asleep in this position.

I awoke with Blackbeard shaking me. He said, 'We're here babe.'

I looked through the side window and could see a large wooden house painted black with a very steeply pitched red-coloured roof. Some of the snow was sliding off it. The only thoughts that were going through my mind at this moment were of me standing under a hot shower and getting off all this dirt, then sliding under clean sheets and resting my poor body. I need a good night's sleep then I'll feel better in the morning.

Blackbeard opened his door and stood on the footplate.

I grabbed my pack and jacket and followed him out to the door. I asked looking up at him, 'This your house?'

He replied, 'Yeah, summer house. Lots of folks in Iceland have them babe.'

He opened the door with a key and we stepped inside. It was open plan with a spiral staircase leading to the bedrooms on the left; wood panelled walls throughout. Kitchen on the left too. It was roomy but cold, since there hadn't been any heating on in here for some time. The house was well insulated from the cold, so frozen pipes weren't a problem he said. A TV and a hi-fi unit stood in the far corner. A tall bookcase and desk with a PC on the right opposite the window. A circular gas fire stood in the centre of the room; how unusual. In different circumstances this could be nice and cozy. He went over to the fire and turned it on. 'Soon get this place warmed up.' He disappeared into the kitchen and turned on the electricity.

When he came out again he said to me, 'Babe, you can have your shower now, and I'll just turn on the heating in the bedroom. It's all done with electricity here in the mountains. There are solar panels at the back of the house that provide *all* of the electricity I need here. No piped hot water either.'

Where does he get all the money to buy this stuff? If this is a summer house, then he has another one elsewhere? I know it sounds ridiculous, but I think I'm beginning to warm to him a little, although I still don't trust him fully. I now know that he is completely different from the other two. Who is he anyway? And the other two creeps....?

He led me upstairs; I followed at a discreet distance. He showed me into a small bedroom where I dropped my pack and jacket on the floor, then to the en suite bathroom with the shower. I was so tired and exhausted, I couldn't even face taking off my clothes first. I voiced this fact to Blackbeard whilst he turned on a radiator. The heat, I noticed was coming through already since I was standing with my back to it. He pulled a couple of bath towels from a cupboard beside the shower and put them on the radiator.

'Oh no,' I thought suddenly. *'Two bath towels? I hope he doesn't think....! No way! There's not a chance that I'm going to let him shower with me! Such a thing is unthinkable!'*

I said, 'Can you leave now please? I want to take off these clothes and shower.'

He just stood there and watched me as I kicked off my wet sneakers and took off my socks. I reached up to the shower controls and turned on the pressure to high and the temperature to hot! Then I stepped in backwards and just stood there under the water. I reached up behind my head and removed my hair clasp and put it on the soap dish behind me.

Blackbeard just stood there with a question mark above his head. He's probably thinking I've taken leave of my senses, and maybe I have! I could feel the hot water seeping through my filthy clothing. It was indeed a strange feeling to shower in this way. I reached round and picked up the soap and began to lather my clothes with it. The muck was coming off with the water anyway, but the soap also helped. Blackbeard turned on his heel and left the bathroom without saying a word, no doubt convinced that he now had a madwoman to contend with! Now that he had gone, I started stripping off my clothes and then the showering started in earnest.

Later, about thirty minutes later in fact, I finally left the shower, suitably wrapped in a towel and clutching my wet clothing, then I dropped them in the sink. I'll wash them later. I changed into fresh clothing; blue jeans with a tight-fitting blue t-shirt on top that doesn't tuck in. I felt a new woman already. The once pink cotton socks and my sneakers too, went into the sink with the other clothes. I only have one pair with me, so it's bare feet for the rest of the day. Well, time to catch up on some reading. I lay down on the bed and propped myself on one elbow, together with my current good read; a photography book that I had bought back home.

I must have dozed off for a while because the next thing I knew, there was a knock on the door. 'Yeah?' I said sleepily; my head still on the pillow.

The door opened and Blackbeard came in. He approached the foot of the bed.

'We're going out for supplies babe. If we're not back here by one o'clock, just make yourself something to eat.'

'Sure,' I replied absently without looking up.

He hesitated as if waiting for me to say something else. 'Well, I'll be off then.' He turned and left the room.

I looked at my watch: 11:30. I spent the next ten minutes brushing out my hair then fixed the clasp on my ponytail. I was thinking, I'd just throw my clothes into the washing machine. I went to the bathroom and took everything from the sink and made my way downstairs. I could feel the heat from the gas fire rise to meet me as I descended the spiral staircase to the living room. I made straight for the kitchen and the washing machine. I found an instruction manual in a drawer and after consulting it, just threw everything in including my sneakers and turned it on.

'Good; that takes care of that,' I thought contentedly.

I turned on a portable radio that I found on the windowsill. There was classical music playing; it was ballet, from Romeo and Juliet I think. I began to hum along with the music and dance around the room like a ballet dancer, now and then going up on tiptoes and pirouetting on the spot. Round and round the kitchen I went, until the washing machine interrupted my 'mid-summer's night dream' with its racket. The machine stopped briefly and I began to waltz out of the kitchen and into the living room; once round the gas fire and across to the hi-fi. I looked at the controls there and chose the radio. I found the same station and turned up the volume. I waltzed around again and again on the spot and pirouetting here and there, then round and round the fire several times. That was me thoroughly exhausted now. I was tired enough as it was.

Presently, I heard a sound outside; I couldn't think what it could be. I stopped abruptly and listened carefully. Was that from outside the door? I went to the hi-fi and turned down the volume. I crossed to the front window and looked out. Nothing! I definitely heard something out there; I'll try the door.

I opened it. 'Oh *no*!' I exclaimed as I suddenly realised who it was!

Scarface stood there grinning at me! He held onto the doorpost for support. He was drunk again. He put his hand on my chest and pushed me backwards into the room.

'Now bitch,' he hiccuped. 'Time,' he hiccuped, 'for my revenge!'

I said frantically, 'What the hell are *you* doing here?' I was backing away from him.

Several wild thoughts connected with self preservation were running through my mind at this moment. At the top of my list; running very fast in the opposite direction. I turned to run but he tripped me up and I fell heavily on the floor on my front. Before I could recover he was on top of my legs, and was pulling my two hands together round my back. He bound them with tape. His hands went under my t-shirt and he unclipped my bra, then he pulled me up by the arms and all but dragged me to the kitchen table. He's going to try to rape me, but he's in for a few surprises. I watched my bra fall down and onto the floor. He forced me onto my back on the table. I kicked out quickly with my right foot towards his groin area. Would bare feet have the same impact as my sneakers? Unfortunately they didn't! He groaned a little and stepped back from me, but recovered quickly and resumed where he had left off. Next he went for my jeans. Down came the zipper, and then he began to pull my jeans down! I'm wearing a thong. Now he had the jeans completely off me! I performed a backwards somersault over the tabletop and landed on my feet; my gymnastics training kicking in here.

He went to one of the worktops and began to search for something in a drawer; I suspected a knife! He had to support himself on the worktop. I ran from the kitchen and into the living room, heading for the stairs. I was well ahead of him, but I had no intention of going right up. I don't want to get trapped in a room where he can rape me. I have other plans forming. I stopped in my tracks and turned to face him. I watched him approach me slowly, holding onto the bannister as he did so, and when he was within striking distance, I jumped at him with both feet hitting him full in the chest and knocking him backwards down the stairs again. I landed on the tail of my spine; the pain was excruciating. I let out a loud gasp, and I think I screamed too! My bottom will be bruised for a month.

As he hit the deck, he dropped the knife. I got up and ran down towards him and retrieved it. I ran upstairs again and made for my room. Thank goodness I had left my door open. Once in, I sliced the tape on my hands with ease then locked the door. I stripped off the t-shirt and replaced it with a grey t-shirt from my pack. It comes down passed my waist. I don't have another pair of jeans to wear; one is down in the kitchen and the other in the wash.

I looked at my watch; almost noon! Another whole hour before Blackbeard returns. I'm wondering why Scarface wasn't made to go with them? He's not going to stop till he gets what he wants. Who is this guy anyway? What's his relationship to Blackbeard? So many questions!

I could hear him coming down the hallway towards me; then the door handle was turned.

He shouted, 'Come on out,' he hiccuped, 'bitch,' hiccup, 'and I'll go easy on you! You know you've,' he hiccuped again, 'got nowhere to run to!'

I shouted back, 'Go to *hell*! You'll have to come and get me!'

He was absolutely right; I didn't have anywhere to run to, but I have this knife and I'll use it if I have to.

'Do I have to break it down,' hiccup, 'or are you going to come out?'

I have a plan forming. I went to the bed and got under the duvet with my knife at the ready.

There was a terrific bang as Scarface hit the other side of the door with something heavy; hammer, axe? I couldn't be sure. Whatever it was, the whole door shook, then it began to splinter in places. Blackbeard is going to be very angry when he gets back and finds this mess. Presently, the door shattered and Scarface came almost stumbling into the room. He carried a two handed rock-breaking hammer in his hands. He dropped it onto the floor. When he saw me lying there, my eyes looking over the duvet at him, he hesitated, then kicked off his shoes, dropped his pants, and stepped out of them. He jumped onto the bed and pulled down the duvet slowly, and was greeted by a long-bladed knife at his throat and a broad grin plastered across my face. He stared at the knife in disbelief.

'Hi!' I said brightly, just before I kneed him in the groin.

He cried out in pain and I dived out off the bed, and as I darted from the room, I heard him curse my back. I headed downstairs as fast as my legs could carry me, still clutching the knife. When I reached the kitchen, I made straight for my blue jeans that were lying next the kitchen table and pulled them on first. Then I took out my sneakers and socks from the washing machine. Next time he comes at me, I will be able to disable him good.

He has to get his pants on first after he's recovered. I could hear him coming downstairs slowly. He shouted, 'You've got nowhere to go bitch,' he hiccuped. 'Might as well give up now!'

Sounded as though he was limping or something. I hope it hurt; if it didn't, the next one certainly will! Will he have the hammer? I have this knife and also my own in the back of my jeans. I slammed the kitchen door closed. There's no lock here so I jammed a kitchen chair under the door handle. This is not going to keep him out very long. I can slow him down however. He tried the doorknob, but it wouldn't budge, so then he tries his shoulder. That doesn't work either, then he hits it with the hammer! It starts to splinter then another blow, and another. It's just a matter of time now. I put the knife between my teeth and picked up a kitchen chair and held it in front of me; legs pointing towards the door. I felt like a lion tamer, although I think I'd prefer to take my chances with a lion than this brute. I was now standing on the opposite side of the table from the door with my back to the kitchen window.

Just then, the door caved in and Scarface stood there brandishing the hammer! It's heavy-looking even in his hands.

He dropped it on the floor at his feet and said, 'OK now, *hic*, give me the knife.' He hiccuped again.

I thought, *'Yep, you'll get it alright; in the guts if you come near me.'*

He said, staggering towards me, 'You can't go *anywhere*,' he hiccuped again. 'You know that.'

I kept backing away from him towards the window. I've decided on one-to-one combat; it'll disable him good. I put down the chair and worked my way round to the worktop from where he had first taken the knife and opened the drawer. I dropped it in and closed it. I'm now on his side of the table. He's got a question mark above his head now. Probably thinks I'm crazy disposing of the knife, but he's in for a surprise. He made a lunge at me and grasped me by the arms. I immediately threw myself onto my back on the floor, grasping his sweater and the shirt that he wore under it with both hands, and at the same time, drawing my knees up to my chest, then I threw him backwards over my head. He landed heavily on his back. It knocked the wind out of him temporarily, then, as I jumped to my feet and stood facing him lying there, he started to get up slowly. I kicked him viciously under the chin and this knocked him backwards. He fell to the floor and just lay there moaning.

'Now to finish the job,' I thought as I picked up the hammer.

Jesus it was heavy, but this next action was going to be *very* satisfying. His right hand was lying flat on the stone floor. I trod on his arm briefly to keep it from moving, then lifted the hammer as high as I could and brought it down hard on his hand.

Bones shattered while blood splattered across the floor. He screamed out, then appeared to lapse into unconsciousness! Well, I guess he got his just deserves at last. Satisfaction? You *bet*!

I looked at my watch: 12:45, then I heard a vehicle pull up outside. Blackbeard? I ran to the front door and flung it open wide. I just broke down and cried. Those tears were the real McCoy! I just fell to my knees. I'm not sure what happened next. I think I may have passed out with exhaustion.

CHAPTER 9

I awoke suddenly and sat bolt upright. I wasn't immediately certain where I was, then, after a few seconds it all began to fall into place. I looked at my watch: 5:15! I was in my room, sitting up in bed and fully clothed minus my shoes and socks on top of the duvet. I noticed that the door had been replaced by a heavy curtain.

I got up out of the bed and went to the shower. I turned the temperature to cold; I'm trying to waken myself up properly, and I want some answers. I stayed in there for about fifteen minutes then came out and dried off. I wrapped myself in the towel and was just about to put on my nightshirt when I heard someone knocking on the doorpost. I got into the bed quickly just as a figure emerged through the curtain. My heart missed several beats. I snatched up the duvet quickly and covered myself with it. It was Blackbeard! He came over to the bed.

I just sat there looking up at him. 'Did *you* put me here?'

'Yeah. Be a good idea for you to get some sleep now.' He was about to turn away from me.

'I'd like some answers please.'

'Like what?' he asked.

'Like why you went out leaving me alone with that animal? He tried to rape me you know – twice!' Tears started flowing down my cheeks.

He sat on the edge of the bed and stroked the hair at the side of my head. 'The bastard was drunk out of his skull babe, and didn't get back when he should have. I know I should have gone out looking for him, but... ' He trailed off. 'I didn't have time to wait for him.... '

I interrupted, 'Who is that guy anyway? What are you doing mixing with his sort?'

100

'The two of them were in jail. They're out doing community service. I had them doing work for me, breaking rocks out there at the back of the house.'

'So that's where he got the hammer from?'

He nodded, then stood up from the bed again and began pacing the room. 'I'm supposed to be keeping an eye on them.'

'Jesus,' I thought. *'I could have been killed!'* I said sarcastically, 'Looks like you failed then.'

'I didn't fail. Everything was going fine until *you* showed up.' He started shouting at me.

I shouted back, 'Excuse me! So *I'm* to blame am I?'

'Yes!' He was shouting louder now. 'If you hadn't showed up, *none* of this would have happened!'

'You've got a nerve! You're so full of bravado and putting on the macho air!' I shouted back at him as I got out of the opposite side of the bed. 'You're *pathetic*! I could have been killed you know.' I screamed at him.

'Killed? That's not likely. You might lose your virginity though!' He laughed.

'I beg your pardon? So you think it's funny do you? When you took them on you must have known what they were like, yet despite the danger, you let me go ahead and ride with you.' I was now backing off towards the bathroom, and almost collided with the dressing table on my left. 'There's only one reason why you agreed to take me. You've already been into my jeans and under my top.....!' I trailed off feeling the tears again. One of them ran down my cheek. 'That's why you wanted to see me with my jacket off! To look over the goods.'

'Listen babe,' he said. 'If I wanted to do anything, I would have done it before now.' He had a wicked look in his eye, or was that his normal look! He started moving towards me, and in a couple of strides was standing directly in front of me. He put his hand onto my towel at the front where it was tucked into my cleavage. 'Well babe, don't you feel vulnerable now? One yank and it's off before you know it.' He laughed and laughed.

'You're *mad*!' I shouted. 'And get your hand off my towel!'

He said laughing, 'Sorry babe, it's *my* towel. Everything here is *mine*, and I haven't given you permission to wear it, so..... ' He trailed off, then he pulled it open.

I screamed at him several times and retrieved it quickly again from his grasp, and immediately clutched it to my front.

He said in a sarcastic voice, 'Listen babe. I think the reason why you decided to come along despite the possible dangers that you thought existed, is because you were hoping that you might get something more than just a hitch.' He was laughing again.

I shouted at him again, 'I beg your pardon? How dare you suggest such a thing!'

'And another thing babe....' He trailed off again, his eyes darting to something behind me and off to my left.

'*What*!' I screamed at him in alarm, because I suddenly realised what he was seeing; my back as reflected in the dressing table mirror! So he's seen me after all! I stepped quickly backwards into the bathroom and slammed the door shut.

I screamed at him through the door, 'I'm leaving. I'm not staying a second longer here! I can't stand the sight of you!'

He shouted back at me, 'Feel free! But you won't see your uncle if you do!'

How did he know it was my uncle that I was going to see? I didn't tell him. I only asked him if he had seen the guy in the photograph. I didn't mention the word uncle!

I shouted back, 'I beg your pardon? What did you just say?' I retreated to the lavatory seat and sat down; the towel falling onto my lap. I could feel the tears forming again. I put my head in my hands and just cried.

He shouted, 'I said you won't see your uncle.' The door opened and he put his head round it. 'And you forgot to lock the door!' He laughed and laughed.

I screamed at him again and crying at the same time. 'Get *out* of here!' I threw a lavatory brush at him, narrowly missing his head.

He retreated out of the door again laughing.

I screamed, 'I don't know what you think is so *funny*!'

'Your antics.' He laughed again. 'Oh, and another thing babe. Since you want to be out of here as soon as possible, you have approximately five minutes to get dressed.'

'*What*?' I screamed back. 'You'll have to give me time to get showered first!' I stepped into the shower and turned on the water. '*He's only bluffing of course; he won't throw me out, will*

102

he?' I thought as I adjusted the temperature.

He said, 'Well it's up to you babe.' I heard him leave the room and disappear downstairs.

I hurried my showering and lathering, but I have no idea how long I had been in there, but the next thing I knew, the bathroom door was opened.

'Oh Christ,' I thought in alarm, *'he's back already!'*

As I opened the cubicle door slightly in my search for the towel, I was still mostly covered in lather.

He said to me, as he stood in front of the door, 'Is this what you're looking for babe?' He was grinning at me. He also had the towel in his hand.

I snatched it out of his grasp intending to dry myself off.

He shouted at me, although I was only inches from him, 'No time for that babe. Your time's up.' He took me by the hand and said, 'Come *on*, let's go!'

I shrieked at him. 'I have to get some clothes on first!' The tears were falling fast now!

He shouted back, 'Make it quick then!'

He left the bathroom door open behind him, then he threw me my discarded jeans and t-shirt. My skin was still soaked as I pulled on the t-shirt and struggled into the blue jeans. I could feel foam sliding down my back, and I dripped water onto the carpet. I watched him stuff all my clothes into my pack, including my sneakers and threw it to me as I went into the bedroom, then he grabbed me by the right wrist and all but dragged me from the room, then it was downstairs. I was screaming at him now to *stop it*! My bare feet had no grip on the carpet, and as a result, I stumbled and fell down several times. Whenever I fell down, he yanked my wrist viciously and dragged me onto my feet again. I'm getting scared; the anticipation of what was going to happen to me now! In minutes, we were downstairs in the living room and heading for the front door. Just before we reached it, I caught a glimpse of the conditions outside; snow! It was thick, and still snowing! He *is* throwing me out!

I screamed at him, 'No! You can't *do* this to me! You can't put me out in the snow dressed like this!'

He flung open the front door angrily and said, 'Now babe, is this what you wanted?' He pushed me out onto the step.

I was ankle-deep in snow, and I was freezing, standing there wearing only my jeans and t-shirt, and without shoes or socks.

I shouted and cried and screamed at him, 'No! You can't *do* this!' The tears were running fast down my cheeks!

He slammed the door closed and I just stood there screaming at it. I dropped my pack onto the ground and pounded the door with my fists. I stood there on the doorstep crying in frustration. I hugged my chest with my arms in a futile attempt to keep warm. I turned my back to the door and stepped off the doorstep. I just broke down. I'm losing control again. I was freezing all over now and feeling ill! My skin was still wet and my teeth were beginning to chatter. It was then that I spotted a figure standing on the far corner of the house in the snow staring at me! It was Stubble Chin.

I yelled at him, 'What the hell are you looking at?'

I retreated towards the opposite corner of the house away from his gaze. I pulled off the t-shirt intending to put my bra on, and that's when I noticed a vehicle further up the road moving fast towards us.

'*Damn*!' I said under my breath.

In seconds it had materialised into a car, and was increasing speed. I put on my thong, and had just started pulling on the jeans, when the vehicle was about to pass the house. I had to improvise with my criss-crossed arms across my chest as the bastard actually slowed down to have a good look at me! I turned my back and put on my bra then a t-shirt, then another, then a sweatshirt, sweater and finally my jacket, oh, and my baseball cap. My socks and sneakers followed.

'Oh God,' I thought with chattering teeth. '*This is turning into a real nightmare.*' I'm starting to warm up a little now thank goodness. Well it's a start anyway.

I have a plan forming of sorts. I grabbed my pack and ran out to the road and the truck. I opened the driver's door and climbed inside, closing it behind me. The keys were still in the ignition! Is this one of his little games? Am I supposed to take off in the truck? Where would I go? I can't get to Uncle Pete without his help; how would I know which house belonged to him? Maybe I'll call his bluff anyway; rattle his cage a little! I kept looking to see if Blackbeard was coming out, but so far there was no sign of him. I turned the key; the engine started first time, then I suddenly realised – it's a manual shift! I've never driven one of those before. I stole a glance to my left through the window; still no sign of Blackbeard. I found that my foot wouldn't reach to the clutch pedal! *'Move the seat forward,'* I thought quickly.

I reached under the seat for the adjuster bar that would move it forward; it wouldn't budge. I tried again, pulling on it as hard as I could with all my strength. It's not moving! Then, the passenger door opened and Stubble Chin climbed into the cab.

I thought with sinking heart, *'Oh God, not again! Just what I don't need right now!'*

He just sat there with a stupid grin on his face.

The driver's door opened.

I shook my head. *'Oh God, here we go again.'*

Blackbeard stood there on the footplate. 'Now babe, where do you think you're going? You can't go anywhere without me, so get out of the truck!' he shouted at me.

'I'm damned if I'm going anywhere,' I thought.

I ignored him and refused to move. He grasped me by the hand and started dragging me from the cab. I tripped and fell heavily onto the ground.

'*Christ*, what are you *doing*?' I yelled.

He yelled back, 'Behave yourself and get back into the house!'

He pulled me up by the arm and pushed me forward towards the house. I stood my ground and refused to move. He pushed me again but I just stood there rooted to the spot and stubbornly refused to be intimidated.

I screamed at him, 'First you want me out of the house, and now you want me back in!'

He shouted back, 'Shut up and get back inside *now*, or I'll be forced to do this the hard way!'

I just looked at him with contempt and refused to budge. I was still clutching my pack when he picked me up bodily and carried me under his arm back to the house.

I screamed at him, 'Put me down immediately!'

He shouted back at me, 'As you wish babe.' He dropped me onto the ground.

I hurt my arm as I fell. 'Ah!' I cried out in pain.

When I got to my feet he pushed me through the door and into the warmth. I made immediately for the gas fire and the welcome heat. I dropped my pack onto the floor where I stood and was just about to warm my hands at the fire when he steered me by the shoulders towards the kitchen. I noticed that the shattered door had been removed, but had not been replaced.

He pushed me towards a kitchen chair and said, 'Sit down.'

I said, 'Why should I?' I just stood there staring at him in defiance.

He pushed me down into the chair, but I stood back up quickly and attempted to move away from it, but he only pushed me back down into it again.

He said threateningly, 'If you don't behave babe and do as you're told, I'll be forced to put you over my knee!'

I yelled at him, 'Don't be ridiculous! I'm not a kid!'

He shouted back at me, 'If you act like a kid, you'll be treated like one! Now, sit down and behave!'

'You go to *Hell*!' I yelled back, but I just didn't have the strength to fight him any more.

I can feel myself losing control again. I've taken about all I can for one day; I'm too exhausted. I have no fight left in me. I wish I was with Tómas and cuddled up in his embrace.

'Oh God,' I thought with resignation. *'What the hell?'* I slipped off my jacket and sat down.

He ignored me and went to the cooker with a bowl that he took down from a cupboard above a worktop and filled it with something from a pot. I'm wondering what's in it. He brought the bowl over to the table and placed it in front of me without saying a word. It was soup. I looked at it and suddenly realised that I was hungry. It looked like he made it himself. A smile appeared on my lips. There were leeks and onions in there and no doubt lots more too.

I looked up at him and said, 'Thanks.' Hey, where did that come from? I actually thanked him. I added, 'A spoon would be useful though.'

He brought me a spoon and I tucked in. It was delicious. I finished it off in no time.

I said almost sarcastically, 'So, what's an American doing

in Iceland then? And your friend that I put in the hospital is American too. He *is* in the hospital isn't he?'

I'm hoping he is, and not prowling around somewhere outside, ready to attack me in my bed!

'Yeah. Well it's a long story as to how I got here babe, but as far as the guy you put in the hospital is concerned; first, he's not my friend, and second, he did go to the hospital alright and the police will be wanting to interview him later. He won't be back here again.'

He went to the cooker again with another plate and put something from a pot onto it. I watched him put potatoes and some veg on there too.

He brought the plate back to the table and said, 'Sorry I lost my temper there babe.'

It was stew. It smelled appetising, and I was hungry.

'I should think so too,' I thought. *'What's he at? Now he's apologising.'*

I started on the meal. 'So, how do you know my uncle?' I said looking up at him standing there on the opposite side of the table.

'That's a long story too babe.'

'I'm listening.'

He turned his back to me and stared out of the window again. 'We were both stationed at Keflavík. That's where we met.' He turned to me again. 'Want anything to drink?'

My mouth was full of food. I just nodded.

He crossed the kitchen to make coffee, filling the pot at the sink.

He said, staring out of the window, 'We hit it off immediately. We were drinkin' buddies to start with. We'd go round all the drinkin' dens especially when we went to Reykjavík. That was usually at weekends. We got pissed a lot.'

He crossed to the cooker and fixed the pot with coffee.

Through a mouthful of stew I said, 'What's he like?'

He ignored the question.

Without turning he said, 'The booze was beginning to affect him. He changed.'

'In what way?'

'He had mood swings. Broke a guy's jaw in a fight once.

Nearly killed him, and would have too if I hadn't waded in there and broken it up.'

'Jesus. And I'm going to stay with him?' I thought quickly. 'So what's he like now?'

'God knows babe. Haven't seen him in years.'

The coffee pot was bubbling.

'Didn't he seek help for the problem?'

'Yeah. Don't know if it really did much good though. Takes will power too. Didn't seem to have much of that.'

He poured coffee into two mugs and brought them to the table.

'Was he in the USAF?' I'm finishing off the stew now. I thought, *'Gosh that was good.'*

'He was at first.'

I had a frown on there for a second. 'How do you mean?'

He crossed again to the cooker and brought down sugar from a cupboard, then came back to the table with it. 'Milk?'

'Oh, no thanks.'

He pulled out a chair and sat down opposite. 'Like I said babe, we were drinkin' buddies. We met in a bar. I was in the USAF. He was ground crew – maintenance, that's until the drink took over, then he was moved to a desk job. Then he was out of the Force for good. He found a job dishin' out drinks in a bar.'

I thought, *'What? And I thought he was in the military doing something useful with his life.'* I almost choked on the coffee. I coughed to clear my throat. As I recovered I said, 'And that's *it*? He served *drinks*?'

'Yeah. That's about it babe.' He stared at the tabletop and played with his mug.

I began to stare at my mug too. Something in the water? I almost giggled out loud. I coughed. 'Anything else?'

'He got interested in a woman, babe. You know how it goes?'

He took a swig of his coffee and fixed his gaze on something behind me.

I laughed and said, 'Don't tell me. She was the cleaner, right?'

I was still laughing when he said, 'Yeah.'

Coffee spluttered from my mouth and I almost choked on

it. '*What*? You're joking?'

'Yep.' He laughed too.

I thought as my smile returned, *'Gosh. He's got a sense of humour too.'*

Now that I had a chance to see him up close, I thought he could look quite handsome without the beard and a decent haircut. Hmm, I like tall guys, but I digress. His eyes were hazel, just like mine.

He placed his hand on my arm briefly and said, 'You're going to see you uncle tomorrow babe. You should get some sleep now.'

He pushed his chair back and stood up.

I just nodded and smiled but didn't say anything to him. Instead, I got up from my chair and went into the living room clutching my jacket and backpack. I stood at the fire warming my hands, then I spotted Stubble Chin sitting across the room.

I thought with some disgust, *'God. Is he still here?'* I turned my back to him and the fire. It was lovely and warm here. Nice and cozy. I visualised myself cuddled up in Tómas' arms..... Oh *God*, I'm dreaming again. *'But such pleasant dreams though,'* I thought sighing contentedly.

I crossed to the staircase and sprinted up to my room. Blackbeard hadn't fixed the door yet of course. He'll have to find another one from someplace. Get it from town, wherever that was.

Once in, I drew the heavy curtain closed. You couldn't see through the fabric at all thank goodness; a girl needs her privacy. I stripped off everything and just dropped them onto the floor where I stood, then I went to the shower. I stayed in there for about twenty minutes; I needed a good wash and heating up after my ordeal in the snow.

I need some sleep now; I'll feel better in the morning. I stepped out and dried myself off, then I put on my thong and nightshirt. I made my way back to the bed, towel in hand and dropped it onto the bed, then I lay down on top of the duvet on my front and cried myself to sleep.

I was lying on my front on a sun lounger and sweltering in the heat on some tropical beach. I'm wearing nothing but my watch and a smile. Oh it's so relaxing here; all my worries draining away. My towel is lying at my left side on the sand, just in case someone should come by. I felt a hand on my hair at the back. I looked to my right; it was Tómas. He was standing there looking down on me. I smiled at him and tried to see his face properly, but the sun was getting in my eyes. I blinked several times and then realised that the face that was looking down on me was that of Blackbeard! What? I was still blinking hard when the face became that of Stubble Chin!

'No! Get away from me,' I shouted at him.

I grasped both sides of the lounger with my hands and rolled off onto my back, clutching it to my front. Then I stood up to face him. All he would see were my eyes over the top of the lounger.

'Sam,' he said.

It was Tómas' voice, then it was his face that I saw. I relaxed then. I replaced the lounger on the ground and lay face down once again. He was stroking my neck at the side, then my back between the shoulder blades. It was nice to have Tómas touch me again. Then his hand was on my back at the base of my spine.

I think that is when I awoke, at least I thought I was awake. It took me a few seconds to work out where I was, then it all came back to me. Then I suddenly realised with horror that I wasn't alone. I turned my head quickly to the right. 'Jesus *Christ*!' I exclaimed as I realised who was sitting by the bed on an upright chair; Stubble Chin! I snatched up my towel, covering myself as I did so.

I shouted at him, 'What the hell are you doing here!'

I rolled out of the other side of the bed and stood up quickly to face him. He made a dive at me and tried to snatch the towel from my grasp, but I was too quick for him. I made a run for the curtained doorway, and, just before I reached it, I grabbed my jeans that were draped over a chair back. I could hear him running after me, but I had a head start. I ran down the hallway towards the stairs stopping briefly to pull on my jeans, then I headed straight for the top of the stairs, but as I started down them in a run, my bare feet, which have no grip here on the carpet, let me down badly – literally! I fell headlong down the spiral staircase tumbling over and over several times, screaming out loud as I did so. I was only able to prevent myself from falling farther by grasping hold of the handrail. By this time, I had lost my towel. I must have dropped it at the first tumble that I took at the top. Stubble Chin came running down after me with my towel in his hand. He was laughing. I just lay there flat on my stomach on the stairs. I screamed for Blackbeard to come. He did. I could hear him running into the living room and heading my way. When he had reached the foot of the staircase, he almost ran up them, taking them two at a time until he reached me. He must have been preparing to go out because he was wearing his red-chequered jacket. I turned and looked up at him as I lay on the staircase on my front. Stubble Chin had stopped in his tracks and was looking down on us from just around the bend in the stair. Then I stood up. He shouted to Stubble Chin to get back to his room immediately. He obeyed and I sighed a big sigh of relief. I followed Blackbeard down the stairs into the living room and made immediately for the gas fire to warm up.

He said to me as he put his arm around my shoulders, 'Come and sit down here babe.' He led me to the couch which faced the TV and sat beside me. I still don't fully trust him yet.

'Thanks,' I said to him with a smile, but I wasn't feeling myself. 'I'm feeling ill. Must be the shock. I need some sleep.'

'It's OK babe. You can sleep here with me.' He smiled as he handed me a couple of cushions.

I just stared at him with a shocked expression. 'I beg your pardon?' Surely he doesn't think I'm going to sleep with him!

'It's OK. I'll just get you a travel rug. You're not going back to your room tonight babe.' At that, he rose from the couch and fetched a woollen plaid rug from somewhere across the room. He handed it to me.

'Thanks,' I said and returned to the couch. I just sat there and watched him as he returned to the couch himself and sat beside me.

I suddenly remembered my backpack was lying on the bedroom floor. I said to him, 'Could you get my pack please? It's on the bedroom floor.'

'Sure babe.' He went up to fetch it. By the time he had come down again, I was lying with my head resting on the couch back.

He said, 'Want something to drink babe?'

'Sure. A cup of tea would be nice, thank you.' I was feeling very sleepy now and safe too. *What*? In his company? What am I thinking? No, I have to relax. I'll be riding with him tomorrow, all the way to uncle's house, wherever that is.

Just before he went off to make the tea, he said, 'I locked him in his room; he can't get to you now babe.' I just smiled back at him and nodded. I'm feeling even more sleepy now. My eyelids were closing and..... I must have dozed off for a second because I suddenly awoke with a start as I felt someone sit down beside me. I guess I'm getting jumpy all of a sudden. No wonder, with the company I've been keeping recently. It was Blackbeard again of course, and he had a tray with a teapot and two mugs. There was sugar and milk there too. Just before he sat down on the couch, he pulled up a coffee table. He sat down beside me and helped himself to the tea, at least I thought this is what he was about to do, then he poured it into my mug.

'Thanks,' I said as I took the mug from him. I helped myself to the sugar.

I did sleep soundly that night with Blackbeard for protection. Well I could relax now and look forward to meeting Uncle Pete and his Icelandic wife.

CHAPTER 10

I alighted from the truck and waved goodbye to Blackbeard, then I just stood there staring at the house that was to be my home for the next two weeks. It was a cabin, although not of the North American style. The roof was reminiscent of a Swiss-style chalet, steeply pitched into a strong inverted v-shape to shed heavy snow in winter. Here again as in other places that I had passed through, was another house with no garden, just rocks with the odd tuft of grass and very little else.

As I walked up the path towards the house, I saw a figure walking towards me with arms open wide. It was Uncle Pete. There was no doubt about it. I remembered him from the photograph. He was in his mid-fifties and sported a full, once-black beard now turning grey, that seemed to emphasise his oval-shaped face. He spent a lot of his time fishing these days, and no doubt had another job besides as most Icelanders do.

I dropped my pack on the ground and ran to meet him, then I threw my arms around his neck. I had to go up on tiptoes to do this as he is taller than me; most people are.

He said, 'Sam you're here at last.' He hugged me tightly and kissed me on the left cheek. I started to cry happy tears. They ran down my cheeks and down my front too.

He said, 'You've grown up fast bárn.'

I drew away from him briefly. 'Sorry?' I didn't understand what he said.

'Bárn means child,' he said smiling.

I hugged him again and said, 'I'm not a child any more uncle. Dad calls me his baby.'

'You are too. Anyway let's get you inside and you can meet Lei,' he said walking back to the house.

I'm thinking, *'Lei? Who's that? And that's not an Icelandic name surely?'* I retrieved my pack and followed him up the path.

The door opened and a Chinese girl in her late teens or early twenties stepped out to meet us. She was about my height – 5 feet. She wore red slacks and an orange, loose-fitting blouse. She's Chinese? But I was told that he married an Icelandic girl. Oh well; my dad must have got that wrong. No matter; I'm sure we'll get along just fine.

I could hear a dog barking from somewhere inside the house. It sounded like a small one. Then, before I knew it, it had appeared from behind the door and was running towards me. It was a little shaggy dog belonging to no particular pedigree that I could name. It began to jump up and down excitedly. I bent down and petted him. I straightened up as Lei approached me.

She put out her hand for me to shake, then gave me a big hug and a kiss on the left cheek. 'Come on in Sam and make yourself at home. You'll be tired after your long journey.' She added, indicating the little dog, 'Oh, this is Petra.'

I bent down and petted Petra then followed the three of them into the house. I dropped my pack on the floor and Lei pulled up a kitchen chair for me to sit on. I just fell into it with exhaustion. I removed my clasp from my ponytail and ran my fingers through my hair.

I said with a sigh, 'I'm very tired. Been through a lot in the last few days.'

'That's OK. I'll show you up to your room shortly and you can have a good sleep. Look as though you could do with one too.'

'Thank you,' I said, then added, 'Oh, do you think I could have a shower Lei?'

'Of course you can. It's en suite so you can have one any time you wish, thanks to Pete.'

Uncle Pete pulled up a chair and sat down beside me. I could detect the smell of alcohol from him. He said, 'D.I.Y. is a hobby of mine.'

I just smiled at him and turned back to Lei. She asked if I wanted a drink. I just nodded and smiled.

She asked, 'Coffee or tea?'

'Oh, it doesn't matter Lei. Whatever you're having thanks.'

Uncle put a hand on my arm. I turned to him then with a look of curiosity on my face.

He said, 'Can't believe how fast you've grown. Bet *you've* had a few boyfriends?'

I blushed. 'Well..... ' I broke off as Lei interrupted with, 'Of course she has.' She smiled at me.

I was just about to mention Tómas when the kettle interrupted with its whistling. The little dog jumped up and onto my lap. I petted her again and kissed her on top of the head. She licked my face several times before jumping back down onto the floor.

Lei poured the tea into three white mugs and brought them to the table. Sugar and milk was already there. She sat down opposite me.

As I helped myself to the sugar I said, 'I'll show you some family photos.'

Lei smiled over her cup as she watched me go into my pack.

I rummaged around for a bit but I eventually found them. I opened the little leather photograph album and showed the first picture to Uncle Pete. 'That's my dad with mom in the shop.'

He smiled and nodded then passed it across to Lei. She nodded too then turned the page. She asked, pointing to the page, 'This your sister?' She passed the album to Uncle Pete. Charley and me are standing together on a bridge. She has a big smile on, in fact we both have.

I said, 'That'll be Charley, my girlfriend.'

'Very nice,' he said nodding. 'Nice girl. You should have brought her along too.'

'Well I did ask her but her mom got sick and she had to back out of the trip.'

Uncle handed the album to me and I flipped over the page again.

I said, 'That's uncle Tom and his new girlfriend.' I spent the next fifteen minutes going through the album.

When I had shown all the photos to them I said, 'Like to go up now Lei. I could sleep for a month.'

'Sure,' she said rising from the table. She led me upstairs and into a small bedroom where two single beds stood on either side of a window with blue curtains on the wall facing the door. A small blue lamp stood on the bedside table between the beds.

I dropped my pack on the floor and made straight for the window. It looked out onto their back yard. In the distance was a mountain range with large quantities of snow still on there. I turned to Lei excitedly. 'Oh Lei. It's beautiful.'

She joined me at the window. 'Yeah, it is. One reason why I liked it here.'

I'm *thinking, 'She "liked it"? Doesn't she like it now?'* I considered asking her what happened to Uncle Pete's wife. If dad did really get it wrong – oh, I don't care. Does it matter anyway? I'm here to enjoy my vacation; not nose into their private affairs. I sighed as I sat myself down on the bed on the left of the window.

She turned to me. 'You'll like it here Sam... ' She hesitated.

My smile vanished for a second. I had a frown there too. *'What is it Lei?'* I thought as I studied her face.

She saw my expression. 'Oh, it's nothing.' She turned away towards the door and said, 'Have your nap and we'll see you whenever you feel like coming down.' With that, she opened the door and disappeared into the hallway.

I'm still wondering about that hesitation. Oh well. I shrugged and took off my hair clasp. *'Think I'll have a shower first,'* I thought as I stripped off. I threw my clothes onto the opposite bed, then made for the bathroom. There was a tub here under the window and a separate shower cubicle in the corner on the right. I elected for a soak instead. I began to run the water. I wondered why the hot wasn't warming up. I was just about to turn the water off again when I heard a male voice shouting my name. I had noticed there wasn't a lock on the bedroom door as I came in. I grabbed a bath towel and wrapped it quickly, then closed the door over. As I stole a peek round it, I shouted back, 'Hi there.'

He was standing in the centre of the room, then he approached the bathroom door. 'Heard you running the tub. No point running the water. No hot water yet.' He was now standing with his hand on the door handle intent on pushing it open farther.

I held onto it firmly as I said smiling, 'That's OK. I'll have a shower instead.'

He was still pushing the door as he said, 'Just want to check the radiator.' It was just inside the door.

I said quickly, 'The radiator is cold.' I had to step back to let him in as he was practically already in the room anyway. 'Em..... ' I broke off.

He smiled at me when he spotted my towel, then he put his hand on the radiator. He bent to turn the controller at the foot. 'Have to have a look at that later.'

'Did I detect slurred speech?' I wondered. Maybe he's been hitting the bottle again.

I was shivering standing there in this cold bathroom wearing only my towel. I said, 'Something wrong with it?'

'Think the central heating system needs attention.' He backed out of the room, with his eyes still fixed on my towel. 'There's a fault somewhere in the system too.'

I'm thinking, *'What's the matter with him? What's so interesting about my towel? Maybe it's not the towel, but what's inside it....!'* I shuddered.

I snapped out of my dreaming as he said, 'You cold?'

I nodded. 'Yep,' I said quickly with a sharp intake of breath. I looked at the floor avoiding his gaze and feeling a little embarrassed.

He said nodding, 'You'll soon warm up in the shower.'

'Yeah.' I blushed. *'Hurry up and get out of here. I'm freezing,'* I thought as I looked forward to my shower.

He left the room closing the door behind him. I locked it hurriedly and threw my towel over the cubicle partition. I stepped inside and turned on the water hard.

Once I had the temperature just right, I stood with my back to the wall and thoroughly soaked myself, then applied the soap. It had a lovely peachy fragrance. Beautiful. I slid myself down the wall and sat on the floor and let the water warm me up. I stayed in there for about ten minutes. When I came out, I felt a new girl already.

I thought, *'Gosh, I needed that shower.'* I'm looking forward to a proper soak in the tub though, after Uncle Pete fixes the heating out.

I stepped out of the shower and dried off, then, as I entered the bedroom, the temperature dropped significantly. Jesus, it was like stepping into an icebox. Still no heat in the radiators. *Oh well, guess I'll warm up in the bed.* I went into my pack for my nightshirt and panties. Once in, I began to warm up good and the feel and smell of clean sheets – I don't remember much thereafter.

I awoke with someone knocking on my door. I propped myself up on both elbows. 'Yeah?' I said sleepily.

'Sam? Supper's ready. We're about to eat.' It was Lei.

I got out of the bed then sprinted to the door and unlocked it. As I opened it, I could smell curry. Gosh I was hungry. 'Hi Lei,' I said smiling. 'Nice smell. I'm starved.'

'OK, just come down when you're ready.' Just as she turned to go she said, 'Pete has the hot water fixed. You can use the tub if you like.'

I said brightly, 'Oh, thank you Lei. I'll have it later.' I sighed contentedly. 'I'll look forward to it.'

She smiled and headed back down the hallway.

Back in the room, I pulled on my cream-coloured jeans and my short, light blue woollen top, my navel on show here, oh, and my California tan. I sprinted downstairs and made straight for the kitchen where Lei and Uncle Pete were already seated; in the same positions as earlier.

I seated myself on Uncle Pete's left, tucking my right leg under me and the other dangling over the edge of the chair, my legs being too short to reach the floor. It's one of my favourite sitting positions. As I sat with straight back there on the chair, I could see Lei's eyes were fixed on my short top. She said, 'Like your tan.'

I just smiled across the table at her. I could see too, with peripheral vision, Uncle Pete's eyes on me, drinking in the view.

Lei crossed to the cooker and brought a saucepan back to the table. As she began to dish out the meal she said, 'You sunbathe a lot or is it fake?' She laughed.

'Oh it's real alright.' I turned to Uncle Pete and back to her. 'I sunbathe and also belong to a fitness club where they have a sun bed. Have to top it up a little in the winter months.' I gave a short embarrassed laugh.

Uncle Pete reddened before he said, 'You have an all over tan then?'

Lei gave him a look.

I said, 'I do.' I continued, 'It's OK. I get asked that a lot.'

Lei pushed a large dinner plate in front of me with what

118

looked like chicken curry on there.

'Thank you Lei,' I said. 'It looks delicious.'

She just smiled and sat down.

We all tucked in.

I coughed as something went down the wrong way. I concentrated on my meal again but I need a drink now. This was a good curry.

Lei read my thoughts. She crossed to the fridge and produced a wine bottle. She held it up for me to see.

I couldn't make out the label but I nodded my approval anyway. It's wine. I don't care where it's from.

She opened it with a corkscrew and poured our glasses to the top.

I nodded my thanks. One small drink and my throat had returned to normal.

CHAPTER 11

I awoke with strong sunlight streaming in through the curtains. I just have to see how this morning looks. I stood up on the bed and pulled one of the curtains aside then looked out. *'Beautiful day,'* I thought. Blue sky and not a cloud to be seen anywhere.

I also needed some air in here. I wanted to open the window, but I'm too short to reach the window catch when I stand on the floor. I can manage it from the bed though. I reached up without too much effort, and, was just about to push it to its 'open' position, when Uncle Pete appeared with Petra. He looked up at my window as he passed.

'Damn,' I said under my breath. I pulled the curtain closed again quickly in case he saw me there at the window. I just hope he didn't!

After going through my usual workout routine, I headed for the shower. Yep, you guessed right; the familiar fragrance of sulphurous water! I'm getting used to it and it doesn't bother me at all now. I could live with it. It's supposed to be good for the skin too.

I stayed in the shower for some minutes, not wanting to come out at all. The thought of going outside in the cold didn't exactly thrill me either. I turned off the water and stepped out of the cubicle. It was then that I was aware of my goosebumps. It was cold in the bathroom. I picked a cold bath towel off the radiator and bent to turn it on, then strolled into the bedroom. I dropped the towel onto the bed. My skin was still soaking from the shower, as I made my way over to the window. I just stood there looking out at the wonderful mountain scenery. I went into my backpack that lay on the floor. I took out my camera and took a few shots through the window.

My goosebumps are more prominent now and I'm shivering a little. I dried myself off, then started on my hair. Today I'm wearing my hair long. It flows over my shoulders.

Is it cold outside? It's impossible to tell from in here. I elected to wear my blue jeans and two t-shirts on my top half plus my green polo-neck sweater. I finished off with my baseball cap. I don't want to get caught out again with the cold. Satisfied with my dress, I made my way downstairs to see Uncle Pete and Lei, oh, and of course, Petra.

Lei was dressed in blue jeans and a green polo-neck sweater. Snap! She copying me or something?

She said to me, 'Góðan daginn.' (good morning).

I wished her the same as I approached the kitchen window.

I looked out and said, 'What a beautiful morning it is Lei. What's it like out today – temperature-wise?'

She said as she placed plates on the table, 'Actually it's quite warm, and the temperature is supposed to rise. It can be very warm here you know even though we're just under the Arctic Circle.'

'Yeah, it's amazing isn't it? You expect it to be cold every day here.'

'We get a lot of snow because we're in the mountains, but when the sun comes out it's beautiful.'

She started scraping bacon, fried egg and sausage onto plates on the table.

She said, 'Pete will be in soon, but we can start without him.' With that, she sat down at her place and I followed suit opposite her. I removed the baseball cap.

The table was well furnished with breads and preserves; cold meats and strange 'things' I didn't recognise, let alone put a name to. I helped myself to a slice of wholemeal bread – my favourite, and some of the nice jam there.

I heard footsteps outside the door and a dog snuffling. The door opened and Uncle Pete stepped into the kitchen. He was wearing a thick green sweater which he pulled off as he entered.

He said, 'It's warm out there Sam. I think it's going to be a hot one. We've been having a few hot days recently – somewhere in the eighties I believe, was the last thing I heard.' He sat down at his place just beside me on my left.

Petra came up to me looking for a titbit. She put her two paws onto my lap and looked up into my face. She was pleading with her eyes. I cut the end off one of my sausages and dropped it into her open mouth.

Lei said, 'Petra; come here like a good dog. You'll get yours later.' She pointed to the far corner where a dog basket lay. 'Go lie down Petra.' The little dog ran across the room and bounced into the basket.

I clapped my hands at her and said, 'Hey, good dog.'

Uncle Pete had only just started on his sausage and bacon, when he leaned over and whispered in my ear, 'You should keep your curtain closed in the morning girl. You never know who's watching.' He gave me a wink. He was smiling too. I wasn't. I blushed instead!

'What?' I thought suddenly. *'Out here with no visitors about? Who was he kidding?'*

So he did see me, but how much? My nightshirt reaches well down passed my waist, so hopefully not much. Then I remembered; me standing there in my birthday suit, taking pictures through the glass. Surely not. He wouldn't, would he? There wasn't anyone out there; or was there? I reached out and lifted the teapot and poured myself some, if only to hide my embarrassment.

There were cartons of milk there on the table too. Why there were three separate cartons there I had no idea, but then maybe Uncle Pete liked semi-skimmed while Lei liked homogenised. I picked up a carton marked 'skyr'. It had a picture of a cow on the front. I poured it into my cup. When I saw what it was doing to my tea I said, 'What the *hell...?*'

Uncle Pete just sat there laughing.

Petra started barking; joining in the excitement. I'm glad she's amused too.

I said, rather annoyed and failing to see the joke, 'What's so funny?'

Lei said laughing too, 'Oh Sam. You've just taken the skyr. It's Icelandic curds; sorry.'

I asked her with a smirk on my face, 'Did you do that *deliberately?*'

'No; honestly!' She laughed and laughed. I thought she was going to throw a fit.

Uncle Pete asked picking up a small bowl from the centre of the table, 'Have you tried this harðfiskur?' He placed it in front of me.

I looked at it. Little brown, brittle-looking pieces of something – flakes of fish maybe? I didn't dare touch it. I shook my head and made a face.

I said, 'No. I'll pass on that one, thank you.'

'It's hard dried fish,' he said with a grin.

'Whatever,' I said and turned away. I looked again at my spoiled tea. I held up the cup for Lei to see. 'Em....?' I hesitated.

She said, 'I'll get you another cup Sam.' She got up and found me another one. I poured more tea and settled down to some cold toast instead.

Later, after breakfast, Uncle Pete asked me if I wanted to go out. I agreed, but where to? He suggested that I go to the beach. There's beautiful black volcanic sand there. I'd love it, he assured me. I'm not sure why he thought I would like to go to the beach, but I guess he was thinking of the photography angle.

I thought that maybe I could go for a swim in the ocean, and catch up on some relaxation at the same time. That's what vacations are supposed to be about. Would the water be cold? Yes, but it's OK once you get used to it. Famous last words – we'll see! It's very refreshing to swim in the Arctic Ocean on a warm summer's day, so he said. I'll take his word for it then.

I fetched a towel from the bathroom and stuffed it into my pack. My camera is there too. Can't leave that behind.

I met Uncle Pete downstairs as he was ready to go. Petra was too. She jumped up and down excitedly as we made our way outside to the car. It's another four-by-four. They're invaluable here. Good for the gravel roads especially here in the highlands.

We drove for about thirty minutes then we began to see the ocean as we rounded a bend in the road. It was oh-so blue, but then the sky was too. Not a cloud to be seen; just blue from horizon to horizon.

'Oh, it's lovely here; thank you for bringing me Uncle,' I said excitedly and touched his arm. I'm looking forward to getting my kit off and my swim.

The ocean is some distance from the road. You can see it

of course from here, but not the beach; it's hidden from view. Just as well for my sake. I intend to swim with nothing on but my watch! This is how I do it back home in California, whenever I can find a secluded spot. Here in Iceland we are about as far away from civilization as you could care to be. Fantastic! It's cool.

He said as I was alighting from the car, 'I'll come back and pick you up later. Take your time; there's no hurry. You're on vacation now girl.'

'Yeah. Em....? I'm wondering how long I should give this?'

'Well, say an hour?'

I grinned at him, 'How about two? I'd like to relax; I want to have a swim too, at least I'd like to give it a go.' I'm thinking about the water temperature.

He smiled and said, 'Sure. No problem.' He got out of the car and said, 'I'll just give Petra her walk now.'

I shouldered my pack and he accompanied me to the beach; Petra running ahead of us. After some minutes walking, we had reached the beach, or rather Petra did. She ran headlong into the waves, jumping up and down excitedly. I took out my camera and began to snap her antics; chasing a rubber ball that Uncle had thrown for her. The sand is, as he said it would be, black, or more correctly, grey, but when the water washes over it, it looks black.

I ran after Petra and fetched the ball for her. I threw it into the ocean. She caught it in her teeth and ran back to Uncle Pete with it. He threw it to me and I caught it and threw it again to Petra. I was beginning to heat up now, so I paused to strip off my sweater. That's better! As I attempted to pull my topmost t-shirt over my head, the other one came off with it. I was now wearing only my bra. Uncle was watching me all the while; I could see that his eyes were fixed on me. I had to separate the two shirts before I quickly pulled one of them on; my red one. I dropped the sweater and shirt onto a nearby rock. After a few more minutes of this frolicking, Uncle suggested that he leave me to it and departed with a disappointed Petra. I watched them disappear over the crest of a hill before I was satisfied that they had completely gone. I want to bathe alone and in peace, just like back home.

I just stood there on the shore and looked at the beautiful blue colour of the ocean. It looked so inviting, but I think it's deceptive. It's going to be cold in the water, but maybe I'll get used to it in time. I have to test the temperature first. The air is warm, yep, sure is, - 85 degrees, according to my watch, but the sea is another matter. I sat down on a rock and took off my sneakers and pink cotton socks, then I tested the water with one toe. It seemed OK. Now the rest of my foot. *Ah*! That was cold, but I could get used to it though. I went for a paddle, then, when a wave came in fast, I had to run and jump out of its path up the beach. My jeans' legs were now soaked, at least the bottoms were. I paddled again and this time I'm ready for the next wave. I ran up the beach again just before it reached me. I'm a kid again, and why not? You're only young once. Go for it girl!

My feet are getting used to this cold. It's actually quite pleasant now. Not bitingly cold as I had envisaged. I shucked out of my jeans. I'm wearing my thong. I ventured further into the foam. The waves were coming in faster now, or at least that is how it seemed to me. I was now in up to my knees. Yep, I'm becoming accustomed to the temperature alright. Good. Well my legs are anyway. I went into deeper water. A wave came in and almost reached my thong, but thankfully, it didn't quite make it. I have to wear it later. I just stayed in this deeper water, and getting myself acclimatised to the cold.

I'm going to take a chance and go for a swim. No-one to see me here. Not another human being for miles. I stripped off the remainder of my clothes and sat down on the nearest rock. The skin on my bottom is sore as it comes into contact with the rock's sand-papery surface. It's black volcanic rock, well, actually a very dark grey; basalt I think.

I found a flat rock about ten feet high and climbed up onto the top of it. I intend to dive from here, but now I'm having second thoughts about going into the water at all.

'It'll be freezing, won't it? Oh, what the hell? What have I got to lose?'

I stood up and, with arms stretched above my head, took a headlong dive into the ocean. God, it was cold. Well, it's not called the Arctic Ocean for nothing! Well, what do you expect girl? I resurfaced and ran up the beach. My skin had goosebumps, but I wasn't caring; it was *exhilarating*! I turned and ran down the beach again into the ocean, and this time I stayed longer, diving and swimming for some distance.

I stayed out there for about five or ten minutes, then, when I had satisfied myself that I had had enough, I made my way back to the beach. It was then that I thought I had detected something glinting in the sunlight some distance away towards the road. Could it be a vehicle on the road? No, that's impossible; you can't see this beach from the road. An aircraft? Sometimes you see sunlight glinting off them. Someone with binoculars or a telescope, or, a long telephoto lens on a camera? Of course, I could be mistaken. I think I may be getting paranoid; events over the past few days are enough to make any poor girl suspicious.

I dug out my towel and was just about to dry out my hair, when I heard the sound of a boat's engine. I turned in alarm towards the sea, seeking this intrusion into my privacy. I couldn't see any boats at all at first, but when I went back into the sea and rounded some chest-high rocks, I spotted two fishing boats anchored some distance offshore. Something was being transferred in boxes from one vessel to the other. I wondered what they could be doing. I don't know why I thought it seemed suspicious. What were they doing in this secluded cove?

I went back to the shore and took out my camera. I returned to the spot where I saw the fishing boats and got down low, resting the camera lens on my arm on top of a rock to keep it steady. I switched to 'continuous shooting' and fired the camera rapidly; click, click, click it went. I don't know how many shots I got, but if there is anything suspicious going on here, I have the evidence. I stayed crouched behind my rock until the boats moved away – one to the north, and the other out to sea.

I waded back to the shore and tried to decide what to do next. Well, if what I saw just then was indeed suspicious, I'm not going to be able to report it myself. I have to rely on Uncle Pete to get me to where I want to go. He doesn't have a telephone as far as I can see; no phone lines to the house, and I didn't see a telephone either. I can't get help. I can't call on anyone. Would there be any signal for my cell phone? For the moment though, I intend to enjoy the rest of my leisurely day; well, till 11 o'clock anyway. I set my watch alarm for 10:45 and lay face down on the warm black sand. It was lovely and cool lying here. I was well up the beach and I reckoned that it would be some time before the waves caught me up.

I woke up with the first of the waves tickling my toes. I looked at my watch: 10:30; just in time for Uncle Pete's return. I got up and ran down the beach into the sea then dived under the water. I resurfaced some distance away and swam towards a chest-high rock. There I stayed until he arrived. I shouted to him to throw me my towel. He did, and I wrapped it around myself and strode out of the sea. I sat down on a rock and just stared at the sand and the waves coming up the beach. He came and sat beside me on the rock.

He said, 'When you said you were going for a swim - so where's your bathing suit?' He looked at my towel.

How did he know I wasn't wearing any swimwear? Did he see me swimming? Paddling? No; he wasn't nearby so how could he know?

I felt my face redden as I said, 'Oh, I don't have one with me. Didn't expect to be swimming in Iceland.'

I gave a short nervous laugh and continued to stare at the waves. The breeze was blowing strands of hair into my eyes, so I tucked them behind my ears.

Petra was frolicking around in the surf, then she started chasing something in the water.

My smile had long-since vanished when I said, 'I'd like to get dried off now and get dressed please.'

I stood up and collected my clothes.

'Sure.'

He stood up too and moved away from me.

I went behind a high rock just beneath the cliff off to the right and started dressing. Minutes later I stepped from behind the rock and joined him there waiting impatiently for me.

Little Petra came running up to us and started nipping at my ankles. I bent down and picked her up. She licked my face and I hugged her close. He walked ahead and we made our way back to the car.

When I got back into the passenger seat, I turned to look out of my window. There isn't much to see here but sand and rocks. It's a moon-like landscape with monotonous grey sand and very little else. It's treeless and totally devoid of any vegetation. Wildlife exists here, but you'd wonder how anything could survive at all in such a hostile environment. It's depressing.

127

I talked to Petra throughout the journey. I reached into my pack and took out my baseball cap. I put it on her head.

She laughed with her tongue hanging out, and looked from me to Uncle Pete and back as if to say, 'How do I look?'

Uncle said at last, 'That's cheered her up Sam.'

I said more cheerily than I felt, 'Suits her, don't you think?'

I hugged her again and kissed her on the top of the head.

'She'll be wanting one of those for her birthday now. You shouldn't teach her bad habits Sam.' He laughed.

In a few minutes we had reached uncle's house at last. Lei met us at the door and Petra scurried inside first. I followed her, pushing past Lei and making straight for my room. I have plans to make and I need Lei's help. I made for the shower and I stayed there for at least ten minutes and when I came out again wrapped in a towel, I lay down on the bed on my front and had myself a good cry. Have to get the trauma of recent events out of my system quick.

After some minutes of this, I took off the towel and laid it on top of the bedclothes, then slid beneath the sheets and sat up, clutching the duvet to my breast. The sheets had been changed since this morning. Tears were still running down my face and down my front, when I heard a soft tapping on my door; it opened and Lei came into the room and approached the bed.

'Something wrong Sam?' she asked sounding concerned.

I had a large lump in my throat and couldn't speak, then it all came out; the events of the last few days. Lei sat on the side of the bed wearing a shocked expression, but didn't say anything.

The tears are falling again. 'Oh Sam,' she said in a concerned voice. 'You've certainly *had* a very traumatic experience. But what a start to your *vacation*!' She pulled a Kleenex from a box on the bedside table and handed it to me. I took it and wiped my nose and face. I told her about the fishing boats that I saw transferring their cargo.

'It may be nothing; something quite harmless. I'll tell Pete about it and see what he says. He might even know them.'

With that, she left the room and I heard her scurry downstairs.

I looked at my watch; almost noon. We'll be eating lunch soon.

'I have to freshen up before I go down,' I thought suddenly.

I heard arguing emanating from downstairs. It sounded serious! I couldn't hear the words but Lei appeared to be getting the brunt of it. I hope I don't get her into any kind of trouble.

I was trying to decide whether to dress in preparation for going downstairs, so I got out of the bed, then I heard footsteps coming along the hallway from the direction of the stairs. I retreated back to the bed quickly, and pulled on my nightshirt.

I lay on my back, my arms on top of the duvet. It was Lei. She came up to the bed with a glass of milk. That's it! No cookies nor anything else to eat. What about lunch? I just looked at her with a question mark above my head.

'Something for you to drink. We're having our lunch now, but I thought you might like to have a sleep before you have yours.'

She put the glass of milk on the bedside table.

I said as I sat up, 'Lei? What did Uncle Pete say when you told him?' I said.

She handed me the glass and I took it from her with, 'Thanks, but I'm not really sleepy right now.'

She sat on the edge of the bed. 'You'll appreciate it once you have it. Trust me.'

'So, what about the boats then? What did he say?'

'He says it's just local fishermen exchanging catches. It's boxes of fish that you saw. Sorry. Nothing more sinister than that.' She gave a short laugh.

She may be right about that too. Well, so much for my amateur sleuth attempts. I wouldn't make much of a detective. Well I tried anyway. I started drinking down the ice-cold liquid. It was so good and refreshing.

'Thanks Lei. That was nice.' I finished it off in another couple of gulps. Jesus! Milk never tasted so good. I put the glass back onto the table and slid myself down between the sheets. I felt so warm and safe there. Maybe I will sleep after all.

She stood up from the bed, then hesitated before saying, 'I've put a little something into the milk to make you sleep soundly. It'll help enormously, you'll see.'

I just looked at her with a shocked expression.

'*What!* Why...?'

Alarm bells are ringing now! What has she done to me? What has she put in my drink? I'm panicking now! Then I began to relax. Was that the drug? Is it taking effect already? I can feel a calming effect; more relaxed, sleepy! What am I afraid of? What can happen in here? I'm going to sleep, and everything, will be fine, when I waken. No, worries....... no, worries. Then only blackness!

I have just been thrown into a snake pit onto my back! They are slithering towards me and several of them are entwining themselves around my waist, legs, thighs and neck. This is petrifying. I don't know if I will be bitten or not since I don't recognise the species. What's going on here? Surely I have to be dreaming. I have to get out of this pit, but I can't seem to be able to move. My limbs are paralysed. I'm terrified. I feel I'm being smothered by the bodies which appear to be getting more numerous. There are constrictors here too. One of them has just encircled my chest and is slowly crushing it. I can feel someone or something touching my hair at the back of my head. That's when I woke up; it was with a start, and it was then that I realised that Uncle Pete was sitting on the edge of my bed. His hand was on my arm as both of them were outside the duvet. I quickly withdrew it.

'You're back. Good. Did you have a good sleep Sam?'

He was stroking my hair at the left side of my face. Some of it he tucked behind my ear. I moved my head away from him and felt my face redden.

I answered with a sigh, 'No. I had a bad dream. Snakes. It was *horrible!*' I shivered. It was cold in here even under the duvet. 'Why is it always so *cold* in here?' I said half to myself.

'I'll put the heating on.' He patted my left shoulder. 'Anyway you're safe now.'

I could see his eyes wandering over my chest and taking in the nipples that were prominently displayed there as they pressed against the fabric of my nightshirt. I pulled the duvet up quickly to hide them. He stood up off the bed and looked down on me. He went to the radiator and turned it on.

When I looked at my watch it read 9 o'clock! 'I've been asleep all that time?' I said in alarm. That's from lunchtime! 'I'm starved; I've missed lunch *and* supper!'

I pushed back the duvet swinging my legs out onto the

floor and just sat there on the edge of the bed.

He said, 'You can have supper now if you like.'

I smiled and nodded, 'Yeah, OK. I don't want to *starve* to death.' I gave a short laugh and stood up, then headed off to the bathroom. I could feel his eyes on me as I opened the door to go in.

He said to my back, 'I'll see you downstairs.' He departed from the room.

While in the bathroom, I brushed out my hair and fixed the hair clasp on my ponytail. Back in the bedroom, I chose my blue jeans and for my top half I pulled on a blue, close-fitting t-shirt. I left off my socks and sneakers; I have no plans to go out again tonight.

I hurried downstairs to Lei and Uncle Pete. He was sitting in the living room reading a newspaper, a glass of scotch in his hand. He must speak Icelandic then, or at least read it. As I passed his chair on my way to the kitchen, I said to him brightly, 'Hi!' He looked up from his reading and just nodded his greeting with a smile, and, as I opened the door to enter the kitchen, I saw him watching me again. Does he find me sexually attractive, desirable? I hope not, he's my uncle after all. It's the way that he looks at me. What am I thinking? I'm overreacting; too much stress recently. I have to keep my cool. Has the drink really changed him that much?

There was a strong smell of curry as I went into the kitchen to see Lei. She's cooking Chinese tonight. She was just in the process of laying a soup bowl at the head of the table for me. I'm considering asking her about Uncle Pete and herself; their marital status. What happened to his wife if he ever had one, but I don't want to do this within earshot of uncle. I said to her in a whisper, 'Lei, can I talk to you in private?'

She turned to me with a concerned expression, then she closed the kitchen door.

I said to her softly, 'My dad said that Uncle Pete had a wife. What happened to her?' I sat down at my place and awaited her response.

She crossed to the cooker and began to stir a saucepan, then came back to the table with it. As she poured soup into the bowl she said, 'She died. She had cancer. She took the car out one day and just walked into the sea. She couldn't swim.'

My heart missed a few beats. 'How awful Lei. When was this?'

'Couple of years ago.'

I started on the soup. It was mushroom and it was delicious. 'Lei, this is lovely soup. Did you make it yourself?'

She just nodded and crossed to the sink with the saucepan. 'Then I came along just at the right time for him.' She was staring out of the window. 'It's a Chinese recipe by the way. Why open packets when you can make your own?' She turned away from the window to look at me.

'Are you guys married?' I asked. 'Could you give me the recipe for this soup?'

'No we're not, and yes you can have the recipe?' she laughed.

Petra had been lying in her basket when I came in. She bounded up to me and jumped up onto my lap. She smelled the soup and turned her head to face the table.

I said, patting her head, 'No Petra. Get down. There's a good dog.'

She jumped down again onto the floor and just sat there looking up at me.

'How did you two meet?' I'm enjoying this soup. It's yummy.

'My parents died when I was very young, and I was brought up by foster parents, but I didn't like them much and I couldn't wait to get away. Then when I was a student at university, I went on a backpacking trip to Iceland and that's when I met him; at the National Museum in Reykjavík. We sort of bumped into one another.' She laughed.

'He's lucky to find you Lei.' I threw some pepper on.

'Yeah, he is,' she said as she returned to the cooker.

'Don't you get lonely up here on your own away from friends?' I asked as I watched her stir a saucepan.

'No, not really. I have Petra, and Pete of course.' She smiled and turned back to her stirring.

I'm thinking, *'Uncle Pete takes second place?'* 'Of course,' I agreed. I finished off my soup and said, 'That was delicious soup Lei.'

She reached up to a cupboard above the worktop on the

left of the sink and took down a loose-leaf folder. 'This is where I keep my recipes.' She opened it and placed it on the tabletop in front of me. 'It's filed under soups,' she said with short laugh, then she produced a notepad and pen from somewhere and placed them on the tabletop too.

As I flicked through the pages I said, 'Gosh Lei, you are organised aren't you?' I found the recipe and began to jot it down.

'Cooking is a hobby of mine.' She took my bowl away and replaced it with a large dinner plate. As she turned to the cooker she asked, 'You like curry Sam?'

'Oh, yes,' I said as I watched her return to the table with a saucepan.

She poured the contents onto the plate then returned to the cooker. She brought the rice to the table in another saucepan and poured it into a bowl in front of me. Em..... ' I've suddenly realised that I don't have anything to eat it with.

She saw me hesitate. 'Oh, sorry. Can you use chopsticks?'

I hesitated again. Before I could answer, she had found a pair in a drawer and handed them to me.

I said, 'Thanks.' I took them from her and hesitated again. 'Em.... ' I started laughing. I shook my head and said with a short laugh, 'No I can't, but, I'm going to give it a go anyway.'

'You haven't used them before?' she asked again.

I didn't answer. Instead, I put the utensils between the two fingers closest to my right thumb and that's when everything went pear-shaped. '*Oops*!' I giggled when I realised I was making a hash of it; the chicken pieces dropping back onto the plate. I giggled again, then smiled back at her. I copied some more of the recipe.

She laughed too. 'Can't take you anywhere,' she said laughing again, then she handed me a fork instead and stood back to watch me sample the meal.

It was chicken; my favourite. I expressed this fact to her. 'Haven't had a home made meal this good for a while. Thanks Lei.' There was a spoon in the rice bowl. I helped myself to it.

She asked as she stood watching me tuck in, 'So what about you then?'

I hesitated. I wondered what she meant. 'What about me?' I'm enjoying this spicy meal. Yummy, it's good, although I think I'll be smelling of curry for the rest of the week. I finished off my jotting down.

She asked, pulling up a chair to sit herself down, 'Boyfriend?'

'*Oh* Lei,' I said excitedly as an image of Tómas came into my mind. 'I met the most *gorgeous* guy. You just wouldn't believe.'

'Is he on vacation with you?'

'Oh no, he lives here in Iceland..... em, somewhere...... ' I hesitated again as I suddenly realised that I hadn't asked him. I giggled at that; I'm not sure why.

She asked laughing herself, '*What*? You meet someone and you don't ask them where they live?' I just nodded and giggled again, and this time I almost choked on my food. I think it was a grain of rice that went the wrong way.

As I was trying to recover she said, 'You are slow. That's probably the first question that I would have asked.' She laughed, then continued, 'That wasn't him driving the truck was it?'

I screwed up my face. 'Oh God *no!*' I replied as I recalled some of the incidents earlier. 'I like to think I have better taste than that.' I giggled again, then put down my fork. I thought, *'God, this is good,'* and sighed contentedly.

She laughed too. 'That bad huh?'

'You wanna believe it.' I laughed and said, 'He wasn't so bad as his two companions though. A couple of jailbirds.' I giggled again and helped myself to more rice.

She stood up and said, '*What*? You rode in a truck with a couple of criminals? You're *mad*; anything could have happened.' She gave a short laugh then added, 'Something to drink?'

I nodded. *'It almost did,'* I thought as I recalled the attempted rape. My smile had vanished for the moment. 'How was I to know they were out on good behaviour doing community service? And I had to get someone to take me to Uncle Pete.'

'Tea OK?' she asked as she picked up a teapot.

'Yeah. Thanks,' I replied absently. I gave a big sigh and said, 'Thank goodness it's over now.'

She crossed to the sink and began preparing the tea. 'But you're OK now though?'

'Sure. I'm just looking forward to meeting him again at the end of this vacation.' My smile had returned.

'So where did you meet him?'

'Oh, it's a long story.' I gave a short embarrassed laugh.

She just stood there expectantly, then the kettle interrupted with its whistling. Thank goodness. She turned to the cooker and attended to the tea.

I finished off the meal and pushed my plate away. *'She's not going to ask again, I hope,'* I thought hopefully.

She did. 'So how did you meet him?' She came over to the table with the teapot and two mugs. Sugar was already there.

As she poured the tea I said with a sigh, 'Oh, he was staying with his sister, Helga, in Reykjavík. She rescued me from the Sjómennsheim.' I felt myself blush.

I picked up my cup and sipped then realised that I hadn't put in the sugar. I like it black too. I helped myself to the sugar.

She had a question mark there. 'Rescued?' She sat down.

I told her the whole story from the beginning; on meeting Helga in the Bureau to meeting Tómas at her house.

Lei had just sat there with open mouth, not believing her ears, especially when I told her about the incident in the shower room. She said finally, 'So, what happened after you met?'

'Oh Lei.' I got up from my chair and walked slowly round the kitchen; my hands in my front pockets. 'He's so.....' I hesitated, 'Oh, I'm so looking forward to meeting him again.' I gave a big sigh of contentment - again.

She repeated her question.

I said smiling, 'He offered to take me round the thermal areas, and he did. It was so thrilling.'

She looked at me over her mug. 'And he offered to take you for a swim in a thermal lake no doubt?' She had a smirk on her face.

I stopped pacing and said, 'Yeah, he did.' I sat down again and raised the mug to my lips. I looked at her over the rim and blew the surface of the liquid to cool it.

She said with a smile, 'Has he been married before?'

I just shrugged and grinned at her over my cup.

'Don't tell me. You didn't ask, right?'

I didn't say anything and maintained my grin.

'So you don't know if he has a family or not?'

'No.' I blew my tea some more and said, 'Oh, he's nice Lei.'

'I'm sure he is. What about his interests?'

I shrugged again. I still have my grin plastered on.

'Did he show you his..... you know?' She was grinning herself.

I hesitated as I looked at her over my cup, then my grin vanished for an instant. 'Pardon?' I giggled as I took a sip and spluttered through my drink. It's gone the wrong way again and I coughed to clear my throat.

She laughed herself before she said, 'His place of work? You didn't ask him?'

'I guess not. Well I didn't have to.' I smiled and said, 'We were visiting that town with the streets of greenhouses? That's where the tourist agency is where he works.'

CHAPTER 12

In the morning when I awoke, I went into my usual workout routine and then had my shower. My dress wear for today was the same as last night, and again, I left off my shoes and socks. I had a look out of the window to see how the weather was doing; rain by the looks of it. Doesn't look as though I'll be out today. I can't move from here without transport anyway. Can't even go out for a walk as I don't have any rain wear with me.

At breakfast, Lei told me that the two of them were going out for a while and didn't expect to be back before 1 o'clock, and I was to make myself lunch if they weren't back before then.

After they had gone, I was wondering how I was going to keep myself entertained till they returned. I sat down cross-legged on the floor in front of the Hi-Fi and selected 'CD', then had a look at their collection of music. Lots of stuff there, but nothing that really turned me on. I chose the radio instead. I found some music with a funky beat and started dancing around the room. This was short-lived however, as it was soon replaced by a country music number. More dance music. This was a fast one, and as I passed the gas fire, my foot caught the edge of the fireside rug and I found myself falling onto an armchair. This is where Uncle Pete had been sitting last night. There was a newspaper lying there, and my bottom had struck something solid beneath it. My nose got the better of me. I looked under the newspaper and found a digital SLR camera with a long lens attached; a very long lens in fact - 1,000 mm! *Gosh*! Must have cost him an arm and a leg. It was a Nikon. I haven't tried one of those before. Think I'll try this one out.

I crossed to the back window and rested the camera – correction, lens - it was over a foot long, on the back of the other armchair. I switched on the camera and looked through the viewfinder. I pointed it out of the window towards the nearest mountains. *Jesus*! The detail on those rocks; the clarity of the image. Wouldn't mind a lens like this for my camera. I was wondering what he had been photographing with this cool lens. I pressed playback. The first one up was blurred; impossible to make anything out at all. Maybe the camera had been hand-held. No, unlikely. You would mount a lens this size onto a tripod to take photos, not the camera itself. Next one was of a bird of prey sitting on a fencepost. Don't recognise it. Not from North America anyway. Then number three....!

'Oh no!' I gasped with my hand at my mouth. It was of me. Several shots of me paddling in the sea. The following twenty were of me again, in different situations; some clothed, and some in various stages of undress. The next fifteen were of me again, this time on top of the rock preparing to dive. Then, about four or five of me emerging from the sea yesterday; full frontal images of me in my birthday suit! So that flashing that I saw yesterday was him! How long had he been there? I looked through the rest of the photos. There were two more; one was a view of my naked rear and the other was of me paddling naked in the sea. I didn't find any other camera cards there on the chair, but that doesn't mean that he didn't take any more shots of me. So this is why he suggested that I go to the beach. I'll have to be careful with him now. I wonder if Lei knows about this side of him?

'Can I copy this card?' I wondered. Then I remembered that I had my portable digital hard disc drive with me. I ran upstairs and went into my pack to find it.

Back downstairs, I took the card from Uncle's camera and downloaded it into the hard drive. It has a colour screen on the front and will display all the photos on there at the touch of a button. A few minutes and I had the entire contents of the card in my possession! Evidence! Now I have proof. Proof of what? He's a photographer, isn't he? Wouldn't I do the same in his shoes? How often do you get the chance to get such photos? I'll ask Lei if photography is his hobby. If it isn't....!

I forgot the radio was still on. They started playing a Viennese Waltz. I began to hum along with the music as I danced around the room. Round and round I went, pirouetting on the spot now and then. Then, I spotted a small bookcase under the staircase.

I waltzed over to it and began to examine the books. First one I picked up was all about fishing nets and how to repair them, or so it appeared to me. It was written in Icelandic. I put it back and chose another. It was concerned with fishing boats. I was just about to replace it when I heard it; a squeaking sound. It was short but unmistakably mouse-like. Then another sound like something whistling. The wind? No. I went back to the Hi-Fi and turned the volume down completely. The house was deathly quiet now. As I returned to the staircase, I heard it again; that mouse-like squealing. Where was it coming from? I stood under the staircase with my back to the wall and strained my ears for the sound again. Then I heard it; coming it seemed, from a door beside me under the stairs. I put my ear to it and listened carefully. Yes, it was coming from in there. I tried the doorknob but it was locked. I looked around in this semi-darkness under the stairs, searching out the key, then I spotted it lying on the top of the bookcase. I put it into the lock and eureka! It unlocked the door! I opened it and just stood there rooted to the spot. A large metal radio with dials and knobs across the front stood on a desk. All the dials were lit up. He must have left it switched on. I didn't know what to think at first. Maybe this is how he communicates with the outside world. The fishing boats? Radio ham? One large knob with numbers showed what I thought might be for dialling the frequency, but I decided not to touch it. The whistling sounds were louder here of course, and appeared to be coming from a set of headphones lying on the desktop. I picked them up and held one of the phones to my right ear. I could hear voices talking faintly, but I had no idea what they were saying. It could have been Icelandic. Yep, it was too.

'Maybe I'll understand something of this,' I thought as I listened carefully to the voices. *'No I won't; they're talking too fast.'* Then I realised that my stomach was crying out for food. I looked at my watch: 12:30. I'm thinking of making myself some lunch now, so I went to the kitchen and rustled up a flapjack and a mug of coffee from the coffee maker. Grabbed a slice of wholemeal bread from the fridge and spread some of Lei's home made jam onto it.

As I stood at the window looking outside, a snowflake fluttered down across my view; this was quickly followed by more, and, if I wasn't imagining it, getting larger. *'Oh, gosh!'* I thought

139

suddenly. *'More snow? Surely this won't last. Even if it lies, it'll soon melt.'*

I carried my lunch on a tray back to the radio shack. Isn't that what the radio hams call their dens? I sat down at the desk and listened again. A voice speaking in English mentioned something about a shipment, and a boat called the 'Siggi'. *'What?'* I thought. *'Wasn't that the name of the fishing boat that I saw in Ísafjörður at the harbour?'*

I went to fetch my camera and looked through the photos that I took of the fishing boats that day. Yep, I knew I was right. There it was, as large as life. I didn't hear what the shipment was though. Sounds a strange term to use in connection with fish. Well no matter. None of my business anyway. I had my coffee in my hand, and, as I reached out to return the mug to the desktop, I miscalculated and the base of the mug struck a thick volume that lay there close to where I was going to put it down. The result was a spill of coffee onto the desktop. I quickly mopped up the spillage with a Kleenex from my pocket, then realised that some of it had been soaked up by papers that uncle had left there. I don't know if I should be in here or not. Maybe he'll take exception to the fact that I had been using his radio without his permission, although I don't really see why he should. It's not doing any harm is it? I'm forming a plan in my head now. I'll tell him that the reason that I was in there is because I heard noises coming from in there, and it was only when I opened the door, that I realised where they were coming from. I had been drinking my coffee and I spilled it on the desktop. It's all true! I've only omitted the part about listening into conversations. I listened again one last time but I couldn't make them out clearly. I returned to the kitchen and washed up my dirty plates and cutlery.

As I looked out of the kitchen window, snow was falling fast and heavy. Big flakes. I'm wondering when Lei and Uncle Pete will arrive. They'd better hurry or this snow could cause a problem later. I poured myself another cup of coffee and settled down at the gas fire in front of the TV to watch a movie to pass the time. There wasn't any way that I could go out in this weather.

2 o'clock came and went, then I heard a vehicle outside. *'At last; they're here,'* I thought happily. I sprinted across the room to

the front window, and sure enough it was them. The snow had now accumulated to about four inches. Lei carried a large box of groceries up the path to the house.

When she came in through the back door I said to her, 'Have a good trip Lei?'

She nodded. 'I think we're in for a heavy fall, the way the sky's looking right now.' She placed the box of groceries on the kitchen table. Petra scurried in too and bounced into her basket.

I have a plan for a snowball fight. Don't get the chance to do this too often. I sprinted upstairs and put on my socks and sneakers. Back downstairs, I ran into the kitchen making for the back door, narrowly colliding with Lei who was in the process of putting something into the fridge. She stood up quickly.

'Where are you off to such a hurry?'

I turned to her briefly as I exited the door and gave a short laugh..... then I collided with Uncle Pete coming in.

He caught me by the shoulders and said laughing, 'Whoa! Sam. Where are you going?'

I didn't reply. Instead, I ran outside and headed for the far end of the house; Petra on my heels. I peeked round the side and could see Lei standing on the doorstep. She wore a red close-fitting t-shirt and skin-tight blue jeans. I threw a snowball at her; it hit her on the right shoulder. She gave a short shriek as it took her by surprise. She looked around trying to identify the direction from which the snowball had come, then she spotted me bending to pick up another one. She threw one at me, and I ducked - it missed. Lei tried again. This one hit me on my front on my navel. I gasped and cried out laughing as I felt the snow hit my skin. I returned the fire with two more in quick succession; one hit her in the chest and the other on the left knee. She was laughing now and running towards me. I laughed too as I tried to escape from her but I lost my footing and slid on my face onto the snow. Petra ran up to me and began to lick my right ear. Lei was onto me in a flash, pulling my jeans out at the back and popping a snowball down there. Petra was barking loudly, joining in the fun. *Jesus* it was cold! I gasped then I squealed out loud. Turning onto my back, I pulled her down on top of me, and at the same time grabbing a handful of snow. She squealed and cried at me and laughing at the same time as she realised what I was just about to do. I pulled the neck of her t-shirt out at the front and threw the snow inside.

'I'll get you back!' She was laughing.

It was then that a snowball arrived from an unexpected direction. Of course it was Uncle Pete. It hit me on the right leg, and I returned fire, hitting him on the chest. Another two snowballs arrived; one hit Lei on the back, and the other hit me on the chest. My t-shirt was beginning to show signs of wetness around the chest area, and I could feel the dampness seeping through. Petra was chasing and barking at the snowballs that failed to disintegrate when they were thrown. I laughed at her antics.

I felt like I was playing with my dad; he was certainly old enough. He was so lucky to find Lei. She's young enough to pass for his daughter, only she's Chinese.

Uncle was closer to us now. He made a grab for me and managed to catch my t-shirt at the front. Lei grabbed me from behind and held my arms, laughing all the while. Uncle took hold of the neck of my t-shirt at the front and pulled it out; he threw a handful of snow into the space.

I gasped out and squealed and screamed at him, 'No! Stop it.' I laughed and cried as I felt the ice slide down inside. I was soaked and starting to feel cold. It wasn't over yet either! Lei was laughing as she grasped me around the waist with one arm and pulled my t-shirt out at the front again with the other, then Uncle Pete piled snow in there. He was laughing too. Lei lessened her grip on me and this is when I squirmed out of her grasp and broke into a run away from them, and away from the house. I heard Lei running after me, followed by uncle. He was slower of course, but he soon caught her up. She made a dive at my legs from behind and wrestled me to the ground. I made the mistake of turning onto my back after I hit the deck. She was on top of my legs and sitting astride me with a broad grin plastered across her face. Just then, uncle arrived at my head.

I thought suddenly, *'Oh, no. What are they going to do to me now?'* I started giggling as I lay there, my arms above my head, and looking up into Lei's face.

'I told you I'd get you back,' she said laughing at me.

Then I felt uncle grasp me by the arms, pinning them down above my head. Lei pulled my t-shirt right up past my bust!

'What's she doing?' I thought.

Then, still grinning, she pulled my zipper down! I was laughing and crying as she started pulling my jeans down my thighs, then she piled the snow on top of me. Uncle Pete was laughing too as he let go of my arms. I was able to get myself up easily enough though, but now I was really freezing.

I screamed at them and laughing at the same time, 'I'll have to change; I'm freezing.' I pulled up my jeans and ran for the back door, aware that I was still covered in snow. Just before I reached the door, I felt my t-shirt pulled out at the back and snow was piled in again. I gasped. Wasn't I cold enough as it was? This was Uncle Pete again.

I ran straight through the kitchen and made for the stairs, not stopping until I had reached my room. I stripped off everything and turned on the water hard. I just sat down on the floor of the shower cubicle, the beautiful hot water pouring down on top of my head. I looked up briefly to let the water fall onto my face, then I thought I could detect movement through the frosted glass of the cubicle. The door opened suddenly and Lei stood there with a blanket...... filled with *snow*! I shouted and screamed at her when I saw it. 'No, Lei, what are you *doing*?' I covered my head with my hands to protect myself from the snow, but it was no use; she started throwing it over me. I stood up to confront her, but she merely emptied the contents of the blanket onto my front and laughed hysterically. I thought as I pulled her into the shower with me, *'She's mad!'*

Now she was soaked too. As she stepped back out of the cubicle she said laughing, 'Sorry, couldn't resist that. See you for a hot cup in about fifteen minutes?'

I nodded and smiled back then sat down on the floor and let the hot water warm me up again.

She smiled then hurried off to her own bedroom to change.

Minutes later, I dried off and threw on a white t-shirt and cream-coloured jeans. As I passed the dressing table, I picked up my hairbrush and hair clasp and started on my hair, then I went downstairs to Lei. She was just turning from the coffee maker as I entered the kitchen. She looked gorgeous in an orange coloured t-shirt that stopped just short of her navel, and a pair of white, tight-fitting jeans. She poured coffee into two mugs and placed mine on the breakfast bar on my right. I sat cross-legged on a stool and sipped my coffee.

She said with a grin, 'Enjoy your snow fight then?'

'Yeah. I'll get you back. Don't you worry,' I said with a laugh. I put my mug down and started brushing out my hair again. Lei came over and took it from me.

'Thanks,' I said.

That night after supper, I was standing at the sink washing up. I turned on the portable radio that stood on the windowsill; it was classical music that they were playing. I couldn't put a name to it, but I began to hum along with it anyway and trying out my new-found orchestra conductor talents. Every now and then I waved one hand in the air to keep the orchestra in check, and as I was about to place a large plate onto the rack, I failed to hear the kitchen door open. I did hear it close though; that's when I froze! Lei wouldn't enter like that and close the door, so it had to be Uncle Pete. He was at my back now, standing close; very close! I'm feeling decidedly uncomfortable now as I could detect warm breath on the top of my head! I could detect alcohol from him. He was pushing me against the sink, my stomach hurting as it came into contact with the edge of it. *'What the hell's he doing?'* I thought in alarm.

He said softly; it was just a whisper, 'Why were you interfering with my radio?'

I asked quickly, turning my head slightly to the right, 'Pardon?' I reached out and turned down the radio volume; maybe Lei would hear us.

I could feel warm breath on the side of my face and a distinct smell of alcohol as he spoke directly into my ear. 'I'll say again; why were you interfering with my radio?'

I thought in alarm, *'What the hell's the matter with him? Has he got something to hide?'* I said, 'You had left it on and I heard strange squealing sounds coming from the room. I just wondered what they were, that's all. *Oh*, and sorry about the coffee spillage.' I gave a short nervous laugh.

He put both hands on my hips and spoke into my ear again. 'Do not go near that radio *ever* again; do you understand?' He's scaring me now! His right hand was sliding down further. I removed it quickly, then it went onto my chest just under my right breast. I removed that too. I nodded and picked up another plate intending to wash it. He said in a threatening tone, 'You know what happens to pretty girls who go snooping into matters that don't concern them?' His left hand wandered down to the helm of my t-shirt then moved up over my navel.

I said to him slowly and in a whisper, 'Get your hand *off* me.' Just then, I heard Lei messing around in the living room, then turn the door handle. He must have heard her too, because he stepped back from me immediately. I turned to her as she entered, deliberately taking my time to smooth down my t-shirt at the helm. I'm hoping that she'll get the right message; that he was interfering with it. My face was already slightly flushed as it was, so hopefully she would understand. I think she did.

She said with a shocked expression, 'What's going *on* here?'

'That's none of your business!' He was shouting at her, then he strode from the room slamming the door behind him, then I heard the front door slam too.

'Thank God that's over,' I thought with relief.

Lei looked at me with concern. 'You OK Sam?'

I didn't answer immediately, but turned to the dish towel that was lying on the worktop on the left of the sink. 'Yeah, I'll be OK thanks.' I deliberately didn't turn to face her as I could feel a tear forming. Instead, I began to dry the dishes.

She said, 'I'll do that. You get to bed.'

I dropped the dish towel again on the worktop and turned to go. A tear ran down my cheek and I tried wiping it away before Lei saw it, but too late; she spotted it, but just before she could say anything, I was out of the kitchen and making for the stairs.

CHAPTER 13

This morning, I wore my red t-shirt and blue jeans. It was going to be another warm one Lei said. The snow from yesterday was certainly melting fast.

Uncle Pete was, she said, off on business and wouldn't be back for some time. I suggested to her that we go to the same beach that uncle had shown me. She told me that she had never been to a beach since she'd come here. I was surprised.

I said, 'You've *never* been to a beach in Iceland?'

'No I haven't.' She finished up with her breakfast and put the plates into the sink.

'You'd love all that black volcanic sand. It's *beautiful*.' Then I suddenly thought, *'How are we going to get there? Uncle Pete's got the car.'* I needn't have worried though; Lei had her own car, and it was a four-by-four too. Extremely useful in these parts.

I finished off my food too, and as I drank down the last of my coffee I said, 'Well, how about it then? Like to go to the beach?'

She brightened up now. 'Sure. I'd *love* it. And we could go for a jog too. I haven't done that for a while.'

I took my pack along with my camera and portable hard drive too. I intend to show Lei the photographs that uncle had taken of me.

In no time, we were heading off to find the beach that uncle had taken me to earlier. We found it without too much difficulty. She parked the car well off the road because we wanted some privacy. We took along a picnic basket with sandwiches and a wine bottle as well.

It was a beautiful day with the sun shining warmly on our skins. Lei suggested that we go for a jog first. I wondered where Petra had got to, but she said that Uncle Pete had her with him. We jogged along the beach. It stretched as far as the eye could see; a crescent-shaped beach of pure black volcanic sand.

I said to Lei, 'It's a wonder that uncle has never photographed you here.'

She stopped abruptly in her tracks. 'Excuse me? What did you say?'

I repeated what I had said, then added, 'He photographed *me* right here.'

'Did he now? With what?' She was genuinely surprised.

'A camera?' I suggested, teasing her.

She turned to me. 'He doesn't have one. Are you sure?'

'What do you mean am I sure? Of course I am; I've even got the photos he took. They're back there in the car Lei.' I pointed to it.

She just looked at me with a shocked expression. 'I'd like to see them later.'

After our jog we returned to the car. I opened the hatch and stripped off my t-shirt as it was clinging wetly to my back with the sweat anyway. I'm intending to go for a swim here; get this stickiness off me.

She just stood and stared at me in puzzlement. 'What are you doing?'

I smiled at her. 'Going for a swim?' I suggested and laughed. I reached round to my back and unclipped my bra, then dropped it beside my shirt.

She looked at me enquiringly. 'Like *that*?'

I grinned back at her. '*Sure*. It's OK. Come on Lei. Get your kit off and let's go.' I was laughing now and eager to get into the water. I unzipped and shucked out of my jeans. Lei pulled off her t-shirt and unclipped her bra.

I stepped out of my jeans, but just as I was about to pull the cord on my thong, she put her hand on my arm. 'Suppose someone should come along?' She was looking around, searching out for possible peeping toms.

I just laughed and said, 'It's OK Lei, honestly. There's no-one for miles around. Can't even see the road from here.'

We even had our very own 'early warning system'; the dust from vehicles on the gravel road could be seen for miles. I pulled the cord and dropped my thong beside my other clothes.

She shrugged and said laughing, 'Oh, what the hell?' She pulled off her jeans too but she hesitated when she came to her underwear. She looked at me briefly, then she pulled that off too.

I grabbed her by the hand and ran down the beach towards the sea, then I stopped abruptly when we had reached the water's edge. Waves were coming in slowly and as the first of them began to tickle our toes, Lei gave out a loud scream and jumped back a little. I gave a loud gasp as I felt the cold water on my feet and jumped back too. I know it isn't that cold but Lei's doing this for the first time. I stepped forward again and pulled her in with me. She shrieked out and jumped back as though hit by a bolt of lightening!

I said laughing, 'It's OK Lei. You'll get used to it.' I stepped forward again and this time it didn't feel quite so cold. The sun was warm on our skins too.

More waves were approaching now; larger than last time. I reckoned that they would reach up well above our ankles. They did! More shrieking, this time from both of us; this was quickly followed by giggling and laughing. I pulled her in further and this time the water level was well up our legs. She's getting braver now and she's enjoying herself. I'm getting the feeling that she doesn't get out much with friends; if she has any at all. She hesitated before venturing farther, and looked around; back up the beach towards the car.

I said reassuringly, 'It's OK Lei. Just relax. Come *on*.' With that, I pulled her into the water further still and now the level was at the top of our thighs. I cupped my hands and threw water onto her front. She squealed and screamed at me, then she returned the favour. I squealed out too and threw water over her head this time. She turned her back to me and I just kept on doing it, and for the next few minutes that's all we did; threw water over one another. Then I took her by the hand and tried to persuade her to go in farther. She squealed and screamed out loud as I pulled her into the deeper water.

I said to her, 'Dive in. OK, after three; one, two, *three!*'

We both jumped into the deeper water. She made a big splash; well we both did and disappeared under the surface. I came up first and heard her gasp as she too came up for air.

'*Oh, gosh*, it's *cold*!' she said laughing.

We were standing up now with our navels below the surface.

Lei was trying to get water out of her eyes when I said, 'Well, what do you think so far?' I laughed.

'It's *great!* Glad I came now Sam. It's *fantastic!* And yes, I like the sand.' She laughed.

I said, 'Come on. Let's get our towels and lie in the sun.' Then I had an idea. I said to her, 'Wait there.' I'd like to get some photos of her here.

As she frolicked around in the water, I ran back up the beach again to fetch my camera, and as I stood next the car about to take it out of my pack, I wasn't one hundred per cent satisfied that we were alone here. I'm thinking of Uncle Pete and him snapping me. I ran back down the beach again and slid myself down behind a rock. I snapped Lei as she emerged from the waves; her lower half partially hidden by the foaming water. She looked beautiful and nymph-like as she strode out of the sea and along the beach. I just kept snapping her as she approached. Uncle Pete doesn't know what he's missing.

I had also taken my portable hard drive out of the pack with the camera to show to Lei. As she strode towards me she said with a frown, 'What's *that* you've got there?'

I showed her the pictures that Uncle Pete had taken of me.

She just stood there and gasped, shaking her head in disbelief. 'I didn't know he was like that. I don't think he had any right to do that.'

I said, 'It's not illegal to take pictures of people Lei, even if they are in a state of undress, I just question the reasoning behind it. If he was a photographer with a place to send photos to, then that's a different matter. A camera club maybe or magazine?'

She shook her head. 'No, he's not a photographer.' She added surprised, 'Oh, are you into photography?'

'Oh yeah,' I replied with a broad grin. 'That's why I photographed you there. Hope you don't mind?'

'No of course not Sam. Best of luck with them if you think you can win a prize.... ' She hesitated then continued, 'Can I see them?'

'Sure,' I said. 'When we get back to the car.'

We went back to the car to put on our jeans and t-shirts,

then I showed her the photos that I had just taken.

She just stood there flicking through the images; a smile beginning to form on her lips. 'Can we delete *them*? I like the others though.' She showed me which ones she wanted erased. I kept the other ones.

I said as I put away the camera, 'I'll get a copy of those to you at some point. You might want to keep them.'

She just nodded and smiled.

I took out my pack and our towels plus the picnic basket from the trunk. We selected some fairly flat rocks high above the shore to lie down on and sunbathe. I spread our towels on the rocks and sat down on mine then stripped off again. Lei joined me and lay on her front.

I said leaning over her, 'I've got sunblock here. I'll put it on your back if you wish?' I took a bottle from my pack.

'Sure. Then I'll do yours.'

I'm hoping that we don't get an unexpected visitor here. Well if we do, our clothes are to hand. Hopefully it won't come to that. I got on to my knees and started on her back with the sunblock, starting at her neck. I'm using both hands here. It's oil and waterproof.

I asked, 'Do you get out very much Lei?'

'No. Not really. We go to get supplies now and then in the town.' I'm working on her shoulders and back now.

She's trapped in that house; no telephone to talk to friends, if she has any at all, and no cell phone in the mountains, cut off from other people. I said concerned, 'You want to get out more Lei. It's not good for you. You're too young for that. Got the rest of your life to live. When was the last time that you had a good time?' I was now working my way down past her shoulder blades.

'I'm having it now.' She grinned at me.

'Apart from today?' I said moving further down her back.

'Can't remember Sam. Been a while.'

I'm almost at her spine now.

She said, 'You'd make a good masseur. I used to get this done back home.'

'Yeah. Well it's only sunblock Lei. The massage is free though.' I giggled.

She turned onto her back and sat up, then she started on

150

her legs.

I watched her as I lay on my back on the towel. 'Lei. Have you ever used the radio in the house?'

'*God* no. He doesn't like *anyone* to touch it. Why?'

'He threatened me Lei.'

She stopped applying the oil. 'He did *what*? You're scaring me now Sam.'

I repeated what he had said to me last night.

She said, 'Oh *God*. We'll have to watch him carefully now.'

'Did he ever threaten you Lei?' I was concerned for her safety.

'He hit me once for going into the room. I was bruised for a week....'

I interrupted with, 'Yeah, and no-one to see them, right?'

'Yeah, he went into town to get supplies that week by himself.' She lay on her back again.

'Why do you think he doesn't like anyone to go in there?' I sat up.

'I don't know really. What did you find there?' she asked in curiosity.

I poured some oil onto my chest; some of it ran down my front and gathered briefly in my navel, then continued on down. I rubbed it into my skin. I told her about the voices and the Siggi, *oh*, and the "shipment".

She said thoughtfully, 'I know that boat. That's Pete's boat.' She sat up to look into my face.

I had just finished doing my front. 'It is?' I said surprised. I don't know why I should have been.

She said, 'Turn over and I'll do your back.'

I turned over and tried to think of something sensible to say. 'I wonder what else is in there that he doesn't want anyone to see?' I don't know why I said that.

She said as she applied the oil to my back, 'Maybe we should have a look Sam.'

I said in an incredulous voice, '*What*? You're not *serious* are you?'

'I am,' she replied, and applied more oil farther down my back. She was working fast now.

'Jesus,' I said softly. 'You *are* serious.'

She was almost at the base of my spine now, then she started applying oil to my bottom too. It's nice to be touched like this, but I wish it was Tómas who was doing this to me.

She said, 'Almost finished.' Then she was. I turned over and sat up.

I reached for the picnic basket. 'I'm starved Lei.'

'So am I. ' She hesitated, 'Fancy a swim?' she said grinning. She stood up.

I said looking around, 'Can't get into the water from here.'

She pointed down to flat rocks off to our left. 'Down there. Race you there.' She started down slowly; not much of a race really. The rocks felt rough on our feet so we had to tread carefully. In no time, she had reached the flat rocks where she stood at the edge and, with arms stretched above her head, prepared to dive in, but I had other plans. When I had caught her up, I placed a hand on her back between the shoulder blades and pushed her over the edge. I heard her scream as she fell, tumbling over and over till she hit the water with a big splash, then I dived in too. We both dived deep; just going down and down and enjoying the coolness of the water. After some minutes, we swam back to the shore and resumed our sunbathing.

I opened the basket and Lei the wine. She filled our glasses to the top.

I lay on my back and stretched and stretched then relaxed with a sigh. 'This is the *life*. Could do this *every* day.' I giggled and sat up. I drank my wine and helped myself to the chicken sandwiches.

Lei lay on her front, sipping her wine.

We stayed there for at least an hour, just soaking up the sunshine. Lei, I think, had had at least five glasses of wine. I lost count after my fourth. We had finished off the sandwiches and Lei had gone to sleep on her front. I had too.

I awoke with a start and sat up. I looked around for the source of the sound. I looked down and to my left. A row boat had arrived at the shore. Two males dressed in rubber boots and dark polo neck sweaters were climbing out of it. It must have been the sound of the boat hitting the rocky shore that I heard.

I lay down quickly on my back and reached over to waken Lei. I whispered to her, 'Lei. We've got company. Put something

152

on.' I said this as I reached into my pack for a thong. I had just managed to find Lei's t-shirt, when I heard voices very close by. They must have been walking passed the rocks where we lay. I turned onto my front and put a hand on her back, preventing her from rising and being spotted from below.

She awoke now too and looked at me with a puzzled expression.

'We've got company. Lie still,' I whispered. I'm trying to stifle a giggle.

She started giggling herself and then she hiccuped and giggled again. It must have been the wine, and it was infectious 'cause I started giggling too.

I spotted one of the guys passing by where we lay. He turned to look up. He must have heard Lei. His companion looked up too and they both stopped in their tracks and stared.

Lei propped herself up on her elbows to get a better look at them. One was quite young – around our ages; the other was much older. Father and son maybe?

I said, giggling myself, 'Get *down*. Do you want to be seen?' I don't know why I bothered; it was already too late.

The younger of the two waved at us. Lei waved back and giggled again, then she hiccuped. Then the guy turned on his heel and retraced his steps.

I thought in alarm, *'He's coming up here!'* I giggled again then tried to pull myself together and think rationally. I grabbed a t-shirt just as Lei sat up and looked around. I think she read my thoughts. I sat up too and pulled her to me; my legs on either side of her. I pulled the t-shirt over her head and she instinctively put it on. Another t-shirt, the one meant for me, I dropped onto her lower half, so at least we were *almost* decent. She giggled again and turned to look at me. Just then, the younger guy's head appeared over the edge of a rock. He's grinning. I had one plastered on too as I looked over Lei's shoulder at him; so did she. He said something in Icelandic and blushed then retreated back down quickly. We both burst into a fit of giggles.

Lei said that Uncle Pete wouldn't be in for a while yet, so we still had time to ourselves. Cool. Time to have a good look round the place especially the radio room. But, in the meantime, I wanted to get this salt off my skin.

Lei sprinted ahead of me and headed straight for her room. Within minutes, I could hear water hammering down from the shower. She's quick, I'll give her that.

I went to the shower too and stayed in there for a few minutes. When I stepped out, I pulled on a pair of blue jeans and my red t-shirt, then I went to find Lei. When I reached her room, the door was slightly ajar. I tapped it softly. 'Lei, are you ready yet?' I could hear the shower water hammering down still. I pushed the door open and stepped into the room.

She came up behind me and dug her fingers into my ribs. I gasped and started giggling, then I spun round to face her.

She stood there with not a stitch on, and dripping water onto the carpet since she hadn't dried herself off. 'You wanted something?' She was laughing.

'Yeah. Get something on and let's go.' I turned from her and made for the door, and as I did so, I heard her scurry into the bathroom. Before I could exit the bedroom, she was at my back again. When I turned to her, she was wrapped in a towel and her skin was still wet from the shower.

I said, taking her by the hand, 'Come on Lei. Let's see what we can find out.'

As we headed towards the head of the stairs, I noticed that she was leaving wet footprints on the carpet. Well, it's not my carpet so.....

We went down to the room under the stairs. I couldn't find the key. It wasn't on top of the bookcase where it had been last time. Lei saw me looking for it.

She said, 'Maybe we can get it open another way.'

I said in alarm, '*What*? You mean break in?'

She just nodded. I wondered what was going on in that head of hers. What's she planning?

She said quickly, 'Go put the bolt on the door Sam. Both doors in fact.'

I just looked at her in curiosity. 'Do I get to find out what you're planning?'

'It'll slow him down if he tries to come in.'

As I went to put the bolts on, I asked, 'Is he likely to return soon?'

She replied as she went to the kitchen to fetch something, 'He's been known to come home unexpectedly.'

I heard her rummage through drawers as I put the bolt on the front door, then I joined her in the kitchen. Just before I put the bolt on the back door I said, 'What are we looking for?'

I watched her pull out drawer after drawer from the worktops.

She said without looking up, 'You go look around the area of the bookcase again. It could still be there.'

I returned to the bookcase as instructed but I still couldn't find it, then I thought maybe he had it with him. I suggested this to her.

She shouted back from the kitchen, 'Wouldn't surprise me.'

Lei came back with a few tools. She got herself down onto her knees in front of the door, then put them down on the floor beside her and selected one. It was a small metal file. She said without looking up as she put the file into the lock, 'Wish me luck?'

I just nodded and prayed that this was going to work.

She turned the file; twisted it counter-clockwise in the lock..... and *nothing* happened! She tried again with a different file. That didn't work either.

'Try two files Lei.' Well it was only a suggestion.

She tried two in the lock. Eureka! It worked this time. She opened the door and we went in.

I'm thinking; why would he put a key for unlocking a door to a room that he didn't want anyone to have access to, in a place where it could be found easily? I voiced this thought to Lei as she examined the top drawer in the desk. It had a lock, and this is what was taking her attention.

She didn't answer immediately, then after a moment's thought she said, 'He knew I wouldn't come in here because I'd be afraid that he would hit me again, and he didn't expect you would since you weren't suspicious about anything. Now that he knows you've been in here he's taken the key with him. Simple.' Lei tried to open the drawer but it was locked. She used her files again for this job.

'That's *amazing* Mr Holmes,' I giggled nervously.

Lei didn't laugh; instead she said, 'You have a look in that desk.' She indicated another desk to the right of this one with the

155

radio. She tried turning the file in the lock but without any luck.

I got down on my knees and started looking through the top drawer of 'my' desk. After a few minutes, 'Em......' I hesitated as I didn't find anything of any real importance. 'What exactly are we looking for Lei?'

'I'm not sure. Keep looking.'

Then, at last, she had it open. She started pulling out sheet after sheet of A4 and examining each one carefully as she did so, then I saw her hesitate when her hand touched something at the back of the drawer. She took it out. I turned to see what she had found. She got down on her knees beside me and unrolled a large sheet of paper. It was the plan of a boat, well, actually the cross-section of a boat. A caption at the foot read: 'Gúðrun'.

As I held down the right hand edge of the sheet I asked, 'You know this boat?'

She replied with a frown, 'I think I've seen it down by the harbour, but I can't be sure.'

I could see little red squares on certain parts of the ship. There were at least five of them. I pointed to them each in turn. 'What are *those*?'

She just shrugged her shoulders, then she spotted something down in the bottom left-hand corner of the drawing; she pointed to it and said excitedly, 'It's a key.'

I looked to where she was pointing. The red squares indicated a 'consignment'. Of *what*? Looks like it was being hidden away out of sight in different parts of the ship for some reason. I could see what appeared to be a harpoon gun at the front of the boat.

'Is this a whaler Lei?' I pointed to the harpoon.

She just nodded, then she said, 'And they don't carry cargo of any kind.'

Then I heard it; a sound coming from somewhere in another part of the house. We both exchanged glances; a look of anxiety appeared on Lei's face.

I said as I got to my feet, 'You get that stuff back. I'll see what's going on.'

I ran out of the room and made my way towards the front of the house. I went straight to the front window and looked out. Yep, it was him alright and he had Petra with him. He's been trying to get in. I made for the front door and began to unfasten the bolt with as little noise as possible, but despite my best efforts, I could still detect a slight scraping sound, and no doubt he could too. He's going to wonder what we were up to! It was at that moment that I heard Lei close a door and seconds later run upstairs. Thank goodness she got out of there in time. I sighed with relief. I'm just hoping that she put everything back where she found them. We don't want to leave any clues for him to find.

I opened the door just as Uncle Pete was pushing it open. I staggered back and almost lost my balance.

He just came straight in ignoring me at first, then he stopped in his tracks and turned to me. 'Why was the door locked?' He turned away again and looked towards the staircase. Petra ran in and bounced into her basket.

I'm panicking now. 'Em....,' is all I could say as I tried to think of an explanation, then I did. 'We saw a prowler outside and decided to lock ourselves in.' I smiled meekly at his back. Well it was the best I could manage in the heat of the moment.

He said without turning, 'You were in the radio room again,' he turned, shouting at me, 'weren't you!'

I jumped, my hand at my mouth. 'No....' I broke off as I could see I was digging myself into a rather large hole here. My body language was betraying me. I get fidgety when I lie and my face felt flushed and my ears burned.

He said finally as he turned away from me again, 'I'll get it out of *her*.' At that he turned and marched off towards the stairs.

I shouted, 'You had taken the key!'

He didn't say anything.

Well it *was* true, wasn't it? The key *was* missing and he had it with him didn't he? I'm silently praying that he did otherwise this hole is going to swallow me up for sure. Just then, Lei appeared from upstairs. I know this because I could hear her coming down slowly.

'You two,' he yelled at her, 'were in the radio room again!'

By now she had almost reached the foot of the staircase. 'You have the key so how could we get in?' Not a good move Lei. All he's got to do is turn the handle and hey presto, we're *both* lying.

He said with a sneer, 'You think I'm that stupid? I know

you. You'd find a way to get in.' He produced the key and held it up for us to see.

Lei snatched it from his grasp before he could react, and made for the door under the staircase where she inserted it in the lock. She turned it several times just to confuse things. Good thinking Lei. 'See, it's locked,' she proclaimed triumphantly.

I was thinking I could relax now, then another thought occurred to me. The desk drawer is unlocked. The one with the plan of the whaler.

He went to the door and pushed her aside. 'We'll see.' He turned the handle. It was locked.

I sighed a big sigh of relief, if only briefly. My heart was in my mouth as I watched him turn the key and open the door, then he stepped into the room. He went straight to the drawer with the plan. My heart was doing a marathon. He pulled on the handle but it refused to budge.

'How did she do that without a key?' I thought. I could relax a little now.

Lei and I were still standing together outside the room. I looked at her. She had a smile plastered on. *'What's she looking so smug about?'*

He marched out of the room and headed for the living room then I heard him open the front door and slam it closed.

'That was a close one Lei.' I gave a short laugh. I heard him start the car and drive away.

She just smiled. 'Fancy something to drink?' she said walking backwards away from me.

I just nodded and followed her to the kitchen. I sat cross-legged on a stool at the breakfast bar while Lei made us some coffee. I said indicating the front door with my thumb, 'Where's he off to?'

'Pub probably.' She turned on the coffee maker. It was already filled with water.

I giggled. 'Lei, how did you do that; lock the drawer without the key?'

She turned from the sink and started giggling too. 'Glued it.'

My smile vanished for an instant. '*What*? You didn't?'

She giggled. 'Yeah.' She nodded and giggled again. 'It's not permanent. He'll get it open again.'

'But he's going to find out it isn't locked isn't he?'

'There's a lot in that drawer. He'll think it's just something that's sticking it.' She brought the coffee pot to the table.

'There is.' I laughed again.

She brought a couple of mugs to the table.

'What now Lei?' I asked as she poured the coffee for us.

She raised her mug to her lips and smiled at me over it. 'Tomorrow we could look over the Siggi. See what we can find.' She sat down at her place. 'And the Gúðrun too if it's there.'

I gulped, and I don't mean the coffee. 'Sure, if you think it's safe.' I wondered if we weren't making a mistake here.

'I meant photograph it. It'll be OK. Trust me.'

CHAPTER 14

Yesterday Lei had suggested going to the harbour in Ísafjörður and paying a visit to the *Siggi*. We might even find the Gúðrun here with a bit of luck. Uncle was going to be away on more business and didn't expect to be back till late. Good. Just the opportunity that we needed. In the afternoon just after lunch we headed off to Ísafjörður. Petra was with us this time.

The weather was promising to be kind to us. The sun had been shining only briefly in the morning and it had threatened to rain, but the sky was now blue and cloudless.

After about a couple of hours driving, Lei thought she knew of a short cut across country so she drove off the main highway onto a gravel road on the right just before a river. It had rained overnight and what had been snow had turned to ice. After negotiating several tight bends, she had changed her mind about the shortcut. 'I think I was mistaken.' She stopped the car and tried to perform a three-point turn. Unfortunately this was an exceptionally narrow part of the road and she was finding difficulty in manoeuvring the car. She backed it towards the river, then when she engaged first gear, I could hear the wheels spinning on the ice. She employed the four-wheel drive and the car moved a little, but when she applied the parking brake she said, 'Damn! No traction here at all; it's just ice.' The car was rolling backwards towards the river and all she could do was apply the foot brake.

I shouted in alarm, 'We're going to end up in the river Lei.' I kept looking round over my shoulder at the river getting ever closer. There was no fence or barrier here of any kind; nothing at all to prevent us from falling down into the that icy-cold glacial river.

She said, 'OK, that's it. I can't risk an accident. We'll have to get help.' She applied the parking brake but it wasn't holding so well, so she engaged first gear and left it at that.

    I got out and looked around. I could see a farmhouse just across the river. Maybe we could get help there; phone for a breakdown truck or something as my cell phone had no signal here either. I suggested this to Lei.

    She agreed. 'I'll stay here with the car, if you go get help at the farm. I'll be working on plan 'B' just in case you have no luck.' She laughed.

    I didn't. I just wasn't in the mood right now. Let's hope she has one; we may need it. I couldn't get to the house from this side of the river without a bridge and I had no intention of swimming in that icy cold water and there was a swift current anyway, so I started out for the main highway that we had exited earlier. It took me all of ten minutes to reach the highway, then it was another long trek up the track to the farmhouse. Then, 'Oh no.' I could see the telephone company putting the telegraph poles into the ground; there was no phone at this house. Well I was here now so I was determined to get the job done. I went to the door and knocked, and waited and waited. *'Damn, no-one at home,'* I thought quickly. I knocked again; harder this time. I could hear movement from behind the door. At last. The door was opened by an elderly guy with a small moustache and short grey hair wearing a green sweater and yes, you guessed right..... rubber boots! I said to him, 'Do you speak English?' He obviously didn't otherwise he would have said something at least. He just stood there and shrugged! I had to resort to sign language..... pointing! I indicated the car across the river and he knew there was a problem, although of course, not the actual problem. He came out and went around to the back of the house where he jumped onto a tractor and started it up. I wondered what he was doing at first, then I thought, *'He's going to go down the track onto the highway then up the other side of the river.'* I watched him drive the tractor down the track then he stopped. He indicated that I get up onto the rear of the vehicle. *'Well, here goes,'* I thought as I climbed aboard and just froze. I had to stand on a metal something; for pulling a trailer or plough maybe? It started swaying from left to right when he moved forward. Then it began to bounce up and down erratically too. *'I'm going to be thrown off this thing for sure,'* I thought. It was scary. *'This is crazy,'* I thought as I held on tight to those enormous mudguards. We moved on down the track, then he veered off to the left towards the river. *'What the hell's he doing?'* I thought as I could feel myself begin to panic.

He continued down to the water's edge and went right in without stopping. We weren't even halfway across when I noticed that the water level was several feet deep here as indicated by the large tyres. I could see Lei standing by the car, Petra in her arms and with a rather large question mark over her head. I could see it even from here. As we proceeded across the river, I began to feel concerned, because the water level appeared to be rising. It was now almost halfway up the tyres. The metal thing that I stood on was bouncing and swaying about from side-to-side even more now as the wheels ran over rocks on the river bed. I can't afford to fall off into the river as the temperature of the water here is very low, and I'd be swept away by the current to a certain death anyway. It was scary. After a few more minutes, the metal platform was in danger of being swamped by the rising water and wetting my feet. Then, mercifully, it was all over as we were fast approaching the riverbank. Within minutes, we were climbing up the steep bank towards Lei and Petra, and now I'm holding on even tighter as I could feel my feet begin to slide on the metal thing. Suddenly, my feet slid from under me and I had to act fast; I grabbed the metal tow-bar - I guess that's what it's called - with both hands, then found myself hanging vertically from it. By the time we had reached the road surface, I was lying flat on my stomach. The guy jumped off the tractor and came around to the rear. He motioned to give me a hand to get up, but I was already in the process of doing just that. He took my hand and helped me onto my feet. I felt myself redden as I said, 'Þakki.' Well at least I know how to say thanks.

Lei had a big smirk on her face. 'What's with you?' I asked curiously.

'Oh, nothing,' she replied. She was obviously finding something amusing. I think it was probably when she saw me lying there on my stomach and looking rather foolish.

The farmer had by now attached a tow rope on the front of the car and another to the rear of the tractor, then he jumped aboard and waited for Lei to get behind the wheel. In only a matter of seconds, the job was done. We both thanked the guy for helping us, and Lei offered him money but he wouldn't accept it.

Once we were on our way to Ísafjörður I asked Lei, 'What are you expecting to find on the boat?'
'Not sure Sam. Won't do any harm to check it out anyway. Remember the Gúðrun?'
'It will if he catches us at it,' I said. 'Hey, I was just wondering. Maybe the 'consignment' had something to do with drugs?' Well, it was only a suggestion.
She said, 'It wouldn't be for the first time that someone has been caught doing that here. The newspapers were full of it not so long ago.'
I said, 'Oh God. It's hard to believe that anyone would want to do that here.'
'Well, just think of all those hidden coves and no-one for miles around to see you. Remember? On the beach; you and I? "No-one to see us", you said?'
'Yeah, OK,' I sighed resignedly. She's right of course. I said, 'And in broad daylight too.'
'And you were the one who saw the boat transferring crates or boxes and thought it suspicious remember?' she said as she took us down to the harbour and parked on the quayside.
'Well, if it is drugs it's our duty to report it to the police,' I said as I stepped out of the car.
Lei left Petra in the car. She jumped into the driver's seat and watched us through the windscreen with her front paws on the wheel as though about to drive it away.
We didn't have far to walk to reach the fishing boats tied up there. My heart was thumping hard now because I had just spotted the Siggi tied up at the quayside. The Gúðrun wasn't in evidence though. As we approached the fishing boats, I said to Lei, 'I'm not happy about this Lei.'
'It's OK Sam. Just follow me.' With that, she climbed aboard the Siggi then turned to give me a hand to get on board too.
I don't care what she says; I'm not comfortable with this at all. I whispered, 'Suppose someone should see us climbing aboard?' I took her hand and climbed on deck.
She said smiling, 'I've been here before. Pete might be suspicious though if he was to find us here, only he's not goin' to.'

163

I thought, *'Famous last words.'*

She turned and made off towards the wheelhouse. I followed her there, then she turned and grasped my left hand, pulling me into the wheelhouse with her. I stumbled over the wooden something that all boats have at door entrances to keep out deck water. She caught me just before I fell on my face. I just smiled at her as I regained my balance.

She said, 'Close the door.'

I did and just stood there looking around the small cabin awaiting further instructions. A flight of steps led below decks and this is what was taking her attention now. As I followed her down the stairs she turned to me. 'You keep lookout. Let me know if anyone even just *looks* as though they're coming aboard.' She turned and continued down the steps.

I shrugged. 'Sure,' I said to her back. I retraced my steps upwards and looked out of the starboard windows. I watched as a fisherman carried nets down the quayside and another helped a mate load a truck with wooden boxes of fish. I could hear Lei searching around downstairs; pulling out drawer after drawer. Then she switched her attention to the galley.

I was bored just standing there keeping watch so I ventured forward towards the wheel. When I reached it, I began to turn it from left to right and back, pretending to steer the boat. I closed my eyes and thoroughly lost myself in a dreamworld. I was skipper of a fishing trawler. Wave after wave crashed over the bow as we drove forward into the night; windscreen wipers on full speed. It was blowing a force ten gale and rain lashed the port windows.

Someone shouted, 'Captain! Some of the catch has gone overboard!'

I thought with some amusement, *'Gee. Even the fish have taken fright. I think I'm going to join them shortly.'*

I snapped out of my reverie when I heard a footfall on the deck. *'Oh God.'* I thought quickly. *'Waken up girl.'* When I looked out of the starboard window, I spotted a male figure wearing fisherman's gear making his way towards the wheelhouse. I hurried back to the top of the stairs and shouted in a whisper to Lei. I thought she didn't hear me because she didn't respond immediately. I started down the steps just as Lei reached the foot of the stairs. I looked back up at the door just as it opened and the guy stepped inside.

He had a startled look as he saw me on the steps. He said in Icelandic, 'Og hvað ert þú að gera?'

Then I thought I recognised him as the guy I had photographed on this boat a few days ago.

She nodded. 'It's OK. I know him.'

'Thank God for that,' I thought with relief. I looked back to Lei to help me out here. I've no idea what he said.

She said, 'He wants to know what you're doing here?'

'Em....' I'm searching for words. Then, it came to me out of the blue. Of course I knew it all the time. 'Talarðu Ensk?' (Do you speak English?) I know it doesn't answer his question but I'm trying my best.

He shook his head. 'Nei.' (No).

'Ég er að læra íslenzku.' (I am learning Icelandic). I thought suddenly, *'Hey, where did that come from?'* I surprised myself there.

'Hvað heitir þú?' (What is your name?).

I turned to Lei once again for help.

She said, 'Name?'

I smiled at him and said quickly, 'Oh! Sam.' I went to the top of the stairs and put out my hand for him to shake.

He shook it. 'Ég heiti Árnar.' (My name is Árnar [Eagle]).

I thought it was time we made ourselves scarce. Lei hasn't found anything of note, so.... I expressed this to her. She started up the stairs just as I reached out for the door handle.

He put his hand on it first and asked, 'Að hverju ertu að leita? Hvers vegna ertu hér?'

I turned back to Lei for assistance, but she got in first. 'Wants to know why we're here and what we were looking for.'

I said, 'Oh? This could be tricky Lei, you think?'

His hand was still on the handle as he awaited a response from us.

I thought quickly, *'Hope he doesn't report back to Uncle Pete, then we really will be in the "sugar".'*

She came up the stairs and I stood aside to let her pass. She said something to the guy in Icelandic and he took his hand off the door handle. She opened the door and hurried outside onto the

165

deck.

    I followed on her heels and wondered what she had said to him. 'Lei?' I said to her back. She didn't reply as she jumped onto the quay. I struggled to keep up then I jumped onto the quayside too.

    I caught her up as she reached the car. 'Lei? What did you say to him?' I opened the passenger door and got in with a smile plastered across my face.

    She got in too and said laughing, 'I just told him that if he didn't take his hand off the door handle, you'd kick the shit out of him.'

    I giggled and said, 'You didn't?'

    'Of course not.' She laughed again and started the car.

    We arrived back in the centre of Ísafjörður about 3 o'clock. We were more than satisfied that so far at least, the first part our plan was coming together.

    We had parked outside a drug store, nose to the wall, as all the cars were parked in this way. I went off to find a store that sold clothing as I wanted to buy a bikini or just any swimwear that I could find. I did find one at last after much searching, but their selection was very small; small in more ways than one, as the only garment I was able to find that came anywhere close to what I wanted just managed to cover the front of my breasts. That must have been the skimpiest bikini in history. For my lower half though, I found a pair of dark blue shorts.

    Lei had wanted medical supplies. She disappeared into the store whilst I waited for her outside beside the car. I spoke to Petra through the driver's window. She touched my fingers with her paw through the glass, and it was then that I thought I heard my cell phone go off. I went around the front of the car and opened the passenger door, then I reached in for my backpack. As soon as I found the phone, I recognised the number at the top of the screen; it was my dad. I thought suddenly, *'Oh God. I forgot to phone him again.'*

    I sat myself on the seat. Petra bounded across to me and started pawing my arm. I pushed her away before saying, 'Hi dad. How's things?' A good way to start a conversation. Petra licked my face. I pushed her away again laughing.

'I've been worried sick about you Sam. Where did you get to? You were supposed to ring when you got to Iceland.'

'Yeah. Sorry. Just didn't get the chance. My battery...... em, oh, and there's no signal in the mountains anyway.' Well it was mostly true.

'Is that the whole truth? You meet someone darling? Boyfriend?' He's prying.

'Well, sort of..... so, what's that got to do with anything anyway?' I sounded frustrated and annoyed and I was.

'Well you know how you get easily distracted?'

'What's that supposed to mean? Anyway, he's nice and cute with it.' I was smiling now as an image of Tómas came into my mind.

'I thought as much. So is he older than you?'

'Maybe..... does it matter?' I sounded annoyed again, and I was too.

Then Lei appeared on the sidewalk. She just stood there with a grin plastered on. I mouthed 'my dad' to her as I indicated the phone. Then I felt myself redden. She nodded her understanding and put her purchases into the car. Petra bounded into the back seat.

'Is he there?' he asked hopefully. 'Can I speak to him?'

'No he's not here dad; he's in Reykjavík. Oh, and he's the manager of a tourist agency in the south. We're going to meet up again at the end of the vacation. It's so exciting dad, ' I said with excitement.

Lei whispered to me, 'Sam?'

Dad must have heard her because he said, 'Who's that you're talking to?'

I turned away from her and held the phone closer to my ear just as a truck thundered by. 'It's Lei. She's Chinese. She's nice. You'd like her. Uncle Pete's partner. She's around my age too.'

'Chinese huh? Uncle Pete married an Icelander; what happened to her? She's young enough to be his daughter then?'

'Yeah. His wife died. Em.... I'll talk to you later dad. Have to go. Bye.'

'Bye baby,' he said with a sigh.

I wish he'd stop calling me that. I switched off the phone and closed my door. I turned to Lei with a smile. 'Get what you wanted?'

'Mostly,' she replied as she got into the driver's seat. She turned the ignition but it didn't start first time. It didn't sound right either. She saw my look.

'What's wrong with it?' I asked frowning.

'I don't know. Was OK earlier.' She turned it again and this time it started, but it still didn't sound right. She backed the car out.

A musical tone sounded from my pack. It was my cell phone again. My dad again checking up on me? I dug the phone out and snapped it on but I didn't recognise the number. 'Hi,' I said brightly.

'Sam? Tómas here.'

'Oh my God, it's him!' I squealed excitedly.

Lei looked at me inquisitively as we moved slowly down the street.

'What's he doing here?' I thought suddenly and gave another loud squeal. I said with excitement, 'Oh, hi there!' I didn't know what to say to him at first, I was so overcome with emotion. I felt happy tears forming. 'Where are you now?'

'On the plane from Reykjavík? We've just landed at Ísafjörður.'

I squealed again. Then I caught myself and calmed down a bit. I said, 'Why did you.....?' I trailed off wondering what had brought him here.

'Just had to see you Sam. Couldn't get you out of my mind,' he said hurriedly. 'Actually I was worried about you. So you got there OK? No problems?'

'Sure...... oh, well, it wasn't without its moments..... em, the journey I mean.' I gave a short embarrassed laugh.

'I see. Well so long as you're OK.'

'Yeah. So where are you staying? You got a place?' I'm hoping it's nearby. It was!

'I'm staying at Hotel Ísafjörður,' he said.

I'm trying to contain my excitement again.

He continued, 'I've taken a few days off. I tried to phone you but you didn't answer.'

'No; that was due to the mountains,' I suggested.

'So what's he like?'

'What's who like?' I knew who he meant of course.

168

'Your uncle?'

'He's OK.' I wondered if I should tell him the truth. 'Em.....,' I hesitated. 'Can we meet somewhere.... like Hotel Ísafjörður?' I laughed.

'You know where it is?' He sounded surprised.

'I've stayed there.' I laughed again. 'I'll meet you in the restaurant..... em, about 4 o'clock, OK?'

'OK Sam. See you soon.' He hung up.

'So, who was that Sam? Your boyfriend?'

I put my cell phone away and turned to Lei. I just nodded, a little embarrassed. I smiled broadly at her and quickly changed the subject. 'Turned out a nice day after all.'

She nodded. 'Have to get to the hotel quick. Pete could be back at the house looking for us.'

In minutes, we were pulling up outside the hotel. Lei got out and told Petra to stay. She bounced into the front seat and, with tongue hanging out, stared at her through the side window.

When I got out of the car, I practically ran through the front door I was so full of excitement, backpack on my shoulder; Lei at my back. When I pushed through the door into the restaurant, it was empty, just like last time. I just stood there feeling a little disappointed at not finding Tómas there, but no matter, he'll be here soon. I'm not sure why I thought that he would be here already.

Lei sat down at the nearest table to the door and I sat beside her. I took the bracelet from my pack and opened the little gift box. Lei's eyes lit up when she saw it. 'Oh, it's beautiful Sam.' Since she was just about to ask where I had bought it I said, 'Tómas bought it for me.'

She said, holding the bracelet in her hand, 'It's very nice. Are those Norse symbols on there?'

'Yeah,' I replied, then I noticed Þórsteinn approaching. Still no staff by the looks of it, nor clientèle either. How can he run a business like this?

He said to me with a smile, 'Hello again Sam. Enjoying your vacation?'

I nodded and said, 'Yes thank you.'

He asked, 'You want tea or coffee or would you like a menu?'

I said smiling, 'I'll have coffee please. We're meeting someone here.'

Lei nodded and said, 'Coffee for me too thanks.'

Þórsteinn disappeared behind the counter and fixed the coffee for us. He came back almost immediately with a tray, two mugs and a coffee pot. He placed it in the centre of the table and asked, 'Anything to eat?'

I replied, 'No thank you.' Lei shook her head. Þórsteinn disappeared back into his lair.

I went into my pack again and produced my necklace from its gift box. I handed it to Lei.

She took it and admired it closely. 'It's beautiful too. You're lucky to have someone to buy you things like this Sam.'

'Oh, he didn't buy this, I did.' Doesn't Uncle Pete buy her anything? So not only does she not get out to meet other people in her own age group, but he doesn't buy her anything either. What kind of a relationship do you call that?

I heard the door open behind us, or at least I thought I did. Neither one of us turned to look to see if it was Tómas or not. The next thing I knew, two strong arms were grasping me around the waist and I found myself being lifted up out of my seat. I screamed and giggled. 'Put me down Tómas!' I squealed again and was still laughing as he put me down onto my feet. I turned to him and said, 'This is Lei.' She stood up and flung her arms around his neck after standing on tiptoes. I said, 'And that was Tómas.' I giggled.

We sat down at the table and Þórsteinn brought another mug for Tómas.

I sat on his right; Lei opposite me. I said, 'You're staying here for how long?' I poured the coffee into our mugs.

'I'm killing two birds with one stone. Have a business meeting in a few hours,' he said putting his arm around me and pulling me close.

'Oh,' I said a little disappointedly.

'Not sure how long I'll be here for exactly, but you keep in touch.' He continued, 'Remember the photos I took of you beside the waterfall and the geyser? They're going into the brochure.'

I giggled and snuggled closer.

Lei had a question mark there.

'Tourist brochure,' I said.

She nodded.

He said looking at me, 'You'll get paid for it of course. Oh, and I made a copy for myself too; that's the one with the two of us together.'

I thought it was time that I asked him a very important question. 'I should have asked you this before; you're not married and no girlfriends?'

'No,' he replied smiling.

I kissed him on the lips. He kissed me back, then the two of us couldn't stop ourselves. The kissing was so intense, I didn't want to stop - ever!

Lei said laughing, 'Hey guys, your coffee's getting cold.' She giggled.

I turned quickly to her with a smirk. 'Lei, can't you see I'm busy.' I giggled and continued where I had left off.

After a few more minutes of this kissing, Lei cleared her throat to get my attention. 'Sam, time we were moving. Pete could be back by now.'

'Yeah. OK,' I said pulling away from Tómas, then I gave him another kiss on the lips for luck, then another, oh, and another. Satisfied, I stood up. 'We'll have to be going now.'

Tómas gave me a big hug and said, 'Bye for now Sam and I'll see you again soon.'

'Not soon enough,' I thought as we made for the door. I turned and waved goodbye to him then I felt a tear forming. I wiped it away quickly with a Kleenex from my pocket.

Back out on the street, Lei suggested that we get back to the house quickly because Uncle Pete could be home by now. He'll be expecting her to have his supper ready on the table.

We settled ourselves in the car. Lei tried to start the engine but all she got was a clicking sound. She tried again, this time it almost started, then it died again. 'Oh God. What's wrong with it?' she said.

I suggested that she leave it for a few minutes then try again. She agreed. While we waited I asked, 'Uncle Pete hitting the bottle again Lei?'

She turned to me nodding. 'I guess so.' She sighed, changing the subject. 'We'd better get going.'

'I got the smell of booze off of him when we first met.'

She just nodded and turned the ignition again and this time it started first time. I smiled at her and looked forward to getting back to the house.

This road out of town was paved. The car purred like a pussy-cat as we headed north and home. It was when we got back onto the gravel road that things started to go wrong. A car sped passed us like a bat out of hell. A shower of gravel hit Lei's car, but thankfully she has a grill on the front radiator that protects the lights from stones.

'God! What's wrong with these stupid people. No consideration for other drivers,' she said annoyed.

'Small minds Lei. Not a lot between the ears,' I said.

I was looking down when it happened; another vehicle, a sports model I think, sped past cutting in in front of us. There was a loud crack and the entire windscreen suddenly turned completely white. Lei hit the brake then struggled to gain control of the car as the vehicle slew across the road. Petra was barking; I screamed; I think Lei did too, then she quickly knocked the windscreen out completely on her side so she could see out. The car ended up facing in the wrong direction.

'Jesus!' I exclaimed. 'The bastard; he nearly killed us!'

'Shit,' she said in frustration.

'Get the breakdown service?' I asked turning to her.

She shook her head. 'Get it tomorrow. I want to get back home today.' She opened her door and stepped out. I got out too then reached in to fetch Petra. She licked my face several times as I joined Lei there at the side of the road. I handed her to Lei.

'Looks like we're going to have to hitch,' she said with a sigh.

I said with a smirk, 'The way to get a hitch for sure is to show a bit of skin. Like this.' I pulled up the leg of my jeans a little.

She said in a Southern drawl and laughing at the same time, 'OK. Get your kit off and show 'em what you have there girl.'

'I beg your pardon?' I spluttered out and broke down in a fit of giggles.

She joined in and we just laughed and laughed till the tears flowed. When she finally recovered she said, 'May as well start walking.'

I agreed. I reached into the car and removed my purchases. She put Petra on the ground. We walked for about ten minutes; Petra on our heels, then I turned and looked back the way we had just come. I could just make out a vehicle further down the road approaching at speed with headlights blazing and throwing up a large cloud of dust in its wake. I said to Lei, 'Look.' I pointed to it.

She turned and saw it too then she said laughing, 'Well, time to show off a bit of leg girl.' We both laughed again.

We stood waiting for the vehicle to arrive, then, when we could see the white of his eyes, I pulled up the leg of my jeans a little and thumbed at the same time. Lei was standing behind me off to my left so I didn't notice what she was doing. I simply assumed that she was doing the same, then with peripheral vision I could see with horror, that she had removed her top! She just stood there laughing holding her t-shirt in her hand and nothing on her top half but her bra.

I shouted at her in alarm, 'What are you doing Lei?'

Then the car was on us. It came to a sudden halt in a cloud of dust.

'Well it worked,' I said, then I thought I recognised the licence plate.

Lei did too and just broke down in a fit of giggles. I was tempted to join in then the driver got out in a hurry. It was Uncle Pete and he wasn't laughing; in fact he was furious!

He shouted at Lei, 'Get into the car now! You've gone too far this time!' He grasped her tightly by the arm and all but dragged her to the car.

I didn't know what to say or do, so I grabbed Petra and got into the back seat and felt sorry for Lei. I hope he doesn't hit her again. Lei was crying now as she sat in the passenger seat next to uncle. He slammed his door shut and hit the gas hard. We shot off up the road at breakneck speed. Uncle didn't say anything to either of us during the journey back.

When we got back in the house, I made my way to my room and the shower and stripped off everything. I just dropped my clothes onto the floor where I stood and stepped into the cubicle. The water felt like heaven. I was ready for it. I had only just started applying the soap when I saw someone approach the cubicle. I thought in alarm, 'Hope this isn't him!' I turned off the water and wrapped my towel that was draped over the cubicle partition.

The door was opened and Lei stood there wrapped in a towel too. I had a question mark over my head. She spotted it and said, 'I need company.' Before I could respond, she had stepped inside. 'Hold me?' she said starting to cry. She threw her arms around my neck and just hung on tight, then she broke down and cried and cried.

'What's the matter Lei? Has he been hitting you or something?'

She just nodded and cried, then she let go of me.

I stepped around her and out of the cubicle. 'Where did he hit you?' I asked. I hadn't see any marks on her face. She still had her back to me as she took off her towel and threw it over the cubicle partition, then turned on the water again. I gasped when I saw the red marks across her back just above the waist. He's been hitting her with a belt maybe? I've got to get her away from here. This is no way to live.

I said, 'Lei, have you considered leaving?'

She stepped back from under the water. 'What? I couldn't. Where would I go? This is all I have.'

I'm thinking maybe I could take her back with me to Reykjavík and she could stay with Helga, at least until she found a job. Maybe Helga could get her one in the Bureau. I voiced my thoughts to her.

She turned the water off and stepped out of the cubicle. She started drying herself off with her towel. 'I love him. I couldn't just leave him.'

I was just about to dry off when she made that last statement. I couldn't believe what I was hearing. 'Lei, you can't be serious. He's an alcoholic.'

As I started to dry off she said through tears, 'He's not. Where did you hear that?' She finished her drying then wrapped her towel.

'The guy who gave me the ride. He said Uncle Pete had a drink problem and had sought help for it but.... '

She cut me off with, 'OK, he did have a problem at one time, but he told me when we met that he had it under control now.' She went over to the first bed and sat down still sobbing.

174

'Well,' I said as I made my way to the bed too. 'He lied to you, and you know he's changed too.'

'But it's all I have Sam. My life is here. I have no friends in Reykjavík.'

'You have no friends here either, so what's the difference?' I sat down beside her and put an arm round her shoulders. 'Listen Lei. This is not a relationship you're in; it's a prison sentence. Next time he hits you it might not be with a belt.'

She started to cry again.

'You come back with me after we've seen over the Gúðrun. I'll tell Tómas about this and he can meet us at Ísafjörður Airport. Fly back to Reykjavík and you can start a new life. What do you say?' I stood up and studied her expression awaiting a reply.

She looked up at me with a tear running down her left cheek. 'I can't... I.... I need time to think about it.'

I tried pleading with her, 'Lei, this could be your only chance to get away. You don't have time to think about it.'

She replied standing up, 'I could have left any time, but I didn't. So what does that tell you?'

'That you're probably crazy?' I began to pace the room. I tried to keep my voice down in case Uncle Pete would hear us. 'Lei, look at him; he's old enough to be your dad for God's sake.' I almost said 'uncle'.

'So? What's that got to do with anything?' She began to pace the floor too, then she turned to me with a look of anger. 'And what would you know about it?'

This was starting to get personal. I said, pointing a finger at her. 'Hey. I know what love is; I've been there and this is definitely not it. He's using you Lei. You ever had sex with him for instance?'

She said, spitting out the words, 'You know, that's none of your damn business!' She was raising her voice now. She turned to the door.

'You're right. It's your life Lei. You can live it any way you like, but he's going to destroy it in the end.'

She said with venom and on the verge of tears, 'Why don't you just butt out of my life!' She turned from the door. 'You know what? I think you're an interfering little bitch!'

I just lost my cool. I said angrily, 'Excuse me? What did

you call me?' I was standing only a few inches from her.

She said, 'You heard.' She put her hand on the doorknob and was just about to turn it when I slapped her across the face. She slapped me back.

Then it happened; there was a loud knocking on the door. 'What's going on in there?' he shouted, then the door opened. Uncle Pete came in and grabbed Lei by the arm. She cried out in pain and started to cry again. 'Get to your room. I'll deal with you later!' he shouted. He's treating her like a kid.

She obeyed then he slammed the door shut behind him. He just stood there in a threatening manner with hands on hips. There was a distinct smell of alcohol off of him. He said to me, 'I have a good mind to thrash you as well. You come flouncing into our lives and start interfering.... '

I cut him off abruptly with, 'What? You invited me here.'

He threw his head back and laughed out loud. 'Is that what he told you?' He laughed again.

I said, raising my voice and backing away from him, 'My dad, if that's who you're referring to, told me that you invited me here!'

'Do you really think I'd invite a little brat like you here and.... '

I interrupted him again. 'Shut up!' I shouted.

His hand went to his belt buckle and he began to loosen it.

'Oh God. What's he going to do with that?' I'm beginning to panic now. I backed away and felt the back of my legs come into contact with the bed, then I fell backwards onto it.

He approached me lying there and removed the belt. He said, 'Do you know what it feels like to be thrashed fifty times with a leather belt? Did your dad ever thrash you with a belt? If he didn't then he should have, then maybe you wouldn't interfere so much in other people's business.'

I screamed, 'Shut up!' I could feel tears welling up now.

He grasped my left wrist tightly with his left hand and placed the belt on my upper arm. I tried to pull away but it was impossible. He suddenly let go of my arm again. 'I'll deal with her first then I'll be back for you.'

I thought quickly, *'No you won't you bastard. We're not staying around here any longer.'*

176

He turned and left the room banging it behind him, then I heard him go into the bathroom and close the door.

I took this opportunity to dress. Before leaving, I used the toilet and freshened up, then I went round the room collecting all my belongings which I stuffed into my pack. It took me a few minutes to do this, then I put it on my back. *'Now to find Lei. First stop's her room.'* I opened the door and stepped inside. He was there, standing across the room in front of the window but there was no sign of her. *'Shit. Where are you Lei?'* I thought looking around.

He said, taking a swig from a half bottle of Scotch, 'Where did you tell her to go? This was all part of a plan wasn't it?' He put the bottle on the bedside table. Now he was brandishing the belt and tapping his other hand with it. He's trying to scare me.

'Yep. I have a plan alright.' I closed the door behind me and leaned my back against it, at the same time removing the key from the lock which I slipped into my back pocket. I'm smiling to myself now as I put my hand on the doorknob.

He made a move towards me and that is when I opened the door quickly and slipped into the corridor. I slammed the door shut and locked it. I heard him shout and swear at me. Next, I had to find Lei. I ran to the head of the stairs, his voice shouting obscenities from the room behind me. I think I took the stairs two at a time, then I caught Lei sitting on the couch, her head in her hands and sobbing. Petra was crying too and trying to get her attention. I put her into the kitchen. She'll only slow us down. I closed the door then returned to Lei. 'Lei, come on. We've got to get out of here.' I grabbed her by the hand and almost dragged her from the room and to the front door. She didn't try to resist. I flung it open and we ran to Uncle Pete's car that was standing at the roadside. As we jumped in I said frantically, 'You got the keys?'

'No, he's got them.' She sniffled.

'Oh! Great!' I said. Then I had an idea. I reached over to the steering column and pulled the cover from under it to expose the wires there.

She said, still sniffling, 'What are you doing?'

'What does it look like? We don't have a key so..... ' I trailed off. I'm guessing now. I have to get this right first time. If I guess wrong, we could be stuck here for a long time. I looked at the wires and where they appeared to be going. Two went to the ignition, so I tried those. I tugged at them with all my strength and, eureka, they came loose. I heard Lei sigh with relief. Then I touched them together and the engine started. Thank God. I said, 'He can't get to us without transport Lei so don't worry.'

She said, putting the car into gear, 'Yes he can. He has a motorbike.'

'Oh for God's sake. Is there no end to this nightmare?' I thought with a sigh. 'Make for the beach where we were the other day Lei.'

'He'll find us there,' she said concerned.

'He won't see the car from the road. You can't see the beach from the road. We should be safe there and we can work on the next part of our plan.'

She hit the gas hard and we shot off down the road.

About thirty minutes later we found the beach. I shouted, 'Turn off here Lei.' I pointed to the left.

She asked quickly, 'How far?'

'Drive down to the beach. We can park there.'

She did and within minutes we were parked on the sand only yards from the water.

I reached over and pulled the two wires apart. The engine cut out and we both sighed a big sigh of relief. I opened the glove compartment and searched around. First out; binoculars. I handed them to Lei. I grinned across at her.

She grinned back. 'Could be useful I guess. Anything else?'

I found a reporter's notebook. I handed it to Lei. She flicked through it. The rest of the items were of no special interest.

Lei said suddenly, 'Look Sam. Names, addresses, contact numbers.'

I said, 'Now do you believe me about Uncle Pete? He's no good for you. He'll only end up hurting you seriously. The drink's changed him bad.'

I had another thought. Uncle Pete might see the tyre tracks of our car turning left off the road and heading for the beach. I'll go back and erase them. Throw him off the scent. I mentioned this to her. She agreed. I got out of the car and made my way back to the road. I had a look to see if he was anywhere in sight, then I stripped off my t-shirt and began to erase the tracks by dragging it over them. Once that task was complete, I headed back to Lei.

When I had settled myself into the passenger seat again, Lei said, 'Sam, look.'

I looked to where she was pointing through the windscreen and out to sea. There in the distance was a ship resembling the whaler that we had seen on the plan in Uncle Pete's den. 'Do you think that could be the same one Lei?'

'Who can say from this distance? It's a whaler too.' She was looking through the binoculars. 'Still too far away. Wait till it gets closer.'

She handed the binoculars to me but I couldn't make out the name of the ship clearly. I returned them to her again. As I got out of the car again I said, 'I'm going back to the roadside to watch for him coming. With any luck he'll head down to Ísafjörður if he thinks we're planning on leaving the area.'

She nodded with an anxious look.

I returned to the road and got myself down behind a large rock. At only five foot tall it's not too difficult to find places to hide yourself. I didn't have too long to wait; I could see a big cloud of dust someways up the road. A single headlight; it had to be him. As the dust cloud grew larger and closer, the roar of the bike could be plainly heard. Within seconds, it was roaring past me. Was it him? It's impossible to tell who's riding a bike when they're wearing a helmet. I noted that the helmet was black and his black leather jacket had a red dragon on the back. Well, it looked like a dragon to me anyway.

I got up from my hiding place and went back to Lei. As I got into the passenger seat I said, 'What colour is his leather jacket and helmet? Are they black? Does the jacket have a red dragon symbol on the back?'

She nodded. 'Yeah. That's him.'

As she was speaking, I noticed that the ship that we had been seeing through the binoculars was very much closer now and there was no doubt about it, it was the Gúðrun.

'Think it's time we paid a visit to the Gúðrun, Lei. See what they're carrying.' As I fastened my seatbelt I said, 'He's obviously got some connection with the ship, otherwise why should he have the plan of the boat in that locked drawer?'

She turned to me with concern. 'How do we get out there without being seen?'

'Midnight's our best bet. Most of the crew should be resting up, if not asleep.' I added, 'Let's get back to the house and change into our swimsuits.'

'What if he's back there at the house? I'm not sure about this Sam. What happens if we get caught on the ship? And the water temperature? It'll be freezing won't it?'

'We'll just have to be careful when we get out there to the ship. Yeah, the water will be colder but we shouldn't be in it for long.' I added, 'It's unlikely he'll be back at the house. For one thing, there wasn't any meal for him on the table, so he'll find something in town no doubt. That'll give us time to have ours and get ourselves changed.'

She nodded in agreement. She started the engine and engaged the four wheel drive. We backed up the beach and in no time, were on the road and heading back home.

When we reached the house, Lei's car was sitting there on the road outside the house, a new windscreen in place.

'Well look at this!' she said in amazement. 'Who..... ?'

I said, unfastening my belt, 'Let's get inside first and we'll worry about that later.'

Once in the house, Lei found a note that had been pushed under the door. She read it. 'From the windscreen replacement service. They say that the police found the car and called them out.'

'Good,' I said as I made for the kitchen, Lei on my heels. As I opened the door, a small hairy bundle jumped up to greet me – Petra, then she turned to Lei and made a big fuss over her.

'Basket,' she said pointing to it in the corner.

Petra obeyed immediately and bounded into her basket.

'What are we having Lei? Hopefully something quick, ' I said as I sat myself cross-legged on a stool at the breakfast bar.

'Yeah. I've got the perfect thing.' She opened the fridge freezer compartment and took out a packet. She held it up for me to see.

Chicken tikka masala. I feel hungry already. I nodded my approval. She took another one out for herself. She set about preparing the meals for the microwave. They would take about ten minutes to cook she said. She put both into the oven together then turned to the window. She asked with a sigh, 'So what do we do after we've looked over the Gúðrun?'

I got up from the stool and crossed to her standing there at the window. I put my arm around her waist. 'If it is drugs –it could be almost anything I guess – we can take the evidence to the police.'

She turned to me. 'We'll need a camera for that.'

'Yeah, but mine is too bulky,' I said thoughtfully. 'Do you have one?'

'Sure. It's a digital one too, but how do we get it across to the boat with out getting it wet?' Before I could reply, she said, 'I think I have a plastic lunch box that would do the job.' She looked in a cupboard above one of the worktops and rummaged around there for a few seconds, then she took a white plastic box out. 'It's waterproof. I'll just get my camera.' She went off to fetch it.

Meanwhile, I returned to the breakfast bar and sat cross-legged again on the stool while I waited for Lei to reappear. She came into the kitchen with the camera inside a transparent plastic bag. Then she placed this inside the lunch box. 'Fits ok.'

I just smiled at her.

The microwave's bell sounded. She crossed to it and removed the chicken tikka masala. She placed one in front of me together with a fork. 'There you go.'

'So, Lei, after we've been over to the ship and collected the evidence, will you come back with me to Reykjavík?'

She sighed and sat herself down beside me at the breakfast bar.

I peeled back the plastic film that still partially covered my meal.

She did too before replying, 'OK Sam. I'll come back with you. I'll have to collect a few things including Petra first though.'

I tucked into the meal. I didn't realise I was so hungry. 'That's OK. Just don't waste too much time getting ready is all.' I continued, 'We want to get out of here as quickly as possible, and if he's here, not to arouse suspicion.'

She said turning to me, 'I haven't been completely truthful with you Sam.'

I had a forkful of chicken halfway to my mouth just as she said that. I turned to her wondering but didn't say anything.

181

'The abuse has been going on for some time now. He would hit me for not having a meal on the table for him. Sometimes it was with the belt.'

'Jesus,' I said slowly. 'All the more reason then for coming back with me once we've gathered the evidence, if there is any.'

She said, rising from the table, 'Wine?'

I nodded.

As she crossed to the fridge she said, 'Remember the little red squares on the plan? There's something being hidden there for sure.'

'Yeah, looks like it. But who's organising it? Maybe he's part of a gang of smugglers. Or maybe he's the ringleader.' I had another thought. 'Would it help us locate where the consignments are being hidden if we were to see the plan of the boat again?'

She shook her head. 'No. Don't see that that would do any good. We'd have to take the plan with us.' She placed two wine glasses on the table at our places, then started to pour the wine.

'Lei. Why did you stay on here? Why didn't you just leave?' I drank some of the wine.

As she sat down at her place, I could see a tear forming in her eye, then it ran down her left cheek. 'I guess I was hoping he would improve, change.... ' She trailed off sniffling.

I said, finishing off my meal, 'Yep, he did that alright.'

She almost laughed. 'I needed a roof and he a housekeeper.'

I pushed the plastic tray away. 'Housekeeper huh? How about sleeping partner?'

She shook he head. 'No sex. He didn't want a family either. Just wanted someone to keep house and have a meal there on the table when he got home.' She finished off her meal. 'He was hardly ever at home sometimes.' She got up and took our trays away.

I sighed. 'Not much of a life Lei. You deserve more than that.'

I kept listening for the sound of Uncle Pete's motorbike but he didn't come home, thank goodness. We passed the time by watching a movie on TV, but I don't think Lei was really taking in the storyline at all, as she wore a worried expression throughout the evening.

CHAPTER 15.

I pulled on my bikini that I had bought in Ísafjörður, then a light-blue t-shirt that comes down just past my waist, and my dark blue shorts; Lei, her red bikini and a light-blue t-shirt on her top half; her camera in its waterproof lunch box tucked under her t-shirt. We wore sneakers on our feet without socks, and this is how we left the house that night. It never gets dark here in the summer months, so we have to be extra careful and we have to work fast if we don't want to get caught.

We arrived in Lei's car around midnight, and, of course, the sun is sitting right on the horizon. It won't set at all here and shadows are very long. We ran down the beach towards the sea stopping only briefly to take off our shoes, then slipping into the sea; Lei ahead of me. As I entered the water, I gave a loud gasp as I felt the coldness engulf my lower half. I knew it would be colder than during the day, but I wasn't quite prepared for this. She's a strong swimmer. I thought I was fit, and I should be as I workout most mornings.

We swam for about ten minutes. Lei reached the boat's starboard side well before I did. She started climbing up the rope ladder that hung there. When I had reached it, I followed her up. When she had gotten to the top of the ladder, she took a quick look around the deck to make sure the coast was clear, then signalled to me to come on up too. Then, in one single movement, she had leapt over the rail and landed on the deck making no sound at all with her feet. I followed her but managed to make a soft thud with my left foot as it came into contact with the deck. I gave an audible gasp when I found myself shivering as there was almost no warmth in the sunlight; at least not as much as during the day. She put her finger to her lips, hushing me to silence, then she moved cautiously, keeping very low and moving down the deck towards the bulkhead. There were boxes of fish piled on top of one another. Some of them were covered in tarpaulin. I stole a peek under it and beckoned Lei to do likewise. She came over to where I was and looked at the boxes of fish there. I looked under the topmost box closest to me and gasped when I discovered what was stashed away there; little clear plastic sachets of a white powdery substance! Drugs? I glanced around quickly to make sure that we weren't being watched, then went right under the tarpaulin followed by Lei. She held the camera to her eye and snapped the drugs lying there in the box. The light of the flash was overly bright in this confined space and I couldn't see anything at all for a few seconds after. And there were more drugs too. I discovered these when I looked under more boxes of fish. Well we have evidence now. Who are these people anyway?

    I thought I could hear footsteps approach. I squeezed myself into a tight corner and pulled Lei in after me. Gosh it was dark in there but my eyes soon became accustomed to what little light there was. I hugged her close and we just shivered there together in this restricted space. Footsteps were getting closer now and I noticed with horror that Lei's lunch box with the camera inside, was lying on the deck and sticking halfway out from under the tarpaulin. She spotted my looking at it and was just about to retrieve it when I shook my head quickly. Next thing we knew, it had disappeared from view; snatched up by someone. I gasped with my hand at my mouth. *'Oh God; we're in for it now!'* I thought in alarm as I felt Lei move closer to me.

    Suddenly, our small space was flooded by sunlight as the tarpaulin that covered my head was lifted high. A male figure grasped me by the right arm and began pulling me out. Lei held onto my left leg with both hands, but I don't know what she expected to achieve by that, then she suddenly let go. Arms were now around my waist and I felt myself being lifted. I screamed and struggled to get free but it was no use, then he let me down. Another figure dressed in fishermen's gear appeared and Lei was dragged from her hiding place too. I shouted at him, 'Leave her alone!' I'm not sure what good it was going to do though. I watched as Lei was carried, kicking and screaming, down the deck. I heard her call out my name, then a door was slammed shut and her voice was suddenly cut off.

The guy who had discovered me said, 'You're English?'

'I beg your pardon?' I swallowed hard and I had a lump in my throat too. 'I am not.... American..... ' I broke off again. I was so petrified with fear that I could hardly speak.

He ignored me and said, 'You'll answer to the boss.'

He pulled me by the right arm down the deck, then he flung open a door and I was hustled inside. Then it was down a flight of steps and along a corridor where we stopped just outside a wooden door. He knocked and the door opened, then he pushed me inside where I tripped and fell onto the floor.

As I slowly picked myself up, I heard a soft whimpering sound coming from, it seemed, across the room on my right. It was Lei and she was lying curled up on the lower half of a bunk bed. Just then, I heard the door close behind me and strong hands had grasped me by both arms. I was taken to the bed and made to sit on it. Lei suddenly turned to me and sat up, throwing her arms around my neck. I pulled her close and we just huddle together there on the bed. I felt a cold shiver run through me. Our clothes were drying on us, but my hair was still pretty wet. I must have looked a mess with my hair matted against my face, and smelling of the sea too.

The guy who had just manhandled me was about six feet tall and wore a dark green woollen sweater, jeans and rubber boots. I glanced at him briefly; another fisherman by the looks of his dress. He was thirty-something with long black hair pulled back into a ponytail.

He said in broken English to me, 'Get some sleep. Captain see you around 6 o'clock.' At that, he opened the door and disappeared into the corridor, closing it behind him again. I heard a key being turned in the lock.

I got up from the bed and began to look around our little prison. I say little, because it was really quite small; about 15 foot square I reckoned. Just beyond the bunk bed on the right, I found a door leading somewhere. I opened it and stepped inside. Toilet, and shower here too.

If we worked fast, the two of us could get showered if we did it together. I put my head around the door to speak to Lei, but she was already up on her feet and coming to join me in the shower. When she came in, I told her of my plan to shower together. It'll save time in case we get an interruption. I started stripping off my clothes, but Lei beat me too it, then she stepped into the cubicle and turned on the hot water. I was just about to remove my extremely skimpy bikini, when Lei spotted it, then started giggling.

'What's so funny?' I asked although I knew what she was laughing at. I said a little annoyed, 'OK I'll admit it's small, but it does the job.'

'Only just,' she said and giggled again.

'Can I help it if they don't stock enough clothes in the shops?' I started laughing too then I had a sudden thought. Just before I stepped in beside her, I went into the other room and took an upright chair back to the toilet. I closed the door and jammed the chair back under the handle. If we get an interruption, this should slow down any attempt to get in, and allow us time to get dressed.

We stayed in the shower for only a few minutes, but I had to admit that it was tempting to stay longer. But, we don't want to get caught in here. I stepped out of the cubicle first and found a towel and began to dry myself off. There was only one towel, so when Lei came out, I handed it to her. Now I was really cold, in fact I was shivering. Just before I got dressed, I washed my few clothes with the soap in the sink. I did the same for Lei, then I wrung them out as best I could. We pulled on our clothes, then went back into the other room and started forming a plan of action.

'We have to get our hands on a weapon; anything will do,' I said in a low voice as I sat on the edge of the bed and tried to get my brain into gear.

'How are we going to accomplish that?' she asked sitting down beside me.

Just before I could answer her, I thought I could hear footsteps coming down the corridor. I had a plan forming; if I can distract whoever comes in through the door for long enough, Lei can hit him with something heavy. I stayed where I was on the bed and took off my t-shirt. Lei had a puzzled expression.

I whispered, 'Find something heavy and hit him hard.'

Her eyes were fixed on my bust initially, then she glanced across at the bathroom. She said as she stood up from the bed, 'Got an idea.' She went hurriedly to the toilet and disappeared inside.

'What the hell's she doing?' I thought and began to panic as I could hear someone outside the door. The doorknob was turned but the door was locked, then I could hear cursing and swearing in Icelandic. Lei had turned on the shower hard, no doubt to make it seem that she was taking a shower, then she ran back into the room and grabbed hold of an upright chair. She stood behind the door, the chair raised above her head ready to strike. I sat on the edge of the bed with my chest thrust out and my t-shirt draped across my lap. I had my hands in my hair at the back pretending to fix it; it was a dishevelled mess after being dried with the towel. The door opened and the guy..... one I hadn't seen before, entered. He was older than the previous one who had been in earlier. Grey stubble on his chin. His eyes were, of course, fixed on my figure, and my bust in particular. That was when Lei brought the chair down very hard on the back of his head. The guy's knees buckled under him and he fell onto his front; his keys dropping beside him on the floor. Lei picked them up and examined them. There were five keys on the keyring. She tried each key in the lock in turn until she found the correct one then locked the door. She took the key off the keyring and handed it to me, then put the rest of the keys into the guy's pocket.

'That'll keep them out for a while,' I said to her as I pondered our next move.

'Tie him up,' she suggested looking around the room for something suitable to do the job. I saw her glance at the curtain on the window.

I shook my head. 'If someone comes through that door, we want everything to appear normal. Get a sheet off the bed and tear it into strips.' I began to pull the sheet off the top bunk with Lei's help.

It took some effort but we did manage to tear it into strips and Lei bound his hands and feet. There were a few strips left over so I gagged him too. Shut him up for a while if he should waken. It didn't look as though he was going to be able to go far any time soon if the damage on the back of his head was anything to go by. I'm thinking she's hit him a little too hard. Oh well, I did say 'hit him hard'.

Lei said, 'We don't want be to stuck with him all night. Suppose he wakens while we're sleeping?'

'Yeah, good thinking Lei,' I said as I tried to decide where we could put him.

Lei suddenly came up with a plan. 'Hide him in a broom closet.'

I said, not believing my ears, 'What, in here?'

She replied, 'No. There may be one in the corridor.' She unlocked the door and opened it cautiously, then she looked out into the corridor. No-one around and now we have to work fast. I chose the left and she the right. She opened the next door down from ours and eureka, it was a broom closet. We both ran back into our cabin and dragged the guy between us to the closet and left him there at the back of the room. There was practically no light in here..... correction, no light at all because I had the brilliant idea of unscrewing the light bulb, then tossed it into the back of the room. I just wanted to reduce the possibility of this guy being found soon. Just before I closed the door, I had a look quick for a firearm. Yep, there was a handgun in his pocket together with one spare clip.

'Well now, that evens things up a little,' I thought with some degree of satisfaction. I searched his other pocket. '*Oh*, look what I've found!' I whispered to Lei as my hand found what I thought was a cell phone. It was too. Oh God, what a stroke of luck. Lei's eyes brightened when she saw me take it from the guy's pocket, and before I could even get a proper look at it, she had snatched it from my grasp.

'Hey!' I said startled.

'Call the police,' she said.

'You know the number?' I asked.

She nodded.

I thought it would be a good idea to get back to our cabin quick. I suggested this to her, then we made a hasty retreat back to our cabin and Lei locked the door.

Once she had settled herself on the bed she started to dial. She said, 'The sooner we tell the police, the better our chances of getting out of here. You don't know what they'll do to us when they find out we've been photographing those drugs.'

She's right of course. The consequences don't bear thinking about. Then I heard it; the ship's engines were started.

'Oh *no*!' I said to Lei. 'If we get too far from shore we won't be able to swim to safety.'

She told someone that we were aboard the Gúðrun and we were being held against our will, and about the drugs, also that the crew were armed.

I thought of phoning Tómas but I couldn't remember his number. I had it in my cell phone directory, but this wasn't my phone. Oh what the hell! He couldn't get to us anyway. What am I *thinking*?

I pulled myself up and onto the top bunk. 'Now for that sleep,' I said straightening out the duvet.

'Yeah. I could sleep for a month,' she said as she laid down on the lower bunk.

I slid beneath the duvet and that's all I remember.

During the night I awoke suddenly and sat up. Something woke me, that much I knew, then I spotted a movement just beyond the bunk bed. It was Lei. She had just emerged from the bathroom and was still in the process of drying herself off, when there was a soft tapping on the door. Lei and I exchanged glances. I jumped down onto the floor making no sound with my feet. Lei wrapped herself in her towel and stood behind me as I said to the door; it was only a whisper, 'Yeah?'

A young male voice answered in a whisper too, 'Open the door?'

'Why?' I replied. I added, 'It's late and we're trying to get some sleep.'

'OK, but I have to ask something?' It sounded urgent this time.

I just stood there impatiently with hands on hips. 'OK, ask.'
'Can you open the door?'

I thought I detected a giggle and it didn't appear to be coming from directly outside the door, so there was more than one of them. Somebody playing little games? I caught with peripheral vision, Lei offering me something. I turned; it was the handgun that we had taken from the guy in the broom closet. I accepted it and nodded my thanks to her.

'What is it you wanted?' I was still whispering.
'Just open the door. I'll make it worth your while.'
I turned again to Lei with raised eyebrows.
She shrugged.

I said to her, 'Oh, what the hell.' I focussed my attention on the door again and turned the key. I opened it slowly, just enough to see who was there.

A young guy with a full, close-cropped beard in his early twenties stood very close to the door. He wore rubber boots, green sweater and jeans. He was smiling. So was I, and at the same time was trying my best to see over his left shoulder as he was taller than me, and I was convinced that he had an accomplice there.

I had my right foot pressed firmly against the door as I hid the weapon behind my back. 'Well?' I demanded maintaining my smile.

'Can we talk inside?' He had his hand on the doorknob.

I said firmly with my smile beginning to melt, 'No you can't. What is it you want? I don't have all night.'

He said trying to push the door open further, 'Err.... are you available for.... ?' He broke off blushing, then added, 'You know?'

I said, beginning to loose my cool, 'Excuse me?'

He turned quickly to someone off-stage, then back to me. 'There was a rumour amongst the crew that two girls were seen on board. Guests of the Captain maybe? You know.....? He's got a reputation; sometimes has girls on board and we just thought we might get a piece of the action too this time, if you get my meaning?' He had a broad grin on his face. It was in danger of getting broader still!

I turned to Lei who had her hand at her mouth. She wore a shocked expression.

I just stood there, not believing my ears; they've come for sex! I said, 'I beg your pardon?' I said angrily, 'We're *not* guests of the Captain. Get out of here!' I began to push the door closed.

He didn't try to force it open again, but took his hand off the doorknob and stood back into the corridor. He said hurriedly, 'You're not..... but.... '

I closed the door again quickly and turned the key, cutting him off in mid-sentence. I sighed and said, 'Let's get back to bed Lei. I need a good night's sleep. I think we're going to need it.' With that, I pulled myself up and onto the top bunk. I was asleep before my head made contact with the pillow.

In the morning I awoke with someone coming into our cabin uninvited and carrying a tray. Yeah, you guessed right; another jerk dressed in fisherman's rubber boots and sweater. He wore a full black beard and long hair pulled back into a ponytail. I glanced at my watch: 5:30.

'Jesus,' I swore under my breath and sat up immediately. Lei, I noticed, had just wakened too but lay where she was not daring to move. Don't they knock first? I could have been having my morning workout in my birthday suit. I shuddered at the thought.

He said, 'Your breakfast.' He set the tray on the dresser under the window and departed from the room again without even looking at either one of us.

I carried the tray over to the bed and placed it between us, then I sat down too. There was a white teapot there complete with tea-bag; I could see the string hanging out. Sugar in a bowl and two brown mugs, oh, and a small jug of milk. A large oval plate contained several rashers of bacon and a couple of sausages plus two fried eggs and four slices of buttered toast. I said, '*What*? Only one plate between the two of us? Someone saving on the washing up?'

She giggled.

'Well,' I said as I picked up a bacon rasher, 'at least we're having a decent breakfast.'

She picked a up piece of bacon too and placed it onto a slice of buttered toast. 'Make the most of it; it may be our last.'

I elected to pour the tea. I said thoughtfully, 'Do you think the Captain authorised this, or is someone just feeling sorry for us?'

As she drank down some tea she said, 'Probably told someone to prepare breakfast for two without mentioning us.'

CHAPTER 16

It was almost 6 o'clock when I heard what I thought were voices coming from outside the door in the corridor. Lei had a startled look.

I thought suddenly, *'They've come for us.'*

I heard a key being turned in the lock and the door opened. I turned to Lei who, I noticed, had grabbed the cell phone from off the dresser and had slipped it under the mattress on the lower bunk. I put the handgun down inside my cleavage and just hoped my bikini top would hold it safely. A key was turned in the lock and the door opened. There were two of them dressed as fishermen and their manner wasn't friendly. Without saying anything, they hustled us out of the room into the corridor, then it was off to the right and into another corridor on the left. We stopped outside a door and one of them knocked, then he opened it and we were pushed inside. I gasped when I saw who was standing there across the room with his back to us; Uncle Pete!

He said as he turned to us slowly, 'OK, let's see who we have here... ' He broke off as he suddenly realised who we were. 'What the....?' He broke off again. He couldn't believe his eyes.

Lei and I simply exchanged glances. She wore a worried expression.

I said to him, 'What are *you* doing here?'

He crossed the room to a cocktail cabinet and lifted a decanter of Scotch intending to pour himself a measure.

'Jesus,' I thought, *'if he'd just leave the drink alone.'*

He said, 'Maybe I should be asking *you* that question. How did you get on board anyway?' He poured the Scotch and turned to us. His expression was difficult to read.

'The sea?' I suggested. I could feel the handgun slip a little. I crossed my arms across my chest to prevent it from moving

192

further. 'So, what are *you* doing here?' I asked again.

He clearly wasn't amused. He took a sip of his drink. 'I'm asking the questions here. This is my ship and you're here without invitation, so I want to know what you're doing here?'

I turned to Lei and back to him. I suggested, 'Curiosity?'

'Curiosity, about what?' He took a gulp of his drink.

Lei said, 'We saw the boat a few times in the same place and wondered what was going on.' That's a pretty lame excuse Lei, but we can't tell him the truth. Well it's partly true.

The ship started rocking; riding the waves. Lei put a hand on my shoulder.

I turned to her and noticed that her face was as white as a sheet. 'What's the matter Lei?'

'Think I'm going to throw up.' She put her hand to her mouth.

Uncle put his glass down on a table and showed her where the bathroom was. I took this opportunity to push my weapon up a little. I'm hoping it stays put this time. She disappeared inside the bathroom and closed the door.

'You haven't answered my question yet,' he said, then he changed tack. 'Maybe you were here looking for something?' He picked up his drink again and looked at me over his glass.

I ignored his question. 'Why is your crew running around the ship with handguns?' I may live to regret having asked that question.

'Armed, my crew? What would they be doing with weapons on board, and how did you know that they were armed?' He's looking at me intently.

'I saw a weapon,' I suggested. I managed a meek smile.

'Who had it, and how did you see it?'

'He threatened us with it.' I'm a terrible liar.

'Did he? Well let's see.' He thought for a moment then said, 'It could only have been.... ' He trailed off thinking, then he crossed to his desk and pushed a button there. He said something in Icelandic into a microphone. I could hear his voice booming throughout the ship. He's making some kind of announcement.

I thought, 'Oh God, they're going to find the guy in the broom closet sooner or later.'

I heard the bathroom door open and Lei came out. Her face

was still very white. She leaned herself against the door for support and looked across at me.

I could feel the ship rocking up and down as it rode the crest of the waves. I felt sorry for Lei. I went over and tried to comfort her.

A cell phone rang a musical tone from somewhere in the room. Uncle picked it up from his desk and spoke into it. A voice speaking in Icelandic spoke to him for some time before he snapped it off, then he turned to me. My heart sank. What has he got in mind for us? He came across to me and said, 'Now, what did you do with the gun?'

'What gun?' I asked in an innocent voice.

'They found Johann in the broom closet. He also had had a gun and a cell phone.'

I didn't say anything.

He asked again in a threatening tone this time, 'What did you do with the *gun*?'

I still didn't answer.

He struck me hard across the face with the back of his hand. I could taste blood. I was livid; I flew into a rage and spat into his face. He wiped it away with the sleeve of his sweater, then he grasped my right arm very tight above the wrist. It was hurting bad.

I shouted, 'Let me *go*!' I screamed at him and spat again in his face.

Then he twisted my arm up my back, threatening to wrench it from its socket. I screamed out in agony as a red-hot knife was inserted into my shoulder blade.

He shouted at me as I screamed out in pain, 'So what did you do with the gun?'

Lei shouted at him now, 'Let her *go*!'

He turned and hit her across the face too. She fell onto the floor and started to cry.

I bent over almost double with the excruciating pain in my shoulder, then I felt the weapon slip out of its hiding place and drop to the floor with a thud.

'So, what *have* we here then?' He picked it up and was just about to say something else to me when there was a knock on the door. He said, 'Come in.' He tucked the weapon hurriedly into the

194

waistband of his pants at the back.

I'm thinking that only some of the crew are aware of what's going on here, otherwise why should he try to hide it. Lei noticed it too.

The door opened and a tall thin guy with a full black beard – 50 something I guess, appeared in the doorway. He too wore the same polo neck sweater and rubber boots as the rest of the crew.

He said, 'Everything OK Captain? We thought we heard screaming.'

Uncle just nodded.

Satisfied with that, the guy departed from the room.

Uncle turned to us and said, 'Now I have a good mind to throw you two overboard seeing you seem to like the sea so much.' He laughed at his own feeble joke. What a jerk. He continued as he crossed to his desk, 'But instead I'm going to let you stay..... ' He broke off, turned to us again then continued, 'But while you're here, you'll have to work.' He looked at us both in turn as if awaiting a response from us.

Lei was silent.

I yelled at him, 'You can go to hell!' What the hell does he mean?

He continued, 'You're part of the crew now and as such you will take orders from me, so, you'll wash, iron, scrub floors, clean the toilets..... ' He trailed off, then, 'For that in return, you get the chance to eat proper food and you stay out of the sea.' He laughed again, then he pressed a button on his desk

'He's mad,' I thought. 'He's off his head. He wants to see a shrink. Oh *God*, what have we gotten ourselves into here?'

There was a knock on the door and two guys dressed in the now-familiar uniform of fishermen, came into the room. They took us back to our cabin and left us there until lunchtime.

Around one o'clock, the door opened and one of the guys; a tall one with a beard came in. We were hustled outside into the corridor and led down a flight of steps, then it was straight ahead and through a door into a mess hall; a rectangular-shaped room with a long table taking up most of the centre of it. Some of the guys were already seated and had started on their meal. Eyes were on us the moment we entered. As I took Lei's hand and tried to squeeze past several of the crew, some seated and others standing talking, I felt a hand touch my bottom. I turned around quickly hoping to catch whoever it was that had touched me, but I couldn't identify the culprit.

This was a self service. The guy who had taken us from the room showed us where to stand in line for the food. Plates were stacked on top of one another on a table near the far wall and this is where the line was forming. A large overweight guy stood at another table with a large urn of soup. I took a bowl from the table as this is what the others appeared to be doing. Lei was at my back, her bowl in her hand. I picked a metal tray from a pile on a table and put my bowl on it. I put Lei's on it too. When we had reached the overweight guy, he put soup from a ladle into our bowls.

We now had to find ourselves a space at the table. The seats were filling up fast. Lei pointed out two empty ones together, so we made for those. I had only just reached the first one, when a tall guy with a grey beard pushed in in front of me, then sat down.

'Charming,' I thought. *'Some of them at least have lost their manners.'*

Then I spotted another two vacant seats, so we headed there. I sat down with Lei on my right. The guy on Lei's right was giving her looks that even I felt uncomfortable with.

Cutlery was already on the table so we started on our soup. It was chicken I think, but then I could have been mistaken. I hope they observe some level of hygiene in here.

When we had finished our soup, Uncle Pete arrived in the room and sat down at the head of the table. Every now and then, heads would look in our direction, fingers would point and even rude gestures were made.

Lei said disgustedly, 'I don't like it here Sam. I just want to get out of here as quickly as possible.'

I patted her arm reassuringly as it lay on the arm of the seat. 'Me neither. Just try to ignore them.'

I finished my soup about the same time as Lei.

She whispered to me, 'I wonder if anyone has looked at the camera yet? They'll know what we've doing.'

I whispered back, 'Don't worry about it Lei. We're going to find a way out of this.'

I watched with peripheral vision, as another tall guy with a black beard leaned down to whisper in Lei's ear. She didn't say anything to him. She had a shocked expression as she put her hand on my arm.

I asked her with concern in my voice, 'What did he say?'

She shook her head and fixed her gaze on something in the centre of the table. 'I can't repeat it,' she said in a whisper. She wasn't smiling.

I looked around the room and noticed that many were getting up to fetch their next course. I stood up and pushed my chair back, then took Lei by the hand and led her to the end of the line. We picked up dinner plates from a pile on a table and helped ourselves to stew and potatoes from a large metal pot, then we returned to our seats.

I had just started on my stew when I thought I got a glimpse of someone I knew. Blackbeard? This guy appeared momentarily in the midst of a group of others who were standing across the other side of the table, then he disappeared again.

I thought to myself, *'It couldn't be him, could it? What would he be doing here? He's not a fisherman is he, but then I don't really know much about him? I must be imagining it. Just someone who looked like him I guess.'*

Lei spotted me looking. 'What's the matter? Look like you've seen a ghost.'

'Remember the guy in the truck who gave me the hitch?'

She nodded. 'Is he here?' she asked looking around.

'I wish,' I said. 'No, probably not. I must have been mistaken. A lot of these guys look the same; beards, you know? They're like clones.' I gave a short laugh.

'Yeah,' she replied absently. 'Hey, this is good stew.'

I agreed. 'The good life isn't going to last forever Lei. Remember what he said; we'd have to work for it?'

She nodded. 'Isn't he going to introduce us? The rest of the crew will be wondering who we are,' she said.

'God knows.' I sighed.

Once we had finished our meal, uncle gave a signal to someone someways off behind us. Two guys came forward and we were ushered out of the mess hall, then it was down a corridor and back to our original cabin. Once in, the door was locked behind us and we were left alone for the moment.

I said to Lei, 'We're going to have to come up with a plan to get out of here.'

I noticed that there were no chairs in the room now. They're trying to remove any chance of us getting our hands on a weapon. There didn't appear to be anything left for us to use.

Lei sat on the bed, and drew her knees up to her chest and cried softly to herself. I joined her there and put my arm around her shoulders trying to comfort her. We stayed in that position for some time, then I could hear footsteps in the corridor. The door was unlocked and two figures entered. One was tall with a black beard and probably fifty-something, the other was much younger and clean shaven. I held onto her right arm tightly as they attempted to separate us.

I shouted at them as I stood up from the bed, 'Let her go you bastards!'

One of them struck me hard across the face and I fell backwards onto the floor. They took poor Lei from the room. I think she was in a state of shock as she didn't say anything to them or try to resist.

I thought with sinking heart, 'They're taking her off to make her work, then it'll be my turn. God knows what they'll give us to do.'

I didn't have to wait long, as in less than ten minutes I could hear footsteps in the corridor approach our door. A tall guy entered and I was hustled outside and down the corridor. He didn't say anything to me as he pushed me forward ahead of him. We arrived at the toilets, at least that is what I thought. He opened the door and pushed me inside. Yes it was the toilets, with the usual male latrines – four of them along the wall on the right. An extra-large cubicle marked with a 'disabled' sign on the door stood beside the other cubicles on the left.

I thought, *'So this is what I have to do. Clean the toilets.'*

I'm looking around for the bucket or even a mop for the cleaning, but I couldn't see anything.

He pushed me towards the 'disabled' cubicle and inside. I was just about to turn to him to ask where the cleaning implements were, when I heard the cubicle door being locked. I began to panic now, but before I could react, he had grabbed me around the neck with one arm whilst the other hand went under my shirt at the front. I started to scream. That's when he put his hand over my mouth to shut me up. I was screaming in my throat and struggling to get free from his grasp, then, with both hands he pushed me quickly forward and I lost my balance. As I fell heavily onto the floor on my front, I struck my head on something solid; the lavatory bowl maybe? I wasn't knocked out, but I was seeing stars momentarily, then he pulled my shorts down my thighs. He put a foot in the small of my back to prevent me from rising, then he pulled them completely off me. I'm screaming now at the top of my voice. As he grasped me around the middle with both hands and attempted to pull me up towards himself, I twisted my upper body around quickly and elbowed him as hard as I could in the face. I didn't look to see where I had hit him or what damage had been inflicted; I just wanted to get out of there fast. Then, I turned quickly and, with all my strength, kneed him in the groin and that fixed him good. He collapsed on the floor groaning and that's when I snatched up my shorts. As I pulled them on quickly I could hear running feet approach from somewhere. Someone's heard me scream, safety at last. I unlocked the door intending to let in whoever it was who had come to my rescue. My friend on the floor was recovering now and attempting to rise, but obviously still in pain. A tall guy entered the cubicle, then he locked the door behind him!

'Oh God no! He's going to try to rape me as well.' I thought in a panic. *'I can take on one at a time but two together......?'*

He pushed me backwards and I fell heavily onto the guy on the floor, then he pulled his zipper down. The one on the floor pulled my t-shirt right up past my bust and untied my bikini top. I screamed at the top of my lungs, then a hand was cupped over my mouth. The second guy started lowering himself onto me, then he pulled my shorts down my legs. I struggled to get free but the one on the floor had his other arm around my neck. I screamed in my throat but who's going to hear me here? Would they care anyway? The second guy reached out and flushed the toilet, no doubt to mask any screams. I could hear running feet again, then there was a hammering on the door. All I need is a short distraction and I can do this one an injury he won't forget in a hurry.

Then it happened; someone had climbed up onto the top of

the cubicle partition and saw what was happening. My would-be rescuer shouted something in Icelandic. The guy on top of me looked round and up over his shoulder, and that was when I took the opportunity to knee him in the groin very hard. The third one jumped down onto the floor. He was much younger than the other two. He unlocked the door and led me out. We headed down a corridor. I started crying at this point. He put his arm around my shoulders. I said to him looking up into his face, 'Thanks.'

He didn't say anything, at least not in English so it was pointless saying anything further to him as he wasn't going to understand it anyway. I was led down another corridor. I thought I recognised it. Yes I did too. This is where Uncle Pete's cabin was.

I thought, *'Not him. What good would talking to him do? I'd get no sympathy anyway.'*

The guy behind me knocked the door.

I heard Uncle Pete shout, 'Come in?'

The guy opened the door and I was led into the room. He said something in Icelandic to uncle. Uncle just nodded and the other one left the room. He had been in the process of pouring a half bottle of scotch when I arrived. He came around to my side of his desk, glass in hand and sat on it; one leg dangling over the floor and eyed me up and down.

I just stood there, rooted to the spot, tears still running down my cheeks.

He said, his speech slurring, 'He told me briefly what happened. You shouldn't walk around dressed like that. It's attracting too much attention, so what do you expect?'

Just as I thought; the bastard had no sympathy for me at all.

I said, '*Excuse* me? You think it's my fault? They tried to rape me and that's all you can say?'

I was on the point of screaming at him, when I caught myself. What's the point?

He encircled me several times, then he locked the door!

'What the hell's he doing?' I thought in alarm.

He stood at my back and touched my neck at the side; his other one went under my shirt just above the shorts at the front. I stepped forward away from him and that was when he grasped me around the waist with both hands. One wandered upwards and stopped just under my bust; the other one caressed my stomach and was slowly working its way down, then he slipped it down the front of my shorts. Enough! I turned quickly, and with all my strength, elbowed him in the stomach. He doubled up and I realised that this could be my opportunity for escape.

He shouted, 'Ah! You little *bitch!* You'll pay for this now!'

I made as if to run for the door, but he recovered almost immediately. He grasped me around the waist again and lifted me off my feet, then he threw me on my back onto the desktop. Sundry items on the desk scattered in all directions, some of them smashing to the floor. The pain in my lower back was bad as I landed on something solid. This also knocked the wind out of me, and as I tried to recover, he pulled my shorts down almost completely. I was minus my bikini top which was still lying where it had fallen on the toilet floor. I screamed and screamed at the top of my lungs.

He hit me hard across the face. 'Shut up bitch!' he shouted, as he climbed on top of me, at the same time unzipping himself, then he pulled my shirt up past my bust.

I tried to hit him with my fists around the head, but he grasped my right one and pinned it above my head on the desk. With my free hand, I groped around for something solid; anything that would do him an injury. I could feel him trying to pull his underwear down and that is when my hand found what felt like a glass paperweight. I brought it up quickly above my head and, with all my strength, hit him hard on the side of the head with it. He toppled over and fell onto the floor. I got up immediately and pulled up my shorts, then ran to the door and unlocked it.

When I got into the corridor, I just ran and ran; I wasn't caring where. I just wanted to get to safety, then, oh *no!* I had just run into Lei who was being taken somewhere by two guys with beards.

I shouted at them, 'Where are you taking her?'

One of them said, taking me by the arm in a vice-like grip, 'You can come with us too.'

'You can go to *hell*!' I shouted back.

He slapped me across the face and we were pushed along the corridor towards what I recognised as our little prison. The door was opened and we were pushed inside.

I sat on the side of the bed and tried to think what to do next; how to get hold of a weapon was at the top of my list of priorities for sure.

Lei sat beside me and hugged me close.

She said as she burst into tears, 'They made me tell them what our plans were. They've looked at the pictures Sam. We're as good as dead already.'

I didn't know what to say at first, then, 'Did they hurt you?'

'They threatened to take all my clothes off and..... torture me! It was horrible.' She burst into tears again.

We just sat there on the bed holding each other tight and awaiting our fate. Some minutes passed and we could hear footsteps – one set - in the corridor. I exchanged glances with Lei. Could she read my thoughts?

I whispered to her, 'Get behind the door and tackle him when he comes in.'

She looked at me with a puzzled expression, 'I don't have a weapon this time.'

She was looking around the room for something to hit him with.

'You've got yourself Lei,' I said and left it there. I knew she would understand.

She got herself behind the door. I sat on the edge of the bed and waited for him to enter, then I pulled my t-shirt over my head.

I thought, *'This'll distract him for sure.'*

I sat there with my chest thrust out, and, as the door was opened, his eyes went naturally to my bare top half. He wasted no time as he came into the room and approached the bed. I just smiled up at him and that is when Lei ran up behind him and jumped onto his back. As he tried to get her off, I took this opportunity to kick him savagely in the crotch and again in the stomach. I hurt my foot this time. He doubled up, but began to recover a little.

Lei spotted a weapon stuck in the back of his pants. She withdrew it and hit him hard on the back of the head with it. He fell to the floor with her still on his back holding onto his shirt collar, then she hit him again and again and again.

I had to intervene here. I pulled her off him and she started to cry again.

I said as I searched the guy's pockets for spare clips, 'OK, let's get out of here and get up onto the deck. If the police arrive, they'll have to know where to find us. There could be a lot of gunfire too.' I indicated the spare clips.

I took the weapon from her and checked the clip. It hadn't been fired. I pulled on my shirt again, then we went out into the corridor and made our way towards a stairway and what I thought was the stern. It was pure guesswork on my part. I heard footsteps approach – one set, I think. I darted behind the staircase and pulled Lei in after me.

We were well hidden here, and, as the guy was about to pass us by, Lei came up behind him.

'Hey!' she said to him.

It took him by surprise. He turned to face her, about to say something and that is when I made my move. I ran up behind him and stuck my newly-acquired weapon in the small of his back. He put his hands in the air immediately and that is when Lei kicked him in the groin. He doubled up and I hit him hard on the back of the head with the weapon. He collapsed onto his front. I searched his pockets for spare clips; I found two.

I said, 'He doesn't appear to be armed.' I searched his pockets.

Lei had her hand down inside his right boot.

I just looked at her in astonishment. *'What's she doing?'* I thought.

She smiled back at me as she withdrew her hand. She had found a handgun there.

I whispered, 'So *that's* where they're hiding their weapons. No wonder the rest of the crew don't know they're armed.'

As she checked the clip she said, 'And they probably don't know Pete's smuggling drugs either.' She put the weapon into the back of her waistband.

We dragged him between us to just under the stairs and left him there, then we made a dash for 'freedom' up and onto the deck. It was freezing up here, and it didn't help that all I wore was my bikini bottom, shorts and t-shirt. Also, the ship was being tossed around like a cork in a bathtub, and the howl of the wind was deafening. The sky was grey now and every so often, a wave would crash onto the deck, as if we weren't cold enough already.

Lei was ahead of me and making for the starboard side.

'What's she doing?' I asked myself, then I knew; she was throwing up over the side. Poor Lei, she doesn't enjoy being on boats.

We were making our way towards the bow, when a series of shots rang out. Someone was shooting at us. We both ducked behind a metal something, and so long as we kept our heads down here, we should be OK. I tried to identify the source of the fire. Lei pointed forward to a capstan with the rope wrapped around it.

'There,' she said.

I saw where she was pointing and returned the fire. Another shot rang out and whizzed over our heads, and this was followed by yet another. A figure darted from his hiding place and I opened fire at him, hitting him in the leg. He fell onto the deck and crying out in pain, then he resumed his firing. I returned it and as he tried to get back to his original hiding place, I shot him in the chest. I went to check on him. I ran, keeping very low and when I had reached him, I felt for a pulse. Yep, he was dead alright. Good!

'One down, God knows how many to go!' I thought sadly.

As I turned around, I spotted Lei up close to the bulkhead. She was throwing up again. I felt sorry for her and tried to work my way towards her. I'm holding onto anything that comes within reach so as not to lose my balance. It was difficult work, but I eventually made it to her.

'You OK Lei?' I had to shout as the roar of the sea against the ship was deafening.

She nodded.

I wanted to get her to safety; anywhere out of this hell-on-earth. Then I spotted uncle behind the harpoon gun.

'What the hell's he doing up there?' I thought in alarm, then I realised that he had a rifle with him.

He aimed it at me and opened fire. I ducked instinctively and returned fire with my handgun, but I was probably too far from him for an accurate shot, and the swaying of the ship from side-to-side didn't help. The bullet glanced off the harpoon harmlessly. I swore under my breath then took aim, holding the weapon with both hands. I stole a

quick glance over my left shoulder to see Lei standing up.

She had dropped to the deck when I did, but now she was exposed; vulnerable! I screamed at her to take cover as I could see uncle aim the harpoon at me, but I don't think she heard me.

I stood up and grasped her arm to pull her down with me, and it was then that I heard the harpoon being discharged. I threw myself flat onto the deck, but poor Lei didn't realise what was happening until it was too late. Maybe she didn't hear the discharge. The harpoon flew over my head as I lay flat on my stomach and slammed into Lei's middle around the area of her navel, and burying itself in the bulkhead pinning her to it, the explosive charge detonating on impact. The vicious cutting barbs that had now been released from the nose, would cause maximum damage to internal organs and major blood vessels. Her entrails were now trailing down her thighs and blood was pouring from her body and over the deck. She was crying and screaming out for help as she knew she was dying. She was choking on blood now as it fountained out of her mouth and ran down between her breasts. Uncle was shouting and crying out for her when he realised that he had hit the wrong target. That one was meant for me!

There was nothing anyone could do for her now. Lei was in the process of reaching out to me; her two arms outstretched, pleading for help, then her head slumped forward and she was dead. I threw up!

I heard a firearm being discharged from the direction of the harpoon. He was firing at me like a madman; bullets whizzing over my head. Several slammed into the bulkhead. He wasn't even aiming properly. He was hysterical; shouting and swearing at me and crying out for Lei. He had just murdered an innocent girl, and now I was about to get my revenge. As I lay on my stomach, I rested my weapon on my arm and took careful aim.

'I know I can do it,' I thought as I felt my hand shake. I whispered, 'This is for molesting me.'

I fired once, twice, three times, hitting him in the stomach and further down too. He leaned on the harpoon for support, then I took aim again and opened fire; one, two, three shots in the chest. He collapsed onto the deck.

I said, 'And that's for Lei.'

Satisfaction? You bet! But it won't bring my friend Lei back. Poor Lei; she didn't have a chance. I broke down and cried and cried. I lay there for a few minutes on my front not daring to look back at Lei, then I got up on my feet and ran hurriedly to the rail where I threw up over the side. As I hung over the rail, I realised that I was too exposed here and was just about to take cover again when a shot rang out. The slug whizzed over my head and slammed into the bulkhead. I threw myself flat onto my stomach once again. From where I lay, I had a clear view of my adversary. I could see him close to the rail and trying to keep as low as possible, and it was then that another shot rang out. I ducked as the slug flew by on my right and struck something metallic behind me. As he attempted to move from his hiding place, I took careful aim and fired. The bullet hit him in the left shoulder. He cried out as he was thrown backwards towards the rail. He slowly picked himself up by holding onto the rail, then someone grabbed him from behind and he was wrestled to the deck and a fight began. I couldn't hear much for the roar of the sea against the ship, then it was all over, thank goodness. Whoever it was that had done me the favour of taking on my assailant, started working their way towards me. He was tall and had a full black beard. He wore a red chequered jacket and a green cap on his head. He was smiling as he spoke. I know he did say something to me as I could see his lips move, but I couldn't hear his voice at all for the roar of the sea.

'Blackbeard?' I said softly to myself, then I shouted it out loud as I suddenly realised it *was* him!

I just ran to him and flung my arms around his neck. I had to stand on tiptoes to do this. I've never hugged him before.

He hugged me too then he said, 'Oh babe, you're safe at last.' Then he kissed me on the right cheek.

Tears started rolling down my cheeks as I found I didn't want to let go of him. Then it happened; a firearm was discharged and Blackbeard seemed to fall into my arms. Blood came out of his mouth as he keeled over and fell onto the deck on his front.

I screamed out and cried and just broke down. I crouched beside Blackbeard but there wasn't anything anyone could do for him. He was dead and that was that. I got up and began to move forward towards Blackbeard's killer. From my hiding place I could just make out a leg. I think he was lying on his stomach, so I took careful aim and fired at it; once, twice, three times. I think I'm losing control here. I could just make out his cries of pain through the roar of the sea as he tried to move away from me, but I was determined to get my revenge. I don't intend to take prisoners here. I began to move towards him again. I could see him backing away from me and holding onto his leg that was gushing blood onto the deck. I got up onto my feet, keeping as low as I could, and running towards him. When I had reached him, he was lying on his back with his weapon lying by his right hand on the deck, but he was very much alive.

'Not for long you bastard!' I thought as I felt the anger rise in me.

Just as I was about to reach for his weapon, his hand moved quickly onto it and that's when I shot him full in the chest, then I lost it completely. I burst into tears and cried and screamed at him at the same time emptying the clip into him. Then I threw it down on the deck and just cried and cried. I got down onto the deck on my knees and couldn't move.

After about thirty seconds, I calmed down a bit and tried to wipe the tears away with the back of my hand. A wave came over the side and soaked me, as if I wasn't wet enough already. It was then that I almost died with fright as a hand was suddenly placed on my shoulder. If this is someone about to blow my head off, I can't defend myself as I've just emptied my weapon. I turned to look at the figure who had knelt down behind me. I gasped and squealed out in delight when I realised it was Tómas! Where the *hell* had he come from? And Blackbeard...... ? Was I dreaming this? Was Blackbeard really dead? Part of me wanted this to be a bad dream, and the other wanted it to be real! He picked me up and hugged me close and then the kissing began. Yep, it was him alright. There was no mistaking those lips. I just hung onto him tight and emptied my sorrows on him, then the crying started all over again.

He said, holding me even more tightly, 'Come inside and get warm. Tell you *all* about it.'

He led me into the warmth and I just broke down again when an image of Blackbeard dying in my arms came back to me. And poor Lei.

I said, still sobbing, 'I want to get warm Tómas. I want to get some sleep. Have to get to our cabin.' I felt so weak I thought my legs would give out any time. I'm thinking, *'If I don't get the chance to lie down soon, I'm going to pass out for sure.'*

He said, kissing me on the side of the head, 'The police have everything under control Sam, and arrests have been made. You're safe now.'

I turned to him and just hung onto his neck, where the intense passionate kissing started all over again.

After a few moments I resurfaced and said smiling up at him, 'Come on. I know where the cabin is.'

With that, and with his right arm around me, we headed straight for it and went inside. No sooner had we entered the cabin and my legs just gave out. I fell, and would have hit the floor, but he caught me in time and I fell into his arms once again. He laid me on the lower bunk and this is when I must have dozed off, because I don't remember what happened next.

I awoke in a sitting position on the floor of the shower cubicle under a torrent of hot water pouring down on top of my head, my back resting against the wall. I still wore my clothes though. I could feel the water's warmth warming me up good. I also noted that Tómas wasn't with me. Thank goodness, because I just didn't have the energy do anything right now. I could feel my eyelids close now and then. I was very sleepy now and the luxurious warm feeling of the water didn't help. Any second now and I'd be in the Land of Nod for sure. Then it happened; the shower cubicle door opened and Tómas stood there minus his shirt, oh, and his pants. He was wearing trunks though. He got me to my feet with my back still pressed firmly against the wall. I rested my head on it and the water now fell directly onto my chest between the breasts. This is where he decided to bury his face too. My breathing was slow and heavy as I felt his hand cup my left breast and caress the nipple. He stopped what he was doing for a second and pulled back from me.

He said, pointing to my chest, 'What happened to your bikini top, or..... ?' He broke off.

I gave a short laugh and said, 'Oh, it's somewhere.... ' I broke off too as I felt his face slide down my chest towards my stomach and there it stopped at my navel which was fully exposed, as my t-shirt doesn't tuck in anyway. I could feel his tongue exploring around there, then he pulled my shorts down my thighs.

'Not now Tómas,' I said through gasps. 'Don't have the energy right now.' I sighed.

He straightened up and concentrated on my chest again, then it was back to my lips. His kissing was now getting more intense and I felt his hand fondle my right breast through the shirt; his other one was attempting to untie my bikini bottom but thankfully, it had knotted itself.

'Tómas!' I shouted and gasped. 'Not now. Just don't have the strength. *Please*, I want to get to bed. Can you take me there?' *'Stupid question really,'* I mused.

He pulled away and said smiling, 'You'll want to get dried now?'

I grinned back. 'I can handle that part thank you. I'll let you know when I'm ready, OK?'

He retreated from the bathroom and closed the door. I had difficulty removing my t-shirt as it clung wetly to my skin, but the shorts and bikini bottom weren't a problem, then I dried off and wrapped the towel. I shouted on Tómas. He lost no time coming in and lifted me up and carried me to the bed. I just lay there smiling up at him, then I wrapped myself in the duvet and removed the towel. I pulled it out and handed it to him. Then I suddenly remembered I hadn't phoned Charley. She'll be worried sick about me.

He saw my worried look. 'What's the matter?'

I told him. 'Do you have your cell phone?'

He nodded and went to fetch it.

I told Charley the whole story and I asked her to promise not to tell mom and dad. This can wait till I get home. I don't want them to worry about me.

When I had finished the call, I asked, 'How did you know where to find us?' I snuggled down further into the duvet.

He sat down on the bed beside me. 'Police got your message.' He stroked the hair at the side of my head as he said, 'Good idea for you to get some sleep now.'

My eyes were already closing as he spoke those words.

CHAPTER 17

Later that day, as I was passing down a corridor, a door opened and someone grasped me by the right arm. I turned quickly to face him and demanded, 'What do you think you're doing?'

A guy dressed in blue slacks and parka stood there. He had a small moustache and black hair, and he was taller than me. So what's new?

He said to me, 'Come with me Miss?' He began to pull me towards the open door.

I asked in alarm, '*Excuse* me?' As his hand was still attached to my arm, I said forcefully to him, 'Could you please let go of my arm?'

He said, rather annoyed, 'Just come with me Miss and....'

I interrupted with, 'Why? I will not!'

He repeated his demand.

I refused to budge and shouted back at him. 'Who do you think you are? Let go of my arm now!' I'm beginning to loose my cool for sure.

He held onto my arm tighter this time.

I said, with my temper quickly fraying at the edges, 'Let *go* of my arm now or you'll regret it!' I meant it too.

He refused to let go and just kept pulling on my arm.

'*Well you asked for it,*' I thought just before I kicked out with my right foot towards his groin area, but it didn't have a lot of impact since I wasn't wearing shoes, so I brought my left knee into play instead!

'Ah!' he shouted as he doubled up in pain.

I turned on my heel and fled down the corridor. I didn't get far, however, as I ran right into Tómas.

'Hey, where are you off to in such a hurry?' he said grasping me by the shoulders.

I turned and indicated the guy I had just disabled. 'He was trying to force me into that room there but I sorted him out good and..... '

He interrupted with, 'You've just assaulted a policeman.'

'Pardon? What did you say?'

The guy had almost recovered by this time. He began to approach us slowly whilst holding onto himself.

'I don't think he'll arrest you for assault seeing it's your first time,' he said laughing. 'It is your first time isn't it?'

I turned back to him and said as I punched him on the chest with my fists, 'Oh shut up.' Then I started laughing too. I turned back to the policeman and, feeling rather foolish and embarrassed said, 'I'm so very sorry...... I didn't realise..... a girl can't be too careful in these parts, you know?' I laughed and felt my face flush red.

He just nodded and almost managed a smile, but I guess the pain was too much for him. He said wincing slightly, 'You can certainly handle yourself well.'

I smiled and said, 'I like to think so.'

He led me through the door and into the same cabin where Uncle Pete had been. Another policeman, I think, sat behind the desk waiting for me.

The first one said, 'This is Sam Winter at last.' He winced again.

The one behind the desk stood up and introduced himself with outstretched hand, 'Páll Magnusson, Chief Investigator. Drugs Division.'

I shook his hand. Tómas came into the cabin at my back. There were two chairs on our side of the desk. He gestured for us to be seated. Tómas sat on my right, his hand on mine.

'Sam, I was impressed by the way you tackled these people and how you put your own life on the line,' he said smiling.

I felt my face redden. 'I was acting out of revenge.'

I told him about my pistol shooting training and the self defence classes that I attended back home.

He nodded, then he said, 'Have you ever considered a career in the police?'

'No.... ' I trailed off wondering.

'We could do with people like you. Criminals are often

armed, even here in Iceland.'

'*Sorry*? I'm not sure what you're getting at.'

'I'd like to offer you a job. What do you say?'

Did I hear right? Did he say he was offering me a job? I asked, not believing my ears, 'I beg your pardon?'

He continued, 'You've plenty of time to think it over. You'd have to be an Icelandic citizen of course before you could do this. I guess you've plenty excuse to stay here and enough to keep you busy for a while.'

He smiled as he glanced at Tómas and back to me.

I said, 'I was only trying to protect myself and my friend Lei. When someone shoots at me I have this uncanny urge to shoot back and I tend to lose my cool ..... ' I trailed off lost in thought.

Do I want to come back here and stay for good? I'd be leaving family and friends back home. I'd have to take a crash course in Icelandic too. I think I could just about manage that though, and Tómas could teach me. I'd have to think about it, I told him. I'd let him know when I had reached a decision.

I heard the door open at my back and someone came in.

'Someone to see you Miss Winter.' It was the policeman I had just assaulted.

Before I could rise, I heard something scamper across the carpeted floor, then it jumped up onto my lap. It was Petra. I squealed and cried when I saw her. She started licking my face and I pulled her close and kissed her on top of the head.

'How did.... ?' I trailed off wondering how she had gotten on board. I turned to Tómas for an explanation.

'I thought you might like to look after him since Lei and your uncle were gone,' he said smiling.

'Her,' I corrected and kissed her again on the head. I asked the policeman, 'How did Blackbeard get on board?'

He shrugged and asked, 'Who?'

'The guy we found on deck with the chequered jacket.' Tómas replied. He said turning to me, 'He came aboard with us.'

'Oh.' I felt a tear forming as an image of Blackbeard falling into my arms came back to me. I wiped it away with my fingers. 'Why should he do that? How did he know we were here?' I wiped away another tear.

'He was worried about your safety, so he paid a visit to

your uncle's house and found the back door open and the dog wandering about barking,' Tómas said, his hand squeezing mine.

'We left her in the kitchen with food and water and the back door open should she need to get out,' I said.

'He also had a look around the house while he was there,' he continued.

I guessed I knew what was coming next. I patted Petra's head.

Tómas said, squeezing my hand again, 'There was a plan of this boat spread out on the desk in the room under the stairs.'

'We've got it here.' The policeman indicated a large rolled up sheet of paper on his desk.

'And the little red squares on there? *Is* that drugs that were being smuggled?' I asked looking at the policeman.

He nodded. 'And we found them in the fish boxes on deck too, thanks to Lei taking those photographs.'

I asked curiously, 'How did you know the camera belonged to Lei?'

'She had left her name and address on the camera menu. A security measure in case the camera was lost or stolen.'

Tómas said, 'Your friend with the chequered jacket....'

I interrupted, 'His name was Jack.'

He continued, 'He found your car abandoned on the shore.'

'But how did *you* know where I was?' This was confusing.

'I didn't go back to Hveragerði immediately. I delayed my return because I wanted to see you again before I left, then I realised that I had no idea where you were, except that you were staying with your uncle.

'I remembered you said that you had hitched a ride to your uncle's house. It was a bit of a long-shot, but I thought I would ask around to see if anyone remembered you. I had the photo of the two of us together with me. I went to a few of the taverns and asked around there. Someone remembered you from the picture, and you asking a guy with a beard and him agreeing to take you. They knew who Jack was and was able to point out the truck that he drove.

'When I found him, I showed him the photograph and he took me to your uncle's house, but of course you weren't there. He suggested that we go to the Siggi and check it out. He knew your uncle's fishing boat. We found it and asked the guy on board if he had seen you or your uncle. He told us that he was on the Gúðrun and that he was the captain. He said that he had spoken to you too. Someone on one of the other boats at the quay remembered you asking about your uncle. They had also seen him on the quay and then boarding this boat.'

The policeman said, 'We found this in Jack's pocket. I think he was going to give it to you when he was shot.'

He got up from the desk and handed me a small gift-wrapped box. The paper was gold-coloured, and it seemed vaguely familiar. It couldn't be, could it? The bracelet that Tómas had given me?

I could feel another tear forming and started to sniffle. I took it from him and removed the wrapper. I opened the lid, and, *yes*, it was my bracelet. There was a slip of paper tucked under the velvet insert that held the bracelet in place.

I was about to take it out, when Tómas asked, 'Is that the bracelet that I gave you?'

I just nodded and sniffled my reply. I must have left it in the house; overlooked it when I was stuffing everything into my pack yesterday.

'I'll read it later,' I thought smiling at Tómas.

Back on shore, I showed the policeman I had met on the ship, the notebook that we had found in uncle's car. The names, addresses and contact numbers would lead to many more arrests, and hopefully put this drug smuggling ring out of business for good.

I returned to Reykjavík and Helga's place with Petra. Tómas has promised to look after her.

On my last day before returning home, we found the most lovely beach to relax on. It wasn't very far from Reykjavík. I had no intention of swimming here though.

I lay on my back beside Tómas, just staring up at the gorgeous blue sky and counting the few clouds that I could see there. He had his eyes closed, I thought at first against the strong sunlight, but I think he was sleeping. I propped myself on one elbow and brushed some hair away from his eyes. I was leaning over him and was just about to kiss him on the lips when it happened; the Earth moved under me and I almost fell over onto my back.

I shouted in alarm, 'What the.... !'

Tómas awoke immediately. 'What's the matter Sam?' he exclaimed.

I was feeling positively sick to my stomach and thought I would throw up any minute.

'What the hell was that?' I said in alarm to no-one in particular.

The Earth just moved an inch or so. Was that an earthquake? Back in California sometimes we get them, but I have no personal experience of one.

He asked sounding concerned, 'What was what?'

'Oh *God!* Didn't you feel it?'

'No, what?' He obviously didn't.

'So you *were* sleeping then?' I asked in a mocking tone.

'No, of course I wasn't. Just closed my eyes for a few seconds,' he said looking at me with tired eyes. He was smiling.

'So why didn't *you* feel it too?' I mocked and poked him in the ribs with my finger. I sat up. I said, 'The earthquake?'

He asked, 'What earthquake?'

'See, you *were* sleeping.' I sat astride him, on his stomach.

He looked at me with a question mark above his head.

I bent and kissed him on the lips, then I straightened up and unfastened his second shirt button down. I kissed his chest there, or what I could see of it anyway. I loosened another button. Furry chest here; interesting!

'No I wasn't,' he said smiling.

I kissed the fur there and loosened another button. I kissed his chest again and now I found a nipple. I kissed that too.

On the Icelandair flight back to Boston I reflected on the vacation and Tómas in particular. He promised to come and visit me in California and I'll pay him a visit too, then if all goes well, I may settle down here. I might also take up that policeman's offer and join their ranks, but first things first.

I sat in a window seat with two empty seats on my right, and, as I looked out onto the Atlantic Ocean far below, I thought about poor Lei. She didn't deserve to die like that, and Blackbeard.

I almost forgot about the note he had inserted into the gift box. I went into the storage bin above my head and found the gift box. Back in my seat again, I began to read the note.

'Dear Sam, Hope you enjoyed you vacation despite the problems you encountered. I hope you can come back to Iceland some day and maybe we can meet up again. I'll look forward to it. Best of luck. Jack.'

I could feel tears forming now. I just let them run down my cheeks before wiping them away with my fingers.

A stewardess spotted me in the process of wiping my cheeks with a Kleenex from my pocket. In a concerned voice she asked, 'You OK Miss?'

I nodded.

'Boyfriend?' she asked smiling.

I smiled and nodded again. I wiped my nose with the Kleenex.

She moved up the aisle.

I laid my head back on the headrest and dozed off with an image of me lying wrapped in Tómas' arms, and all my worries ebbing away.

The End

****

Printed in Great Britain
by Amazon